SHELL GAME

A MEDICAL THRILLER

D.J. LEE

CONTENTS

CHAPTER ONE

Late December, Somewhere in Bend, Oregon

"I've finally figured out what's going on here, angel; unreal. Can't believe I'd find something like this working a temp job...anyway, report's been filed, so those problems are a done deal. I'll pick you up on Wednesday. When's your friend's opening?" James Harris jogged down the mudroom stairs, stopping just short of the bottom. "Yes, I'll be careful skiing; I always am. Love you, babe." He ended the call, and shoved his phone in his parka pocket, whistling and anticipating his reunion with his fiancée. As he launched onto the last step, the garage light went out, leaving only the dim cast of a winter morning streaming through the windows of the garage door. He smelled cigarette smoke and an unusual cologne as he fumbled in his pocket for his phone, thinking to use the flashlight function. James turned his head in response to a gust of air from his left, startling as he saw a man erupt from the recess under the stairs.

"What!?" James shouted in terror and feinted right as he

raised his arms in a futile attempt to evade the savage swing of the Louisville slugger aimed at his head. James gave a cry of anguish as the bat connected; his head exploded in searing pain and he crashed to his knees. Before he could react further, the brutal blow to his head was repeated, and he lapsed into unconsciousness.

SCRITCH-TAP... SCRATCH, SCRATCH, SCRATCH... SIGH... *scratch*

Something to the right made an off-time counterpoint to the regular beat of James' heart. Those were the only things that he could hear as he emerged from the darkness of unconsciousness as if he waking from anesthesia — sounds first. His head pounded as he recalled his last few minutes of awareness with no concept of how much time had elapsed since then. The pounding increased as he struggled to lift his head. Priorities. He needed info about where he was first, then he could figure out what happened. He peeled open his eyes, greeted with double vision, nausea, and a chorus of drums that throbbed in his head in time to his heartbeat — all concussion symptoms. He swallowed convulsively as he struggled not to vomit the bile that crawled up his throat. After a few shallow breaths through his nose, the nausea eased, and he began to take stock of his surroundings. He was bound to a chair, sitting in a pool of light in a musty room lined with rows of boxes. Other than the buzz from a failing fluorescent light, all he could hear was that curious, irregular grating noise. This was not his garage. After his stomach settled, he risked return of the drum concerto in his head when he turned toward the sound. He saw the blinking red eye of a mounted camera and a figure in the shadows — a man of his size, who shifted constantly. The scrape of his shoes on the floor was the sound he heard. His head still pounded and every degree he turned his head made the pain worse, but his vision was improving. His cautious survey of the room was interrupted by a raspy twang of a Texas drawl from behind him.

"Well Doc, bout time you woke up. Shame on you, keeping comp'ny waiting. Anyways, you and me already done said howdy. You stirred up some trouble, yessir, but we fixin ta get it back straight; s'all good. If'n I'm right, we ain't gonna get no answer from The Big Chief bout this little meetin'. That would suit me good, all right...real good." The man behind James cracked his knuckles and whistled, "Hey! Flip that switch, Junior; let's get this done."

"Who...who are you? What do you want? Why...I don't understand..." As James spoke, light glinted off the watch on the right arm of the man in the shadows as he reached toward the camera, and the blinking light went to solid red. The man behind James rounded his chair, bringing with him a hint of the same mingled odor of cigarette smoke and cologne that he had smelled in his garage. James shifted his focus from the man in the shadows to the one standing in front of him. "You?? What are you up to? What would I know..."

"Harris, you know plenty, and we bout to find out exactly what." The man in front of James was around six feet tall with carelessly styled brown hair and could have been as young as thirty-five or as old as fifty. He wore a mocking expression as he assessed James. His only distinguishing feature was a colorful tattoo of what might be a dragon, which twined its way around the right side of his neck before disappearing under the collar of his shirt.

The tattooed man smirked as he swaggered to an open tool chest sitting on a nearby table, and shrugged out of his jacket, tossing it on a stack of boxes. His worn, flannel shirt stretched over his shoulders as he flexed his arms before removing items from the chest, systematically arranging them on the dingy towel that covered one side of the table in a macabre parody of instrument preparation for a surgical procedure. James swallowed against a rising lump in his throat while watching the process of a surgical scrub tech preparing the Mayo stand for an...operation. His pulse raced as his focus narrowed to the rows of gleaming instruments, precisely lined on the filthy towel. His attention was wrenched from the instruments when the door was banged open, revealing a man wearing a sweater and khakis. The glow from a bare light bulb outside the room gave James a glimpse of what appeared to be a corridor in a storage facility with corrugated steel walls and a numbered door across the way, before the man cursed and slammed the door shut. As he strode into the room, he snatched a Bluetooth device from his ear and snarled.

"No emails, and no one's bothering to answer their phones back East...typical...Fuck those assholes! Let's get some answers." Almost before he finished speaking, the tattooed man stepped forward and backhanded James so hard that his head snapped back. James retched and groaned as the throbbing agony in his head ratcheted yet a bit higher. There was an ungodly screech of metal on concrete as the man in the sweater dragged a chair to the edge of the tarp under James's chair. He pushed up the sleeves of his sweater as he sat, leaning forward and clasping his hands, resting his elbows on his knees. His casual pose was at odds with the violence being inflicted; his forced smile never reached his eyes.

He briefly glanced at the man with the tattoo and nodded. Immediately, the man went behind James and loosened the ropes binding his arms to the chair. James gave a sigh of relief as he was now able to move and ease the spasms in his arms. But his relief was short-lived as his left arm was retied and the right forced palm down, onto a mobile stand that the tattooed man retrieved from the shadows. The man hummed as he reached for something off the table of instruments, and turned back, snapping the jaws of a shiny, double-action plier shut on the base of the small finger of James's right hand. The bone gave a sickening snap as it was crushed. James gave a bellow of pain and shock, contorting his torso in a vain attempt to withdraw his arm. His vision tunneled in as he danced on the brink of unconsciousness from this new source of excruciating pain. After the echo of his scream died down, the room was quiet except for his anguished moans as he fought to cope with the searing agony now radiating from both his hand and head. He heard only the pounding of his heart as he panted and felt sweat pour down his face and spatter onto the tarp. As James struggled for composure and brought his mangled hand to his chest, his assailant tossed the pliers back on the table, lit a cigarette, and casually walked over to lean on a stack of boxes. When James could finally focus outside himself, he saw that the tattooed man was across the room, leaning on more boxes, legs crossed, with an eager, almost lustful expression on his face as he blew a cloud of cigarette smoke into the air, then removed the cigarette to flick ash on the floor.

"Didn't graduate, but anatomy is fascinating. Ten fingers, 28 li'l pieces a bone; lotsa nerve endings means lotsa pain. We'll work our way up to your arms. We got a long way to go, Doc, and I got all the time in the world." He hummed as he continued to smoke, obviously savoring thoughts about what was to come.

The seated man looked bored as he flicked imaginary lint

from his pants before he crossed an ankle over the opposite knee and leaned back in his chair before focusing on James with a sigh.

"Dr. Harris, we're going to have a chat, exchange some information, and then go for a journey." James panted and struggled with his bonds, feeling the edge of panic as he spat out a mouthful of blood, and tried to focus his once again blurred vision first on the man with the tattoo, then the man asking the questions. Through the haze of pain and nausea that engulfed him, his face grew slack and his heart stuttered as he realized he also recognized the man seated before him.

"But I don't know...why do you think that I..."

"Let's start at the beginning, shall we?"

CHAPTER TWO

Taryn struggled to separate waking from a great dream when reality, in the form of her Newfie pup Maxx, licked her in the face. She blinked the sleep from her eyes and focused on his grinning face, inches from hers.

"Maxx!! I thought you were still at the boarders!" She threw back her braids to hug her canine best friend, who slapped his paws on her shoulders in a big doggie hug, then flopped down and took up the remainder of the space on the bed.

"Well, T, after I busted ass getting your damn dog to you, the least you could do was say thanks," growled Taryn's totally fine and mostly naked roommate, Cody, who came into the room with two mugs, a smile, and a towel slung around his hips. "Here's your coffee, babe." With her dog and a wakeup coffee delivered by her best friend, and probably the hottest man in Seattle, Taryn thought her first day, post vacation, was starting out right.

"Hmmmm," she savored her first sip. "Cody, you're the

best...thank you! This mocha totally hits the spot...and thanks for Maxx, too."

"Soooo... gimme a vacay recap." An unholy light lit Cody's eyes as he claimed a corner on Taryn's bed. "Girl time, watersports, guy sports? Usual stuff?"

Taryn mentally rolled her eyes at Cody's ongoing perverse interest in her social life as she attacked her mocha, petted Maxx, and ignored his innuendo.

"R&R, catching up. And you're interested because?"

"Just curious...You were *out there* when you left. You finished work, dumped your boyfriend on the way to the airport, and then went off grid for two weeks. That's harsh even for Walter."

"Walter's a wuss."

"Emo friendly, maybe a douche; wuss is harsh."

"Semantics. Why'd you set us up again?"

"He's the opposite of your ex; thought that's what you said you wanted."

"You know me....why'd you think that Walter and I would work out? Especially since Maxx hated him?"

"Make your mind up about what you want, T-baby."

"Whatever. I was so tired before I left, I couldn't see straight." Taryn frowned as she reran her pre-vacation insanity. She *had* been running low on tact by the end of the holidays. "I'll clean things up with Walter...eventually. My biggest issue's that my Mom's gotten worse since Thanksgiving. I'm planning on heading to California to see her as soon as I unpack and get organized."

Although Taryn's mom had battled Grave's disease to an uneasy truce successfully for years, she was currently in a months-long period of more debilitating symptoms and medication side effects. Despite the team of experts caring for her, Taryn felt she needed to be doctor-daughter in person rather than by checking in long distance.

"You'll figure out how to see your folks. And I'll believe you'll circle back and make nice with Walter when it happens...meanwhile I have to listen to him whine." Taryn launched an on-target pillow at Cody in retaliation for his ongoing critique of her non-existent conflict resolution skills. After some imaginative cursing that she'd have to file for future reference, Cody recovered and saved his coffee. He resettled himself and the towel that defied gravity on the part of Taryn's bed not occupied by Maxx. As she looked at all six-foot-two of tatted up hard body man inches from her, and considered whether to call in emergency FWB privileges, she shook her head to break off from perving on her roommate.

"When did you grab Maxx? Weren't you supposed to still be in L.A.?" Maxx put his head in Taryn's lap and looked adoringly at her, simultaneously thumping his tail on the bed as she played with his ears. Maxx was hands down her best friend.

"I took the early flight back and grabbed him on the way home. Figured I'd save the monster from another day in purgatory." Cody ran a hand over his beard stubble and yawned widely before returning to his coffee.

"That kennel is cushier than some houses...and I was gonna pick him up by noon. Why the special delivery service?" Despite the innumerable perks and bennies of roommate life with Cody, she also knew his methods. Coffee/and or breakfast in bed was his favorite suck-up move he used when he had annoyed one of his numerous girl-friends. Even worse, it usually worked. As Taryn contemplated his true motivation, her bullshit alarm blared when Cody's grin turned sheepish. He looked away while rubbing his biceps and the tat covering his right arm — a 'guilty' tell, if there ever was one.

"Shit, Code, what have you done, and how's it involve me?" Taryn narrowed her eyes as she ran over the possibilities, totally forgetting her minutes ago pinch hitter during the drought fantasy starring Cody.

"T-baby...see you've got too many scheduling and January AR...

"AR? How's augmented reality got anything..."

"Anal Retentive" Taryn scowled "rules, so..." Cody flicked his green-eyed gaze at his suspicious roommate before mumbling the punchline. "I accessed your work email and signed you up for a job with Marsha's agency starting the end of January." After his confession, he thumped his empty cup on Taryn's nightstand, re-tucked his towel, and hustled away from ground zero as Taryn blinked in shock.

"As in accepted some assignment for me in *January* before I could regroup? What the hell were you thinking? I need to visit my Mom! You ass, you've wrecked everything!" Taryn shot off the bed, pushing Maxx out of the way; vacation afterglow was officially over. She dug through the pile of travel crap on the floor to find her backpack and fumed as she realized that Cody's actions had assured that January would be as hectic as December had been. While a typical December was all about work, with no time for family or mental sanity, January was Taryn's catch up with life and family time. That overdue visit with the parents in Santa Monica was now looking even more unlikely, courtesy of her wonderfully infuriating roommate. And, as much as she thought Marsha was the best recruiter she'd ever worked with, sometimes she was too commission oriented. This being January, she must have hefty Christmas bills.

"Dammit, Cody, which job, which rep? Marsha's been after me for this god-awful job in northern Arizona..."

"Relax!" Cody rolled his eyes and smirked, "I signed you up to go to Bend in Eastern Oregon." Taryn looked at Cody with her mouth agape as what he had said sunk in. Bend? In January? She located her backpack and extracted her laptop to survey and contain the damage Cody had wreaked on her life.

As a traveling anesthesiologist, Taryn Pirelli was the medical equivalent of a baseball pinch hitter. When hospitals were short an anesthesiologist due to sickness, vacation, or just a temporarily open job, they hired her to step in to fill the shortage and save the OR schedule. It was a job with lots of perks, like being able to see the country on someone else's dime, while racking up frequent flyer and hotel miles. It had been four years of Taryn-creates-her-perfect life since she started traveling for work 4 years ago, after a short sentence working as an Assistant Professor in the Anesthesiology department at UCLA. The change sparked by dumping her ex fiancé turned to be total lifestyle good luck. The Hollywood fable of the magnetic, gorgeous hotshot surgeon was not even close to reality in her book; her pet name for her ex was 'Asshat in Chief'. Taryn traded emotional and breakup trauma for a new city, a customizable schedule, new friends, and a great new life.

She had met Cody through mutual friends while skiing, years before she landed in Seattle. They'd turned into travel and adventure buddies, then roommates after Cody had suggested that she stay with him when she decided to relocate. A temporary landing place after her move had turned into one of the best decisions she ever made. Other than an annoying tendency to manage, manipulate, and otherwise orchestrate the lives and outcomes of his friends, Cody

Jennings was all that she could hope for in a roommate and best friend — loyal, honest...well, *responsible*...and due to his day job in marketing, seriously loaded. He was also connected with the most interesting (and colorful) people she had ever met. However, all of the upside was in serious jeopardy if he'd trapped her in the hinterlands of Eastern Oregon in late January.

"There's a ski mountain there, but why Bend during ski season and not Whistler or Park City?" she snarled as she flopped back down on the bed and booted up the MacBook she'd extracted from her backpack. "I'm not even going to ask how you got into my email, hacker-ass, but what's the scoop with this damn job that they're looking for help in the slowest time of year?"

By this time, Cody had wisely taken himself and his towel back to his room to get dressed. On his way out, he stuck his head back in, "According to Marsha, Bend's off the chain fun in winter...*and* she's desperate. Something about the previous doc she placed there not working out; folks at the hospital are pressuring her to provide a replacement. It's not all downside; they're paying a sign on and short notice bonus." With that last bit of detail, Taryn knew she was cornered. Taryn's work with Marsha over the past year had led to some amazing niche temporary jobs local to the Northwest that she might not have otherwise found. Taryn was big on friend loyalty believing that friends were your family, and you were there to help your tribe. In the short time she had known Marsha, she had become part of Taryn's tribe. Unfortunately, Marsha's call for backup had come at the absolute worst time for Taryn. She believed in taking care of her tribe and network, but this setup just smelled like a cover for a Cody wager gone bad.

"Cut to the chase; who do you owe and why? Hacking,

forgery, accessing my credentialing files are your activity short list. Was there *possibly* a lost wager before that?" Cody came back clad in jeans and a long-sleeved black tee, and a suspiciously innocent facial expression.

"Why do you assume this is about me and who I owe? The hack's retaliation for November when you screwed with the alert functions on my work laptop." Cody smirked as he ran a hand through his hair and leaned on the wall closest to the door.

Taryn flipped him off and continued to scroll through the emails relevant to the job in Bend. "November was payback for August, when you switched languages on all my devices. You're the worst gambler I know, yet you can't stop making bets. Where's the acceptance file for this cursed job?"

"Such a bad attitude right after vacation!" Cody shook his head in mock disapproval as he dropped down on the patch of bed not occupied by Maxx. He plucked the laptop from her hand, located the file in question, then presented the laptop back to her before walking to the window for a weather check. True to Seattle in January form, it was raining steadily, and hovering just above freezing as well. Taryn skimmed the file. Everything for the job was in order, but if she took it, she needed to be in Bend by next weekend, which meant no family visit time.

"T-baby, it's just a little schedule change. If you'd checked your voicemail and emails while you were away, you would have seen that Marsha was trying to tag you."

"Marsha knew I was on vacay; and I seriously doubt she tried to contact me...this goes deeper than that. Who. Do. You. Owe?"

"You know Marsha's tight with my bud, Ryan..."

"Which is how we connected."

"Getting you to take this job was the price for..."

"Losing to Ryan in your latest poker game. Dammit, Cody! Why can't you just learn to play poker for real, and not just bluff?" Cody crossed his arms and shrugged as he turned, quirking a smile at her.

"C'mon...it's the roommate rule...You know, all for one..."

"Not a Musketeer. You're the one who makes poor wagering choices"

"You're being a real hard-ass for such a normally nice woman."

"Stop whining. And I'm not sure that was even a complement... and your poker dysfunction is mind-boggling. My time trying to teach you's been wasted."

"Well, I ..."

"I'll do Marsha a favor in a heartbeat, but I've had enough of your missing poker gene." Cody sighed and shrugged, as he tried and failed to look tragic. Taryn muttered under her breath as she shook her head; how could someone so smart not be able learn how to play five card stud?

Cody sheepishly held his hands up. "Guilty! I suck at poker. I'm working on it. C'mo-o-on T-baby, it's just a three-month stint, and you even score two weeks of vacay." Cody wheeled as he gave her his patented, lopsided smile. "Bachelor's right there; we could ski weekends. This'll be a chip shot! Great money, time near a ski mountain, close enough I can come visit. You might even like the place well enough to stay put for a while. Not like you stay here more than two weeks at a pop anyway."

"Bend is *not* Seattle. Are you trying to get me to move out? And tell me again how this isn't about YOU? You're angling for free ski vacay lodging after losing your fricking bet! You'd best figure out a way to pay me back for saving your butt...and quick."

"T-baby you're permanent here...I just..."

She frowned and considered her always obtuse room-mate, and her own issues. Well, she could always take it outta his hide...or other parts. She gave him a speculative look. The skinny from her girlfriends who had actually dated Cody was that he was as good in bed as the packaging promised. She knew for a fact that he was genuinely a nice guy...and if they did get entangled, she wouldn't have any angst about waking up, or sleeping in a strange place. But how do you go back to just friends and roomies after banging boots? She knew from the cold shoulder she got from many of Cody's girlfriends that many of them already assumed that she and Cody were much more than roommates. In a true sense of irony, those were the women who didn't last in Cody-land; she had to admit the man did have good taste. She shrugged; she was overthinking, as usual. Why not just go with it, and have some uncomplicated fun? Gorgeous hot man; shared well; not clingy...and she was long overdue for some some benefits without strings...and little more morning coffee in bed.

"Whatever, you suck at poker. You would owe me." Taryn held Cody's gaze. With a glint in her eye, she decided nothing ventured, nothing gained. "What would you say to payback in the form of Friends With Benefits nookie? At a future date to be named, of course.

Cody pushed away from the wall with a leer. "Payback accepted; I'm down for boy toy duty... even if I know you're using it... and me... as a handy solution to avoid getting back..."

"Swipe left and bug off. Not your issue"

"It's really time you fixed your boyfriend malfunction, decide what you want... less bite, more kiss and make up, might be a start." Taryn tilted her head as she glared at her roommate, and Maxx nuzzled her. Sometimes, friends took one for the team and each other, just because.

"All right... I give." Taryn sighed and shrugged as she rolled her eyes in surrender. "I'm in for the job...you're helping me and Maxx drive there. We'll work out the rest later."

"T-baby, it's winter; no way would I let you and Maxx do that drive by yourselves."

"You know, when you're not being a pain in the rear, you're a good man, Cody."

"I'm glad you've come to the only logical solution for this little problem; my persuasion skills work again."

"Don't push your luck."

CHAPTER THREE

Bend, Oregon
Taryn

"I thought the best thing I could do was take you two to dinner. Figured I could give you my recommendations for places to go and things to do in person, and at one of my favorite restaurants. Lots of fun stuff to do here." Charlie Post, the real estate agent for the condo where Taryn was staying, was a ruggedly handsome man with thick, dark hair with a hint of gray, a goatee, and a tan that belied them being in the depths of winter.

"I wondered if you'd heard any gossip about why my predecessor left? This being a small town and everything. My recruiter had no details, other than the hospital held her responsible for finding someone to finish out the contract." Charlie gave Taryn a funny look as he set down his glass and ran his fingers through his hair.

"Not surprised that your recruiter didn't have any details. Your predecessor, James, Dr. Harris, didn't leave... he's missing. We became friends during his time here; we've skied together."

"So now I have the job opening mystery answered. When did Dr. Harris leave?"

"Dr. Pirelli..."

"Call me Taryn, please...Charlie."

"Taryn, this wasn't voluntary. He disappeared sometime over the weekend after working on a Friday three weeks ago."

"Wait, he disappeared? No message, no warning?"

"There are no clues, no leads, and he didn't notify anyone. All hell broke loose the following Monday when he didn't show up for work. It's an open missing person case. I sent the last of his effects to his family in Colorado a few days ago. No idea if James will come back, or why he left," Charlie shrugged before taking a swallow of his drink. Cody's expression was thoughtful as he studied Charlie and played with his glass.

"That's not the story the recruiter got...or told me...us."

"Would you want to advertise that the previous doc in the job had gone missing?"

"Marsha wouldn't have put T in a bad situation; I'm sure of it." Cody placed the call as he spoke.

"Well... sorry to say, but people flake...unusual, but..." Taryn shrugged. "You sure there were no clues the last time you saw him?"

"James wasn't a flake, and I heard nothing of concern when we last spoke...which is why this whole situation is so maddening."

Cody clicked off his call. "Marsha knew nothing of this... said she'd verify with the client first thing Monday."

"It sounds like you're the only one pegging this as disappearance." Charlie snorted.

"That's rich...how're you an authority on that after a few hours in town?"

"I checked online info — newspapers, message boards. There's no mention of even a search party looking for someone who went missing after a day of skiing... that's not the usual."

"Nothing here's the usual, and for the record, I've participated in some of the on-mountain search parties for James or evidence..."

"Which found?" Charlie glared at Taryn, then sighed. "Nothing in the back country; no new avalanches, no evidence or markers of anyone in distress."

"None of which is consistent with Harris getting in trouble skiing. I'm betting he just ghosted for personal reasons."

"James Harris is not a flake — or likely to go AWOL. I've got a sense for people. And trusting my gut has kept me out of a world of hurt over the years."

"Army?"

"Navy...twenty years active. I've trekked with James, cold weather and warm. He isn't a man who can't 'handle himself' in the back country."

"Isn't...so you think he's alive."

"He's a survivor; take my word for it."

"I'm not convinced. How does a man disappear on a busy ski mountain?

"And how's it gonna impact T? Taryn?"

Taryn frowned; Cody had an annoying tendency to orchestrate things when there was a any hint of mystery or danger. Luckily, she had years of practice shutting down those tendencies.

"I can take care of myself, just like always. Seeing that

Charlie's my first contact here, and is bringing up all of the backstory drama, I'm hoping I can trust him."

"You can...absolutely. I'm a man of my word. But my biggest suggestion is for you to keep your eyes peeled at work. Look at what you see, and what you don't see, then let's have a chat."

Taryn frowned at Cody, who shrugged as he slung an arm over the back of his chair and absently turned his phone end over end on the table while watching Charlie.

"That's a weird directive..."

"Because I don't want to bias you. You should keep your mind and your eyes open." Taryn was silent, then looked towards the bar where a large group of après' ski revelers gathered. "Look, I've got a daughter a bit younger than you. If she was in this situation, I'd sure as hell hope someone would help her." Charlie looked away from Taryn, while rubbing the worn pewter Celtic knot on his keychain. He closed his eyes briefly before scooping up the keys and shoving them in his coat pocket.

Taryn raised her eyebrows at Cody, who sent her a look before shaking his head. Before either could speak, their server came to take their orders, and Charlie dropped the subject to return to tour guide information for the rest of their meal. The only additional pertinent info they got out of Charlie the rest of the night was that he had been the nursing director four years previously at the hospital. Taryn saved her comments until she and Cody were headed for her car.

"THANKS CODY...JUST WHAT I NEEDED. THIS IS A SHIT-storm. I need facts; there's something Charlie's not telling us." Taryn snatched her keys out of his hand before she stalked off to her SUV, scowling as she considered the options and implications of everything she'd learned. Cody, recognizing her growing ire, was still searching for a way to mollify her when he slid into the passenger's seat.

"Okay, new plan...you need to gather everything you can find about Charlie, and anything else you can find about this place." Data analyzed, decisions made; Taryn was in anesthesiologist rapid decision mode.

"But..."

"If I know more about Charlie's background and motivation, I'll know what to trust of what he says and thinks. Mean's I'll have to wait until I get to work to get the real scoop on James Harris."

"So, now you're interested in *Harris?*"

"No! I'm just trying to figure how to avoid landing in trouble. He obviously got on someone's bad side. Whoever contracted with Marsha knew that disappearing without finishing a job was a red flag. Hence the rush to hire with bonuses."

"Marsha stuck to her story; they told her Harris left."

"Who's they?"

"Marsha said the hospital contracted her...and yeah, the original contract was through the anesthesia group."

"Exhibit one of something stinks; that's not the process. Why the change in contracting entities? Start with getting what you can on Charlie. I need an ally, and he's a logical choice." Taryn thought about the short list of reasons why someone on a locums assignment might disappear without notice. The common reasons encompassed everything from mental issues to family crises to physical incapacitation, but she needed to chat with someone at the hospital for those details.

"You think you're gonna be okay 'til we figure out what's going on?"

"I'll deal...but now I'm wondering if my pepper spray's gonna keep me safe here. A community hospital in Eastern Oregon in the dead of winter's not exactly a war zone, but something's fishy here."

"Agreed. And now I feel bad that I roped you into this."

"You should...but I'm perfectly capable of taking care of myself until we get more info. Not like this is some clandestine op; it's passing gas at a community hospital. As long as you can get me info on Charlie, and I nose around the hospital, I'll figure out how to navigate the assignment."

"Maybe you should wait until I get more info."

"If I need help or backup, I'll call. A predecessor who bailed on his job, and an ex-military, ex-nursing director who jumped to conclusions because he'd seen bad stuff in the past. What on earth could be that dangerous in a little ski town in eastern Oregon?"

Blake

BLAKE MYERS DUMPED THE LAST LOAD OF HIS PERSONAL gear in the great room, leaving the balance of his work supplies in the garage. After time with a willing playmate at his private club the night before, he was focused. His flight to Bend was uneventful, and his admin had found lodging that met his specifications; game on. He popped in his Bluetooth earpiece to make a call to his best friend and business partner, Steve Harris, as he continued to rummage through his luggage. The call connected just as he found the case he'd been searching for.

"I'm in the condo." Blake tossed the case he'd searched for on the coffee table before sprawling on the couch. "Gonna review what we've got so far. Got a week to poke around before I start work."

"That's a week to piss people off."

"We've had this conversation."

"I get that you want to help, but you're a shit when people get in your grille. You've also got no backup, on top of no tact. Maybe we can..."

"Look, nothing here's gonna get easier to find with time. Jimmy's been missing over three weeks. So-called authorities don't have jack." Blake frowned and ran his fingers through his ragged, below shoulder length, black hair. "No more waiting. Jimmy's as much of a brother to me as he is to you; you don't abandon family."

"I get it...but I could..." Blake snorted.

"*You* have the wrong last name. I'm just a company sup checking out his reps and territory."

"Well..."

"No better cover than partial truth." Blake opened the case he'd taken from his luggage, removing items and placing them on the table, the random clicks punctuating the silence.

"It's just crazy enough that it might work," sighed Steve finally. "I honestly don't think you can swing this without going ape-shit with someone at the hospital...operating room's not our company."

"I've got this covered..."

"Doubtful...you can't keep it together when you get into it with people you like. No one there's gonna make exceptions for a visitor being an asshole."

"I will always play nice..." said Blake with a half-smile as he inserted the clip into his 9mm and chambered a round, making sure the safety was on before he slipped it into his shoulder holster. "Until it's time to not be nice." No sense being stupid or naïve; everything about the details surrounding James Harris' disappearance screamed foul play to him, and he never walked into a fight unprepared.

"That's a movie...not gonna work for real," said Steve with a bark of laughter. "How's H&K gonna help with fact-finding and questions? Ever hear of diplomacy and patience?"

"I'll manage." Blake picked up the TV remote and flicked through channels. "I'll look through Jimmy's records again. Monday I'll...hell, I could go see what I can find tonight."

"Bend's not Denver, my man."

"Thanks mom...you gonna give me a fuckin' curfew?" grunted Blake as he tossed the remote onto the coffee table and rose to pace. "Look, it's been a shitty week, shitty month. Even this hell hole's gotta have something doing on a Saturday night. I'll call you," he ended the call without waiting for a reply and settled his suit jacket over his shoulder rig before shrugging into his overcoat. He headed to the garage, mentally cataloging the bars about town that he had noted in the dossier he reviewed on the trip out. Tomorrow would be soon enough to start unravelling the puzzle that had brought him to Bend.

CHAPTER FOUR

"Doc, patient's moving"
"Again? Sorry...but he's had a ridiculous amount of drugs."

"Maybe...but he's still moving." Taryn frowned as she increased the gas flows on her anesthesia machine, incredulous that the drugs she had given the patient seemed not to be working. She was on her second case, first day of the new job. First case had been equally frustrating — moving patients, drugs not working. After a tour of the operating room, she had been pressed into work to cover for an anesthesiologist who had called in sick. Although she excelled in hitting the ground running, unpredictable drug potency and patients trying to walk off the OR table during surgery were the anesthesia equivalent of dealing with an earthquake while driving mountain switchbacks with bad brakes during a snowstorm.

"This your first day? Surprised Harry didn't fill you in. Everyone here's needed more drugs for anesthesia the past three months...no explanations why."

"I didn't get a briefing...but I'll deal. I think you can start now, Dr. Sellars."

"Maddie's fine...and welcome. And make sure the other folks in the group give you an accurate summary on things around here. Sucks that they've thrown the new person in the deep end without a lifesaver."

"Traveling anesthesia's what I do for a living...I thrive on change and new places. I'll make this work." Taryn and Maddie Sellars exchanged eye smiles over their surgical masks, then Maddie made her incision.

Taryn re-checked the gauges and exhaled percentages of anesthetic gases on her monitors. Everything seemed to be within expected parameters for an adequately anesthetized patient, but the patient moved again. She swore under her breath and gave more drugs in the IV before the problem resolved. After tidying up her work space on the anesthesia machine and cart, she willed the interventions to continue to work. With the patient settled, she dealt with charting on the computerized electronic record, filling in dosages of medications that she had administered. She gave a speculative look at the syringes of the drugs she had given and shrugged. Maybe it was just a coincidence. The computer interface recorded the relevant vital signs and administered anesthetic gas levels, and she filled in the amounts of the drugs used. By the time she had filled in all of the blanks on the electronic record, the vitals and patient seemed rock steady. Not the way she would have picked to start her time in Bend, but at least she had averted a potential crisis.

"Sorry again for the mix-up with the patient moving."

"No worries, and not a surprise. Most of patients these days seem to be a bit twitchy when I get started."

"Have you heard any explanations about what's happening from the other anesthesiologists?"

"Last I heard was that they had a bad batch of Sux; left out on the loading dock too long at the factory or something. No worries on my end; everything's fine now, so all good." Taryn thought of her drug choices. Sux or succinylcholine had not been the muscle relaxant she used on this patient. The routine induction or sleep drug had been Propofol, a medium acting muscle relaxant, and Fentanyl, a narcotic agent. The patient had seemed to need more than the average dose of Propofol to get off to sleep; maybe that was the problem. If it was something that kept occurring, she'd report it since it could potentially impact anybody getting the drug.

Taryn settled in to watch the patient and the laparoscopic video of the surgery on nearby monitors. Anesthesia was one of those professions that could go from soothingly routine to frighteningly critical in seconds. Much like air travel, the takeoffs and landings, or in anesthesia terms, the induction and emergence from anesthesia, were most critical — provided things went well with the actual surgery.

Today, she'd been lucky. Maddie Sellars was a slick surgeon. The scheduled laparoscopic chole or gall bladder removal and the rest of the anesthetic were uneventful. Taryn was on her way back to the OR after giving a status report to the PACU nurse when she was hailed.

"Hi Dr. Pirelli...I'm Shannon, your anesthesia tech. I've been tied up with other rooms, but I'll get your room cleaned up for your next case." Shannon was talkative and sounded like she had just stepped off a street in Dublin. She filled Taryn in on details unique to Bend, pushing the supply restocking cart as she walked with her back to the room. "Has everything been Okay?"

"Um, well... equipment was good, and everything was well stocked." With that they launched into a lively discussion of the OR. It turned out that Shannon had worked at the hospital for almost seven years. Housekeeping was done with room cleanup and the nurses were taking a break before readying for the next scheduled case.

"Well, the surgeons are all good...and quick. They just had a doc retire from the anesthesia group, it's why they're using temps." Shannon chattered on as she cleaned, refilled supplies, reset the anesthesia machine. As Taryn asked more in-depth questions, the nurses for the room came back to open the sterile supplies for the next case.

"Bye, Doc" said Shannon, as she pushed her cart out of the room. "Call me if you need anything, or a hand." Taryn gave her a wave and smile, just then seeing a note on her anesthesia cart with Shannon's name and number, and the message 'Call me whenever'. She smiled, then shoved the note into her pocket and finished setting up.

"LET'S GET THE PATIENT INTO THE RECOVERY SLOT AND on the vent," Taryn sighed as she pushed her last patient of the day into recovery. Any ideas of a calm remaining day disappeared as she began inducing the third patient of the day. After induction of anesthesia with Propofol, the patient had almost jumped off the table when she began to insert the endotracheal tube. The same outcome with slight variations happened all day, but oddly, no one in the operating rooms seemed surprised. Taryn rounded her shoulders in a vain attempt to relax while rubbing her forehead. Time for Tylenol, now that the day was finally over. She collapsed into a chair at the bedside computer terminal to complete her charting.

"What ventilator settings do you want, doc?" asked the respiratory therapist as her fingers flew over the control screen of the ventilator, entering the values Taryn rattled off. The recovery room got the patient connected with the monitors as she finished computer charting and gave the nurses' report. In keeping with the flavor of the day, the patient began waking up on the ventilator, setting off a cacophony of alarms as he began to struggle to breathe on his own while the ventilator continued delivering the ordered respiratory volumes and rate. The respiratory therapist was luckily still present.

"Let's put him on demand ventilation and see what he does." After an entire day when nothing went as predicted in the patient's responses to the medications she had administered, why on earth had Taryn assumed that the last case would be different? The patient's uncoordinated, unconscious thrashing as he fought the ventilator slowly decreased as the new settings became effective.

One of the nurses gave her a smile. "Oh, it's pretty typical for what we get here, doc...the operating room nurses told me you handled everything in there just fine. Finish your report; we'll take it from here."

Taryn finished with post op due diligence as she replayed the day's minor disasters. Unpredictable patient reactions may have been usual for them, but not for her. She was careful and vigilant. Well controlled, stable anesthetics, great patient outcomes, and no surprises were her work style. She frowned as she shoved her hands in her pockets and replayed the day. As she arrived back in her room to clean up her workstation, she realized that she still had the scrap of paper with Shannon's name and number. At some point, she should call and see if she could get some unofficial information, non-MD perspective on issues in the OR pertaining to abnormal drug reactions. If this was how everyday was going to be, the next three months would suck.

After gathering her gear, Taryn went to the main desk, and asked the unit secretary about other of anesthesiologists who might still be around. The other scheduled cases were done, leaving the on-call person as the only other anesthesiologist in the facility. As luck would have it, he was busy bringing an emergency case up from the emergency room. She sighed as she went through the empty outer lounge to the locker room and changed into her street clothes. As Taryn finished, she heard a hum of voices and the beep of a monitor — that had to be the emergency. She re-entered the lounge, to find the anesthesiologist on call, Michael Downing, there wolfing down a sandwich. He gave her a smile, as he talked around his food.

"Taryn, right? Thanks for helping us out. How was today? Sorry we kinda threw you in the fire; we'll get you oriented tomorrow."

"Well, things went well. I found what I needed, and didn't get lost, but I don't think I've ever seen so many patients with medication reactions in my life."

"Really?" he replied, as he continued to shovel food in his mouth. "Not something I've heard from the other partners or noticed, but okay, you're allowed your opinion." Taryn ate her reply and shrugged as she pasted a smile on her face and fled after wishing him a quiet call.

SHE WAS STILL DEEP IN THOUGHT AS SHE HEADED FOR the hospital exit, passing through the doctor's lounge that led to the parking lot. The head of the anesthesia group, Harry Lam, hailed her to join his conversation with a fireplug of a man in a suit. Harry was geared up for the outside like Taryn.

His grim expression relaxed into a smile as he waved her over.

"Taryn...I'd like to introduce you to our hospital CEO, Wyatt Cook. Wyatt, this is Dr. Pirelli, the locums doc who so graciously helped us out and filled our vacancy on short notice." Wyatt Cook was a rather florid faced man with thinning, blond hair and brown eyes, and appeared to be around 50. The pungent aroma of smoke enveloped him like a thick, winter coat. His eyes shifted to the left as he extended his hand.

"Nice to meet you Dr. Pirelli." After they shook, Taryn shuddered and fought the urge to wipe her hands on her jeans while edging back a step. Cook gave her the creeps, but she needed to be a professional and play the game.

"Did you get your questions answered about our OR protocol? Adherence to it is vital for your success here." Before Taryn could answer, Cook continued his monologue. Or was it a lecture? She struggled to find the hidden significance in his words as he droned on.

"Please consult one of the regulars if you have questions or problems with the equipment or facilities. We're quite concerned about the untimely and unprofessional departure of your predecessor, Dr. Harris, where ever he's taken himself to. Leaving without notice is just not done. Your recruiter assured me that you *will*, at least finish out your contract as agreed. Our evaluation will, of course, be contingent upon your successful completion of your contract." Taryn opened her mouth to respond but Cook forged on. "I want to make sure that you're comfortable with everything concerning your stay and work here, and also willing to be a compliant, albeit temporary member of the CHG Bend team." It was an obviously prepared monologue.

Taryn got the feeling that he was speaking to make a

point. "I've got no problem being a team player, or following hospital guidelines, and feel confident that my work quality will compare favorably with that of your other anesthesiologists."

"Good. After Dr. Harris' unsatisfactory tenure, it's vital that you demonstrate that you're onboard with both our culture and our hospital motto and eager to help our team accomplish its goals. We'll be watching you closely."

Taryn couldn't decide if she needed to get pom poms and cheer, or just curtsy. She shoved a hand in her parka pocket, flexing her fingers rather than letting her irritation show. James Harris had obviously not generated a fan club during his stay in Bend, and that seemed to be the primary concern, rather than the man being missing. It would be tricky to successfully navigate the politics while caring for her patients.

"Well my housing is awesome and the schedule Harry's shown me seems pretty straightforward...I think I'll be fine."

"Yes, housing... Charlie Post does a great job, but just take his rantings with a grain of salt, hmm? He's a bit of a loose cannon — has some personal issues that, unfortunately, he continues to air. You'll want to stay clear of him and his influence if you want to be successful here." Wyatt's smile was more of a grimace. Charlie's admonition to 'watch and listen' rang in Taryn's head, as the stilted, medically-related conversation lurched along, before Wyatt took his leave a few minutes later. Taryn filtered her experiences and observations about the first day as she and Harry walked out together, discarding several summaries of the day. They were in the doctors' parking area before she went for it.

"I had a decent day, Harry, but honestly, I saw some strange drug reactions with most of my patients." Harry frowned, and crossed his arms, nodding as she related the basics of the most disturbing of her cases.

"Well, Taryn, I'm glad that you came to me directly. Report your findings to Mike Downing; he's Q/A chief. He'll follow our protocol on problems and complications. I think that would be the ideal way for one of our locums folks to deal with complications and issues. I'd like to caution you against mentioning anything you observe to anyone other than Mike Downing or myself. I'm afraid we would look quite negatively on any deviation from this rule. Please don't do anything which might force me to take further action if report your findings further." She blinked as she looked at Harry, discarding words before choosing a reply. "So, you want me to..."

"Consider the fact that you're a temp worker here, and that the rest of us will continue as a part of this community long after you leave. Also, you've been contracted by the hospital, and not by our group, as regrettable as that is," he shrugged, adding, "it's just how things are. Keep quiet; keep your job," and turned to walk to his truck. Taryn inhaled sharply, wide-eyed at the implications of what Harry didn't say. She was jerked from her reverie as another doc on her way into work greeted her as she walked past, and Taryn resumed walking to her vehicle. She turned on the radio to distract her thoughts as she drove to pick up Maxx from his doggie daycare, *A Dog's Life*. It had started to snow and got progressively heavier as she drove the two miles to the facility. She trudged in, glad for the relief and company of her dog.

"Hi Dr. Pirelli," Becky had been the attendant on duty that morning. "Let me get Maxx for you. Such a great dog; settled right into our routine." She retrieved Maxx, who gave

Taryn his usual grin and mugging — most definitely the best part of her day.

"Hey, not to be nosy, but watch yourself at night. Last weekend, a woman was assaulted a couple streets from here, behind one of the bars. She's alive, but pretty banged up... concussion, busted ribs, broken jaw...still hasn't woken up after surgery. I've got a friend who works dispatch at the PD; she gave me the scoop. They try to keep that stuff quiet, so they don't scare the tourists, but you're here for a bit...thought you should know. It'll likely blow over, but be careful until they catch whoever's responsible." Taryn looked up, then stammered a thanks to Becky before she led Maxx to the car. So far, her stay in Bend was speeding from unexpected detour to not promising and finally, awful.

CHAPTER FIVE

After her chaotic first day, Taryn decided to call Shannon for non-MD department scoop and coping tips. As she drove Maxx home, she got voicemail. Starved for moral support and counterpoint, she called Cody.

"T-baby! Great timing; great news," said Cody as Taryn pulled into the garage, turning off her car and switching the phone off speaker. "Charlie's history checks out; interesting guy. He currently controls about 40% of the vacation and executive condo rentals for Bend and has for the past three years. He's not just ex-military, he's ex Special Forces. Twenty years active in Navy, most of it with the SEAL teams."

"So opinionated, loyal, super vigilant ex-military guy, now in real estate. At least he might be able to get me a personal protection device beyond pepper spray. I just found out from an attendant at Maxx's daycare that the police are hiding the fact that women here are being assaulted."

"What?"

Taryn gave Cody the short version of what she knew,

along with her overall impression of Bend, the hospital, and the oddities she had encountered on her first day of work.

"Why'd Charlie go from active duty on the SEAL teams to nursing director in a small-town hospital, then local real estate mogul?"

"Transition out of military happened after his wife, Eden, was killed 10 years ago in a traffic accident toward the end of his last tour; 10-year anniversary's actually this week. He got a compassionate reassignment to the Kitsap Peninsula Naval Base, then the Naval Reserves, and finished out his stint with the military. He went into nursing, which allowed him to care for his son and daughter. At the time, they were only 8 and 11. His kids are both adults now; Charlie's an empty nester. That's it; not sure about why he switched from nursing director to real estate agent."

Taryn could hack and worm her way into controlled access computers, but Cody was truly talented on getting inside information on people and places.

"So, career transition to successful, powerful real estate agent from nursing director for reasons unknown. There's a story there, but not sure it's relevant to anything. I guess the only interesting thing is that he's still here in Bend."

Cody had another impression. "His wife's family's here; older brother, who was also his spotter for a time. I don't see a man who's been in the SEAL teams getting scared off by a bunch of suits."

They continued to chat for awhile before signing off, still no closer to figuring out what led to the disappearance of Taryn's predecessor, and how it might impact her. She took care of dinner, letting Maxx do his business in the backyard, instead of going for a walk after the warning from the attendant at doggie daycare. The condo was a distance from the presumed site of the assault, but no sense being careless.

Rather than vegging out in front of the TV, Taryn booted up her computer, using a VPN tunnel rather than doing the direct run through the condo Wifi. Maybe it was paranoid, but no one needed to have a nice listing of the websites she'd accessed or her laptop's IP address. After gaining access to the hospital mainframe, she started nonspecifically poking around for anything she could find about the OR and pharmacy. In all likelihood, anything significant was either going to be in hard copy form or only accessible via the hospital intranet, but a quick check couldn't hurt. Taryn surfed and searched for half an hour before giving up. She needed more time on the hospital comps before she could figure a way into their system. As she mused about how exactly she'd accomplish that, the phone rang — Shannon.

"Hi Dr. Pirelli. How was the rest of your first day? I bugged out around 3:30. When did you finish?"

"Call me Taryn. Please, Shannon." She filled Shannon in on her day.

"Hmmm, drug issues...again."

"Again?"

"Well, I came into the lounge one day last month while Dr. Harris and Dr. Downing were having a shouting match. Dr. Harris was talking about reporting some problem with drug anomalies to the Portland FDA office. Dr. Downing was livid. That's pretty much all I got before they asked me to leave. From what I learned later, Dr. Harris went over Downing's head with his complaint. Downing's the Quality Control officer for anesthesia."

"Anyone give you more info?"

"Not to me. And I didn't dig. It was a doctor issue. I've learned to stay out of things that don't directly affect me."

"Any idea why he disappeared?"

"Can we table this until we meet in person?" Taryn frowned, then stood to pace.

"Why would we need to talk about something like this person?"

"I...well, I don't" Taryn could almost see Shannon wring her hands as she stuttered and searched for an explanation. Whatever was going on in the hospital, caution with everyone seemed to be the best approach. Taryn relented on insisting that Shannon give explain herself fully, focusing instead on solidifying logistics and timing to meet Wednesday and get the rest of her answers.

Tuesday

DESPITE TARYN'S FOCUS ON MAKING TUESDAY A BETTER day, her clinical misadventures kicked off with more patients having unexpected drug reactions. To cover herself, she made a spreadsheet listing all of the drugs she used on each patient, along with drug lot and batch numbers, along with the type of reaction. Although she regretted that she hadn't done so on her first workday, who starts a job expecting trouble? She ran into one of the regulars, Sherry Winger, in the lounge on coffee break after battling through her first two cases.

"Dr. Winger..."

"Sherry, please Taryn."

"Sherry then...I've experienced some problems with patients having weird drug reactions two days, now. I know regional patient populations can have varied responses to drugs, but this wasn't involving one particular drug. Have you had any issues recently?" Taryn had just begun to speak when Sherry grabbed the remote and turned up the TV volume.

"Yes, there're some issues, but I can't get into it now, Taryn...give me a call after work," she added before hustling into the locker room without getting her coffee. As the locker room door closed behind her, the main corridor opened, and the OR charge nurse entered. She frowned as she grabbed the remote and turned down the TV volume before returning to the OR desk enclosure. It was only then that Taryn noticed the camera nestled over the door to the main corridor. She found she suddenly had no taste for the rest of her coffee and tossed it before heading back to the OR.

THE REMAINDER OF TARYN'S CASES WERE LESS unpredictable, but still far from normal. Ray, the fourth group member, who'd had the sick call the day before, was congenial, but seemed oblivious to any drug potency issues when questioned. Taryn's cursory research on his recent cases showed he had multiple patients unexpectedly admitted to the PACU for post op ventilator management. At a loss to explain what she was seeing, Taryn was again faced with consulting the call anesthesiologist for perspective. Promptly at three, Michael Downing came into the lounge, where Taryn was working on her chart completions.

"Hi, Michael...how was the rest of your call yesterday?"

"Pretty routine, after we got the emergency done. Did you have a smoother day today?"

"Yes and no...I still had several patient drug reactions that I can't explain. Has anyone else reported any issues involving drug potency?"

He took his time replying as he checked what appeared to be a database on his phone.

"Nothing's been reported." He paused, then added, "Taryn, you know the hospital's a part of a larger chain of corporate facilities. If there was truly a recurring problem, I'd have received notification about issues at other facilities. Given that fact, I hesitate to be the standout facility bringing unconfirmed quality issues to the fore. Maybe we can just chalk it up to you being new here, and having a few adjustment issues, hmmm?"

She blinked and changed gears. 'Adjustment issues' could refer to anything from just settling in, to being deemed totally incompetent. While there was no stand out drug presenting issues, the pattern of patients with drug reactions was disturbing. Taryn filed it under wait and see, and headed for the locker room to change, increasingly unsettled by her new workplace.

Blake

"I've got shit-all here. Anything new on your end? I got your email with the credit card info." Blake nursed a whisky as he massaged his neck in a vain attempt to release some of the tension from his three-day marathon of combing the journals and files that James had sent to Denver the week he disappeared. Blake had spent most of the weekend, along with Monday and now Tuesday since his arrival in Bend combing through the handwritten journals, looking at pages of dates, with associated numbers that were obviously some type of code. The plus was that the info all seemed to be of similar format, so he decided to enter all of it into a spread-sheet — the significance of which he had no idea.

"Nothing new here."

"I used the charge records and checked out his stomping grounds; no luck....and no computer." He matched up info on local restaurants and bars with the list of charges from James' credit card charge record, but found no clues, although he had a stack of business cards and a few entertaining hours with a woman met during his search. More ominously, there had been no recent credit card charge with the final charge being for dinner Friday night, three weeks previous.

"Damn, we could use a break."

Blake was back to pacing, surprised that he hadn't worn a path in the carpet. He ruled out hurling his empty glass at the brick fireplace since he'd only have to clean it up. He'd gone skiing Monday afternoon, hoping his favorite past time would help him unwind, but was met with only partial success. Local gossip on why James might have disappeared or where he might be had been non-existent. There were no missing person fliers or any references to James or his disappearance in the papers beyond the initial police report. It was as if James hadn't even existed in Bend. Blake's current plan to reconstruct his life in the community would have to occur through the much slower process of waiting until he began work at the hospital, became acquainted with his medical colleagues, and allowed these contacts and their info to direct his investigative attentions.

"We knew this was gonna take time, man."

"I'm not feeling this 'wait and see' shit. Thursday, I'm seeing that rental agent, Post, who sent us the rest of Jimmy's effects...maybe something will turn up there." Steve's non-committal grunt was just as discouraging.

"Hey, man, incoming call from an Oregon area code... lemme get back to you."

Wednesday Afternoon

"SHANNON, YOU CAN'T BE SERIOUS!" TARYN WAS laughing hysterically at Shannon's anecdote about the most recent OR Christmas party. In a welcome break from the anxiety she had felt since beginning work days, she and Shannon focused on commonalities and humor before discussing problems. This was exactly what she needed post vacation.

"Truth! And you're laughing, so you agree. You're funny! We could use some more positive energy/can-do people at work." Taryn shook her head as she held up her hands in surrender.

"Your problems here are deeper than having a positive attitude."

Shannon signed as she nodded. "We have issues right now, but Bend is honestly a great place to live."

Taryn sobered and chose her words carefully to avoid straining her growing friendship with Shannon. "I can tell you love this place, but what I've had is three days of patients almost walking off the OR table, and no logical explanation for it. On top of that, I've gotten evasive, non-answers from everyone, including you, when I ask about the anesthesiologist who had the job before me."

Shannon's silence was her answer.

But Taryn pressed on. "Now that we're away from work, why do you think James Harris went ghost, and where would he go?"

Shannon frowned and glanced over her shoulder. There were a few people scattered around the coffee shop, one of whom had on scrubs. Taryn leaned closer to allow Shannon to whisper a response.

"Look, Taryn, everyone from admin to Harry is pretty serious about no one engaging in idle chatter about Dr. Harris. Last week, one of the nurses got reprimanded about speaking about him to another nurse in the operating room. Follow the rules, stay outta trouble is the ticket here. I talk to my husband, Jonas, about things at home. Don't get dinged for anything so soon after starting." Shannon raised and lowered her coffee without drinking as she darted her eyes about the shop, before adding, "The latest I heard midday was that they found Dr. Harris...his body.... yesterday...on the mountain. Check your hospital email...word from Harry is that's all there is to be said about it. He always looks out for us; he'll take care of you, too." She sat up and added more loudly, "Promise me you'll follow the rules, and won't ask anyone else, even within the department, about Dr. Harris?"

Taryn frowned as she looked at Shannon's earnest expression. There was no way she was going to get any more information.

"I'll drop it, Shannon; thanks for the heads up."

Time to call Charlie.

Wednesday Night

"HI CHARLIE...THANKS FOR RETURNING MY CALL. IT's been an odd week at work. I see what you mean about the hospital. Did Dr. Harris ever mention problems with drug efficacy in the OR? I've had some weird patient reactions and no one seems willing to listen to me, or give any background. Shannon Barnes is the only one talking, and she's told me nothing. What do you know?"

Her question was met with dead silence on the line.

"Where're you calling from?"

"The condo. Pulling together some dinner..."

"Fuck it...I'm coming over." Charlie abruptly hung up the phone. Taryn stopped what she was doing until Maxx nudged her for a piece of carrot. She gave it to him and hoped she had done the right thing by contacting Charlie.

TARYN WAS JUST GIVING MAXX A TREAT AFTER THEIR walk when he alert-barked as the doorbell rang; Charlie as promised. Maxx did the sniff inspection as Charlie shrugged out of his coat. With a woof and a tail wag before trotting off, Maxx gave Charlie his infallible, 'Okay person' assessment. Unlike her impressions, Maxx was always spot on in his ability to sniff out jerks and weirdos. Charlie accepted Taryn's offer of an after-dinner drink, after she ushered him to the great room.

"Taryn, I need to apologize for being evasive with you and Cody last week, but I wanted you to experience the place first hand...and also have time to check you two out. Appearances can be deceiving." Charlie placed his untouched drink on the table, clasping his hands as he rested his elbows on his knees.

"Are you satisfied that my identity is verified...if not my motives?" Taryn sipped her decaf and propped her feet on the coffee table.

"About as sure as I can be." He gave a quick smile. "Hell of an assignment to end up with after vacation. Interesting man, your roommate." Taryn nodded in approval; Charlie had been as thorough as she and Cody had in vetting and research.

"Sounds like we both have enough info to be comfortable allies, if not friends."

"Agreed." Charlie took a sip of his drink, cradling the glass in his hands as he made himself more comfortable, crossing one ankle over his knee. "James and I spent significant time skiing and socializing before he disappeared. He's met all of my friends here. I'd heard he was a good doc and found him to be a straight shooter — honest, solid. Since the beginning of December, he'd been pretty wound up about some of the drugs he was using in the OR."

"What was James' assessment?"

"Said the routine drugs didn't all have the proper actions or potency, and that he had reported that to the powers that be in the operating room. According to him, no one took follow-up action. When he demanded answers, he was apparently met with resistance both within the anesthesia department and from administration."

"From what Shannon told me this afternoon, he's gone from the missing to deceased category."

Charlie sighed as he got up to pace. "Yes...I'm friends with the chief, who told me they'd found his body yesterday morning...and that the family didn't take things well when they were notified. The hospital's pressured the police to keep everything quiet...but that won't last."

"Well, they're aggressively discouraging talk among employees by using disciplinary action threats, so that fits with your observation about admin during your tenure. Did you try to verify the info James shared with you about the drug issues?"

"No way to do that without inside access to the hospital.

I'm an ex-employee and not welcome to visit or be involved in current issues; I'm also restricted by a Non-disclosure Agreement. I've been assured the NDA will be strictly enforced."

Taryn nodded and considered her options and her cold coffee.

"I can say that James' observations were on target. Sums up what I've seen the past three days, and I mean to get answers to confirm what I've seen and figure what it means. I'm working on accessing into the hospital comps and pharmacy records remotely. Also looking at drug lot number on stock in the OR."

"Lot numbers?"

"Yup and batch numbers. That's how drug shipments and groups are ID'd. You know if James kept any records with that kinda info?"

"No clue. The police confiscated his effects, then sent them on to the family when nothing contributory was found. I only packed up and sent what they didn't take."

"You said you found out about the body yesterday?"

"Bruce Peterson, the chief, is ex-military. He's kept me in the loop since James and I were friends."

"Hospital's a big change from the SEAL teams."

"True, but a reality when I was nursing director and now is that the admin at the hospital controls information to spin it to their advantage."

Taryn nodded her agreement. "When I met Wyatt Cook my first day, he essentially accused James of abandoning his post and job. He also made it clear that since the hospital was paying my agency, he and not the anesthesia group chair, was my direct-report boss. A bad evaluation from top of the pyramid in that type of power structure could have high potential to ruin one's career. Harris, if he had turned up at a later date, would never have had a chance."

"Not surprised, and that's typical of the MO of the previous team as well. Keep in mind, *his* boss was Harry and the anesthesia group; they'd have no reason to wish him ill. Although Harry and the group members would be very concerned with James' findings, nothing he shared about drug reliability issues would have been well received by anyone in authority in the hospital administration."

"Other than me looking at the drugs there now, what other issues are there?"

Charlie shrugged, rising to pace. "Given James' personality and persistence, I think that he stepped on some toes. We need to know who he pissed off and why they decided to silence him."

Taryn petted Maxx absently, now. "I honestly think the only concrete thing I can address are the drug issues."

"No chance you'd also look into what you can find about Dr. Harris?"

Charlie stood in front of the fireplace, facing Taryn.

"Charlie, I know he was your friend, but I don't know the man. I'm also taking my cues from the fact that there's active discouragement and punitive measures for anyone talking about Harris at the hospital."

"But you've got prime access by proximity."

Taryn frowned, and paused before shaking her head."

"If you're an ex-SEAL, and won't touch delving into questions about your friend, I don't see how digging around for answers about James Harris will be good for my professional longevity. A bad evaluation from here won't help me get work down the road. Besides, aren't the police doing an investigation?"

"They are..."

"Let's wait for them. It's a safety issue for me."

Charlie sighed before nodding.

"I understand...and agree. I've had my suspicions, but nothing concrete to base them on until James disappeared. That being said, I'll do all I can to help you."

"I need some extra protection. There've been some assaults of women leaving local bars that the police are keeping quiet."

"Bruce mentioned it. I'll see what I can do to get you a firearm surrogate."

"Excellent." Charlie's phone chimed. He checked it, sending the call to voicemail. "We'll leave it there; I'll contact you tomorrow for the personal security upgrade."

Taryn walked Charlie out, with Maxx trailing them to the door. "So where exactly did they find Dr. Harris?"

Charlie shrugged into his coat before answering. "They found him in a tree-well...still waiting on a Cause of Death."

"So a fall? Or Slide?"

"Maybe. We'll see what the post-mortem shows."

CHAPTER SIX

Thursday Afternoon
Blake

T he real estate office door chimed as it swung open,
interrupting Blake mid-sentence.

"Charlie! *Finally!* This is Mr. Anthony, your four o'clock.
He's here to look at the unit James Harris was in." Charlie
checked his watch, noticing Jenna's blush, the quick flick of
her eyes towards Anthony, and that she upset her coffee; just
five after four.

She snuck a glance at Blake as she began cleaning up the
mess. Blake ignored Jenna as he shook hands with Charlie
and gave him his business card. Charlie watched his usually
poised admin continue to fumble, before looking at Blake
more critically. Dressed in Western business-casual black, he
was a few inches taller than he, with an athletic build and
striking good looks that had a hint of Native American ancestry. His casual words didn't match the chill and intensity in
his pale blue eyes.

"Told you earlier, just Blake's fine, pretty lady. Glad you could make it, Charlie. I'm with Summit Investigations...out of Denver. Checking things for the family of Dr. James Harris."

"That's quick work getting here the day after the family was notified about the body."

"I was already here. Had some questions after reading the police reports. Thought first- hand knowledge would be best. I need to look at the unit Dr. Harris was in."

Charlie was silent as he hung up his coat and looked again at Blake's business card.

"Let's talk in my office...Jenna, thanks for holding down the fort," he said while waving for Blake to precede him. Blake gave Jenna a wink before he swaggered into Charlie's office. Charlie backtracked casually to Jenna's desk, noting that she immediately started to shuffle papers. He dropped Blake's card on her desk and murmured,"Check it," before heading to his office where he closed the door pausing only to pour himself a cup of coffee. He took a seat behind his desk. "Coffee?" he offered Blake, who shook his head.

"Nope...had my caffeine quota for today." He sprawled onto one of Charlie's client chairs, crossing a leg over his knee, his clenched jaw belying his relaxed posture.

Charlie sipped his coffee as he made his way to his chair, unsurprised that Blake forged on before he was seated.

"Any objection to heading over to the unit now? Sooner I get started the better."

Charlie settled himself while taking in the deceptively lazy way Blake lounged in the chair and surveyed the room. He narrowed his eyes as Blake continued.

"I need to sweep the condo inside and out; enough time's wasted; I'd like to get going now."

"And why're you looking for something our police didn't find? That was a comprehensive report."

Blake paused, then drawled, "A real estate agent...with access to a police report on a missing tenant, who's just now turned up dead...interesting." Blake slid forward in his seat as he rested both arms on his legs, his hands fisting, his voice a quiet, barely contained growl. "Goddammit my clients and I are done with you hillbillies...it took three weeks to find Dr. Harris...correction...his body... on a ski mountain that operates seven days a week."

"It's a big mountain...with a significant portion out of bounds."

Blake snorted. "That's a lame ass excuse. Man's gone three weeks without a clue, then turns up frozen like a goddam popsicle in a tree-well. I call the whole situation suspicious. What the fuck has your police department been doing other than coffee and donuts?"

Charlie was silent as he put down his mug, leaned back in his chair and took a long look at Blake, who stared back. Their silence ensued until Charlie's office phone buzzed; Blake sneered and swore silently when he answered it.

"Yes? Good enough." Charlie's lips quirked as he hung up and regarded Blake as he adjusted his jacket when he rose and paced to the window.

"As much as I'd like to waste the rest of my evening arguing with an asshole, this interesting chat will have to wait until we confirm all of your info, Mr. Anthony...or whoever you are. Not traipsing around at dusk with an armed stranger who shows up with threats and an attitude late on a Thursday afternoon."

Blake turned, failing to hide his irritation. "My clients and I need answers."

"Definitely...but those will come after we have your info

confirmed through our...how did you describe it...Hillbilly police department. I'll let you know when they've completed their due diligence, and you can call and make another appointment."

Blake swallowed the first reply that came to mind, then gave a curt nod. "Fine...we'll do it your way. Any idea when we can move forward?"

"Whenever the police are done next week. And Anthony?"

Blake turned, anger still evident in the stiff set of his shoulders and face. "Yeah?"

"Don't even think about leaning on Jenna or that appointment will be pushed to the end of never."

Blake nodded again and left with Steve's prophetic words echoing in his head.

Friday Afternoon
Taryn

"Can I help you with something, Dr. Pirelli?" The pharmacy tech found Taryn in the OR satellite pharmacy. After two days of intermittent canvassing, she finally completed inventory for vial Lot and Batch numbers of commonly used medications in the OR and ICU. After she and Shannon had spoken, the idea to inventory the medications in the dedicated operating room pharmacy satellite took hold, since those were at the center of her issues at the hospital. Unlike most areas of the surgical suite, there were no surveillance cameras in the small outpost, which was located around the corner from the OR. She focused on anesthesia drugs, particularly the medications that had been problematic for her.

"I just needed some extra Propofol for my next case. Hey...," she looked at his badge, "Emmett...any way you can tell me what paperwork I need to complete for the permanent pharmacy records? I got an email this afternoon."

"Not sure...you need to talk to one of the pharmacists in central. I'm just pinch hitting this floor. I'll take you there."

"Good enough...let me grab my stuff and change."

After changing clothes, Taryn found Emmett waiting in the OR lounge, where he immediately motioned for her to follow. Given the politics, she had opted for slacks and boots rather than athletic wear, or even scrubs going to and from work.

"Who are you subbing for?"

"Aurielle...no one's sure how long it will take for her to recover. We're just happy she made it."

"Made it?" They were walking towards the elevator leading to the main pharmacy.

"She's the regular OR/ICU pharmacy tech. She was attacked outside one of the bars near main street on Sunday; she's just out of the ICU today. She's better, but I heard she has a concussion — no memory of who hit her. She's got a long road to recovery."

As the tech chattered on, Taryn mentally checked off the possibilities as they took the elevator down to the basement and main pharmacy. When they arrived, Taryn scoped the physical layout as she completed the required paperwork. Taryn was guarded in her responses, even though the head pharmacist was friendly and helpful.

"Glad I'm all caught up with paperwork; thanks for the tour!" Taryn waived at the head pharmacist and Emmett as she departed, and mentally summarized the visual security measures. Access to central pharmacy was via the usual hospital badge plus a keypad. She had memorized the code that Emmett keyed in to enter. The biggest issue when she gained access over her call weekend would be neutralizing the surveillance cams outside and inside the pharmacy. In addition to a camera at the main pharmacy entrance, others were scattered conspicuously throughout the pharmacy suite and in the two interior, administrative offices.

As she left for home, she mused over her observations and difficulties during the previous week. Now she had to add a pharmacy tech who'd been assaulted to her list of woes. Was the assault by design or just coincidence? There was no way she could get into the patient's chart unless she took care of her in the OR. Snooping beyond that would be a privacy and HIPAA violation and could get her fired. There was no leeway to raise further concerns about the patient related drug issues without drawing attention to herself, and Harry and Michael both had strongly discouraged further involvement from her. All she could do was continue to document drug related issues and hope for the best. The best outcome would be that she never had reason to rely on the password protected file on her laptop that she viewed as a last-resort cover in case shit hit the fan.

Despite the lip service on quality assurance that she got from group decision-makers Harry and Michael, she got the feeling that others in the anesthesia group were being actively discouraged from expressing any concerns about drug potency. Too bad she needed facts rather than feelings to be credible. Her biggest hope for answers lay with Sherry Winger, but between work and her family issues with a sick child, they hadn't been able to connect after their chat in the lounge. Everyone was unfailingly polite, but pointedly quiet about issues clearly affecting them all.

Direct pharmacy access for information was the logical next step she would pursue, along with securing extra physical security.

AFTER SHE COLLECTED MAXX AND RETURNED TO THE condo, Taryn switched into hacker mode. She completed the organizational security schematic of the hospital, locating security cameras, mirrored corner nodes, which also likely contained hidden cameras, and anything she could find on the location of the electronic check in kiosks the hospital security officers logged on their rounds. After brainstorming with Cody, she figured how to reverse engineer the data she needed to complete the work that she had begun on Monday. Now that she had an understanding of physical security within the facility, she should be able to covertly search areas of interest, assuming she could erase electronic evidence of her presence. After debating, she decided to call Cody to serve as her sounding board.

"Great...you're done with work. Whaddaya know about altering security cam and badge access records?"

"Hey, happy Friday to you too...sounds like you're up to your usual poking around."

"I have a good reason...something's up with the drugs here in the operating room."

"What are you trying to do?"

"I need a work-around so I can selectively alter the surveillance data tabulated in the security badge and video logs. Most of the sensitive areas of the hospital are accessed via scanned ID badges, with a second level access by keypad in certain areas. There's also video and possibly audio surveillance. I need to make sure I can erase all evidence in any place I poke into. I've sent you files on what I've done so far."

After some silence, punctuated by typing on the other end of the line, Cody launched into techno-geek speak of how to do exactly what she needed done.

"I'm planning on sneaking in on Sunday when I start call."

"You want me to be your wingman and lookout, or just run interference remotely?"

"Remote should do it. Don't want you seen in the hospital.

"Fair enough. What kinda progress did you make last night?"

"I got access to the hospital badge security registry. I can access the badge data — in and out of the hospital — for each employee." As an MD, Taryn had more unlimited physical access to patient care areas like pharmacy and the operating room than lab techs.

"You planning to use that for surveillance? Of whom?"

"Not sure yet...but it's gotta help with something. I also found that patient related records and data are maintained in a separate section with slightly different security profile than the operational information"

"Great...so you won't have HIPAA privacy issues. You find anything else?"

"I know where on-site pharmacy storage is located and have entry access." Her plan was for Cody to come for a skiing and morale visit on Saturday, and also help her with analysis of the data she planned to get on her Sunday entry into the pharmacy. She was winding up her computer efforts with Cody when her phone rang...Charlie.

"Important call incoming. You on the first flight?"

"Yup."

"See you in the morning." Taryn clicked over to Charlie.

"Well someone's interested in the story behind Dr. Harris."

"What?"

"Waiting to check him out, but a PI claiming to be from Denver is here asking to see James' condo."

"Why and how would someone show up so quickly?"

"Exactly my question."

Taryn paused, still torn about her decision to opt out of matters to do with Harris. "I'm concerned, but still not willing to go out on a limb to dig for info on Harris, Charlie. Cody's coming in for the weekend to ski. Can we plan to meet up and talk about what we do know about the drug issues? Maybe Sunday night? I'm going into Main Pharmacy sometime during the day."

"Do I want to know how you're gonna manage that?"

"Probably not...I can cover my tracks. I'm also planning on contact some people in my network for background info on pharmaceuticals practices."

Charlie sighed. "My opinion of amateurs and civilians on intelligence ops is that what you don't know will get you into trouble."

"This isn't a SEAL level op, Charlie. Even Cody agrees that my plan is sound."

"Best laid plans are frequently derailed. Anyway, always here; call anytime. And I should have your protection hardware issue solved by Sunday."

"Sounds good."

CHAPTER SEVEN

Saturday Morning

"I agree with Charlie. There's more than coincidence between what happened to James Harris and your drug issues, but for now, can we just ski? I've had a shit week."

Ignoring the request, Taryn responded, "So now it's two against one in favor of digging into the Harris disappearance." Taryn considered the ongoing intrigue about Harris and her curiosity about the medication potency issues. She was still not convinced of the connection between the two, but it was becoming more difficult to ignore.

"What about some roommate solidarity?" She finally flicked her free hand in a dismissive motion at Cody's long-suffering look of impatience at her ongoing endless loop analysis of the drug issue. "Fine...let's just ski and have fun. We both need a break."

Cody had given her the rundown on his difficulties with a vendor (bad) and the tangle it had caused with his team (worse), and the very strong possibility that he would have a call to sort it all out happening on Sunday, when her on-call day started. Workday Sunday would come soon enough for both of them.

They were gearing up when Taryn realized that she'd forgotten to pack foot and hand warmers. On her way to the combo pro and retail shop, she became distracted by the antics of a group of tweens near the main lift. Before she knew it, she had run into...something and wound up sitting in the snow.

"What...how?!" Taryn was surprised by the unexpected impact and her abrupt seat in the snow. A large gloved hand attached to a blue, red, and black sleeve reached down, and unceremoniously jerked her to her feet. She looked up, and into a pair of forbidding, icy blue eyes topped by a pair of lowered black brows.

"Why the hell don't you look where you're going?" a deep voice growled. "I sure as hell don't want to run into your ass coming into my line on the mountain. Do us all a favor and keep your eyes front on the mountain, okay doll?"

Blake was more annoyed than hurt by Taryn running into him on his way to the lift. He took in her features. She was gorgeous. Her arresting face boasted a flawless, caramel complexion and sparkling hazel eyes...but unfortunately, she was clueless when it came to her surroundings. She was short; probably around 5' 4", with braids cascading from her multicolor knit cap.

"Excuse me...you were the one walking without direction control."

The man's rudeness and patronizing tone infuriated Taryn, regardless of his smokin' hot looks. No manners and a nasty attitude spoke louder than his pretty face as far as quality of character for her. And who the hell outside of a '50s musical said 'doll' anymore?

"I'd have thought my bright green and pink parka would let you know someone was there ...if you'd only bothered to look."

"Sweetheart, you need an eye exam...seriously."

"And I'm not your sweetheart, you Neanderthal...what rude and inappropriate century are you from?"

"You make a habit of being so rude to people you run over? Too bad your manners don't match the wrapping." He bent down to pick up the skis he had dropped at some point during the collision.

"I didn't do the trampling; that's on you, Big Foot. Might try getting some corrective lenses for your goggles. You can't see worth shit. How's that work for you on the mountain? Ski by Braille? You volunteering to be the next organ donor on the mountain?"

Blake gave a slow blink at the string of insults and checked his knee jerk reaction. "If I didn't think it would get me charged and cited, I could suggest some corrective measures to fix that attitude," Blake ground, closing his eyes and shaking his head as he refocused on the reason he was in Bend. "Look, I don't have the time, energy, or inclination for babysitting some bratty ski bunny, so do yourself a favor and stay out of my way."

The unknown man's attitude, coupled with the frustration of the previous week, pushed all of Taryn's buttons. She scooped up one of his fallen ski poles, ending up toe-to-toe with the current obstacle to her ski day, pointing the end at him, javelin style. "So not the woman for the threats and patronizing, asswipe. You lay one hand on me, I'll rip your nuts out through your mouth. Now back the *hell* up outta my space and leave me alone."

Blake put a choke hold on his temper and mouth before he said or did something that wound him in jail...or resulted in a run-in with the ski pole that Taryn now brandished. He held up his hands...in surrender?

"You win...Princess Venom; I'll eat the blame. God*dam*, you're a piece of work! Hell should freeze over before we meet again. Gimme my gear; fuck off and die." Blake snatched his ski pole as Taryn gaped, then collected the rest of his gear. He had no answer for why or how the woman had managed to get under his skin. And, he was even more incredulous that the idea of charming her and getting her in bed entered his mind...*bad, fucking idea*... He shook his head and shuddered; neither the time nor place for that shit...and stalked toward the main ski lift.

Taryn sputtered as she watched him leave. What the hell was *with* the people in this town? She looked around in amazement and frustration, only to see two lift operators had apparently been there for the whole show and were laughing so hard they had to hold onto each other to remain vertical. Such is life...she would hopefully not run into the ass again.

Now she had another reason to hate the assignment and the city. Two months, two weeks, six days, and counting.

———

"Cody, he ran into me, knocked me down, then acted like it was all my fault!"

"Maybe it was...maybe it was both of you. I think, as usual, you're over-reacting. Sounds like your usual 'cut folks off at the knees on date two' temper tantrum when they don't follow your agenda. Might wanna look at that issue."

Taryn glared at Cody. "That sure as hell wasn't a date. You know, you're a great roommate and wing-person...but you're still a man-ass."

"Shoot me...and call your girlfriends when you want a

whine and bitch about men session. Can we just ski...please?" Cody shook his head before trudging towards the lift. Taryn regarded him with disgust before grabbing her gear and following, after checking that the newest boil on her ass was nowhere to be seen.

After a few warm up blue runs, they went to big bowl land, and Taryn forgot about her collision with the man she now thought of as 'Ski Sasquatch'. She and Cody enjoyed their morning break from reality until they ran into Shannon when they broke for lunch. The Shannon version she and Cody encountered was very different from work Shannon. There with her kids, who were apparently on the ski team, she was now eager to volunteer critical explanatory details about the inner workings of the anesthesia group and the hospital. The short version of the politics centered around an attempt to replace the anesthesia group power structure with someone loyal to admin, namely Michael Downing. Now firmly in R&R mode, Taryn was uninterested with the details of the intrigue, and only focused on having a good time skiing the rest of the day. All of the drama had unfolded shortly before James Harris began work at the hospital. Shannon's summary resonated with Taryn's assessment that someone loyal and tractable was needed as head of the group...but why? Taryn shrugged, resolving to push Shannon for a summary.

"Harry's pretty much in lockstep with Downing now...what changed?"

"Not sure, but five months ago the fifth group member quit, and Harry became a big fan of Dr. Downing."

"I smell a payoff," Cody offered.

"I bet he's right. Let me guess...admin forced the fifth group member to retire, then started in on some other medical group or field?"

"How'd you know?" Shannon was wide-eyed. "Since the start of the year, admin has talked of hiring employed docs to replace the pathologist group."

"Admin/Hospital-based physician conflict patterning 101. Gets down to money, power, and control. It's also why I'm trying to stay clear. It's a no-win situation for me and happening everywhere nationwide, not just in Bend. This is why I like temp jobs; I'm not interested in drama. I don't have the capability to fix the problem that is ultimately at the root of the Harris issue."

The only nagging questions that Taryn envisioned pulling her into a James Harris investigation scenario was what other docs might know about the drug efficacy problems she had experienced...and why was it happening now?

Sunday Morning

A LITTLE BLEARY-EYED FROM A FUN APRÈS-SKI TIME that morphed into Saturday night partying, Taryn felt her coffee kick in just as she paused before turning into the hall to the main pharmacy. Cody was her remote assist, generally running interference and tracking her progress, courtesy of the chip on her key fob. She was gratified when he gave her the 'All Clear' text to let her know that he'd deactivated the camera surveillance in the hall outside, intersecting the area where the main pharmacy was located. He also managed to purge her badge access records that documented entry into the suite. After keying in the access code she'd acquired on Friday, she entered, flipping on a light switch so that she could navigate the workbenches, drug compounding hoods, and the control machines for the satellite medication dispensing kiosks. Rather than risk tripping an incursion alert, Taryn decided that low tech access and copying the relevant central pharmacy inventory information with a USB drive would get her the information she most needed with the smallest chance of detection. As she started to ping Cody for help hacking into the comp, she paused, then flipped the mouse pad over to find the login credentials neatly printed on a Post-It note. She exulted in her good luck and recorded the information so that she and Cody could later alter the computer access records. There was no sense in getting the poor pharmacy tech fired. She located and copied all of the pharmacy inventory data for the hospital for the past year including pharmacy overflow storage.

Next, she logged out and was headed to search the pharmacy director's office when she heard noise in the hallway. She scanned her surroundings for a likely hiding place, before realizing that all of the kneeholes for the computer workstations faced the door. Her heart pounded in her ears as she flipped off the overhead light switch and ran for the furthest corner of the office away from the door. Maybe whoever was entering wouldn't come all the way to the back of the office. She found an unlocked coat armoire on the back wall, slipping in just as the outer door opened and the office lights flicked on. She heard the outer door slam, then tuneless whistling, and the jingling of keys. She peered through the sliver remaining when she pulled the door just short of closed. It was a hospital security guard, apparently on routine rounds and in no hurry as he strolled over to the security verification device on the wall opposite the offices. After logging his presence, the guard did a visual inspection of the exterior office, trying the doors to the inner office and controlled substance safe, before exiting.

Taryn blew a breath of relief. She waited two or three

minutes to insure the guard wasn't returning, before creeping out of the armoire. She used the flashlight function of her phone to navigate to the door, sparing a glance at the computer terminal she had used, which was only then going into sleep mode. She thanked her lucky stars that she hadn't been caught, and that the active computer screen hadn't been noticed.

After some inner debate about the potential value of information she could get from the director's office and computer, Taryn opted for caution. She could break in again if she needed specific access only available from the pharmacy director. As she strode down the corridor to the nearest stairwell to an exit, the raucous peal of her pager caused her to jump and realize that she had been extremely lucky. She silenced the pager and bounded up the stairs, checking for people and cameras before exiting and walking to the side street where she had parked. Taryn slid into her SUV, texting Cody to finish badge access and security cam cleanup, before driving to the nearby coffee shop to answer her page.

"Dr. Pirelli for the Nursing Supervisor." Taryn tapped her fingers on the steering wheel and calmed herself as she watched the traffic outside the shop and waited for the Nursing Supervisor to pick up.

"Hi doc...we have an appendectomy booked for Dr. Sellars. She wants to start in an hour."

"I'll come in."

TARYN HAD ONE ADDITIONAL EMERGENCY CASE ON CALL that afternoon, after which she hurried home to work on the information she had garnered. Cody and Maxx were having a rousing game of fetch when she pulled into the condo garage.

When she walked out to the yard, Maxx trotted over and gave his usual paws-on-the-shoulder, enthusiastic welcome, which resulted in her plopping into the snow. Taryn shook her head as Cody snickered when he came over to the garage.

"File the comparisons to yesterday in the screw you bin; don't wanna hear it. Let's get to work on the info I copied."

"Done," Cody laughed, as he hauled Taryn up, helping her brush snow from Maxx's coat before the three of them trudged up the stairs and through the mudroom to Cody's makeshift data center at the kitchen island.

"I covered your tracks with the security cams and badge access plates. Unless you did something stupid..."

"As if..." Taryn breathed a sigh of relief as she shook her braids free of the twist she had put them in for work.

"Well, you're set." Cody tilted his laptop toward her.

"Oh yeah... you need to wipe the record of me using that comp in pharmacy."

"Terminal number?"

"Excuse me?"

"The number of the comp...I need the terminal number to wipe the log in."

"Umm...can't you just get rid of it?"

Cody sighed as he crossed his arms. "I can only wipe access when I know the name of the station or terminal. Maybe I can finesse it...how many comps in the whole office? Do you think anyone was or will be in central pharmacy today?"

Taryn poured them both a glass of wine and gave Maxx a bone before pulling out her own computer with a frown. "Six...no seven comps total in the office. Change of shift's the only time there was likely anyone except the security guard in there..."

"Security guard?"

"Yeah, he came by on rounds when I was in there...scared me to death...I hid, but it was close."

Cody swore as he checked his computer. "Shit...totally forgot to look for a weekend rounds schedule for security."

"Which is actually only the Sunday schedule since Saturdays are usually just another clinical day. Yeah, we...I was lucky. Onward...I'll copy this drive, then let you do the same. How long before you take care of access and security cam erasure?"

"Couple minutes...I've located the pharmacy comps."

The next minutes were filled with the sound of keystrokes and Maxx chewing his chew bone.

"I'm analyzing quarterly totals of drug usage, stock on hand, etc. Nothing seems out of line, but I'd have to see comparable data to say that for sure."

"I'll help you with previous year info once I'm done erasing that login. Any records of defective drug reports?"

"Absolutely nothing, other than the rare allergic reaction."

"Did you file anything from last week?"

"Yes, but it was through Dr. Downing, and the quality assurance, Q/A, process."

"Can we get at Q/A files?

"Not through the hospital mainframe...those are kept separately. Any reports are submitted in each departmental office. I'll have to get into the anesthesia office and chat with our admin on Monday. That's gotta be easier than getting into the hospital's central Q/A office. For now, I'll enter drug data and lot numbers in the spreadsheet I started. That should show us if there's a pattern of certain drug lots with adverse reactions."

"Be nice if we had something...anything from when James Harris was here."

"I agree...but we don't, so we'll just have to work with what we have." Cody leaned back in his chair before rising to pace and run his hands through his hair.

"This whole thing's a crapshoot, T. You're not gonna figure out what's going on without more info...and a whole lotta luck."

"Says the gambling fail. I'm anesthesia good at rapid critical analysis in addition to being lucky. I say the critical issue is that we need to see what happens with the reports I filed last week. That will give me an idea of process, and how Harris' info was likely filed. Get back to work; I really need a hand here."

Cody rolled his eyes, but dropped back into his seat to continue working. For the next two hours, they reviewed the data from pharmacy that Taryn had obtained, focusing on tabulating drug makers and usage of the various medication classifications. Taryn checked the time after finishing everything she'd planned to get done. "We're due at Charlie's in thirty; I'll help you finish up after we get back. I need my pepper spray upgrade, a break...and food."

―――――――――

"Charlie this collapsible walking stick is the perfect solution!"

Charlie's personal security upgrade came in the form of a collapsible, weighted walking stick, which could be extended at both ends and used like a Japanese Bo staff.

"When you told me you had some martial arts training, I figured this was a first stop for an enhanced security measure. Ever use one of these?"

"Not other than the basic lessons and intro with sensei"

"I think you're a natural."

After she got a feel for its weight with the ends at full extension, Taryn spun the stick with increasing skill in Charlie's garage as he and Cody watched.

"Glad it will work out...why don't we head in for dinner? I've got some ideas how to get more info on James' disappearance."

Taryn sighed in resignation as she and Cody followed Charlie upstairs into the kitchen; the discussion would be the obvious price for dinner and her new device. She still wanted to keep her distance from the Harris affair.

"Why do you keep pushing me to look into the James Harris issue? Given what's happening at the hospital, I'm really not interested. There are other issues here. Did I mention that the woman assaulted last week was one of the pharmacy techs who worked the operating room satellite?"

Charlie was placing steaks on the indoor range grill, while Taryn and Cody sat at the kitchen bar and enjoyed the wine he had poured. "What?" Charlie looked at Cody, who shrugged, and let Taryn explain.

"People with an operating room and pharmacy connection like James...and this tech are having bad outcomes. This. Is. A. Police. Issue."

Charlie paused in turning the steaks to look first at Taryn, then Cody. "What if I get info proving that James being in that tree-well wasn't an accident?"

"What, he had a Go-Pro?" The only way she would get roped into this goose chase would be with concrete evidence, that she was sure Charlie didn't have.

"No...just let me get back to you."

Taryn sighed as she spun her wine glass rather than drinking, looking at Cody as he studied his drink. "What's on your mind, Cody?"

"I know you and Harris were tight, Charlie, but with

more people getting hurt, I'm leaning toward none of this being Taryn's issue. Let's figure a way to get what you need without involving her."

"No proof this pharmacy tech is connected to Harris... but let's say it is. If I can make the connection will you two change your minds?"

"That's a big if." Cody finished his wine, then reached for the bottle to top off everyone's glass, and refill his own.

"Give me until Wednesday before you write it off...I should have what we need by then." Charlie smiled as he checked his phone when the new email chime sounded. Cody shrugged when Taryn looked at him. She frowned and considered the previous week at work.

"Who's this person from Denver asking questions about James? How does he fit in?" Taryn was convinced that there was no way Charlie could produce the proof she needed.

Charlie gave a half smile. "I'm working on that too...and it may be the just the thing I need to convince you."

"Show me and I'll decide. Till then, label me from Missouri." Taryn winked at Charlie.

"Any chance Charlie's right and Harris discovered something really big?" Cody and Taryn continued to debate as Taryn drove back to her condo after dinner. Cody spun his phone, his eyes unfocused as he considered what they had just learned.

"Pharmaceutical sales are huge business. I just find it hard to believe that Bend is at the center of some huge scheme or operation." Taryn frowned, more than a little annoyed that the unfounded speculation had outlasted dinner.

"Have you done any research at all on the chain the hospital is part of?

"Honestly no. It's not like I've had idle hours and easy patients."

"Whining, T. My info shows that it's a small hospital that's part of a multi-state, corporate chain. Corporate buying and contracts for a chain would potentially mean billion-dollar, pharmaceutical contracts for in-network hospitals. First rule of war; know your enemy."

"Not at war, and I have no enemies." Taryn recalled her conversation with Shannon as she made a left turn. "You think James found something that big?"

"Maybe...What if...Harris figured out the patient issues were due to faulty drugs...and someone in administration found out?"

Taryn mused about what she knew about the cost of trade name meds versus generics, and also about the culture at the Bend hospital. "High cost is why some patients opt to purchase the medications out of the country."

Taryn thought of the parallels with consumer goods. Sometimes people willingly bought knock-offs. Sometimes they paid top dollar only to learn they had been duped. "I honestly don't believe that's what happening here."

"Say the drugs you've been using are counterfeit. And someone at the hospital is involved in covering it up, or knowingly acquiring defective product." Taryn had to give it to Cody that he always considered all angles of a problem completely.

"Counterfeit, as incorrectly made or poorly functional?" Co had a considering look on his face.

Taryn shook her head. "That would be hard to disguise and harder still to prove."

"Might explain your problems last week. Someone in the

hospital *has* to know there are issues." Cody might have been the original skeptic, but what he was proposing made perfect sense. Suddenly, Harry's silencing of dissent within the department looked more sinister. Taryn stared at Cody as she thought over all that she knew. "That's strange enough that it might actually be true."

CHAPTER EIGHT

Monday Morning

"Everything looks to be in order...Mr. Anthony...may I call you Blake?" The clerk in central processing assigned to check the implants and instruments he was bringing for use in the OR spent more time with hair flips and posing than reviewing his instruments and implants... but, whatever.

"Absolutely, Sheila." Blake winked, and thanked God for name tags. Blake suppressed his smirk at the excited blush of the clerk, whose name he'd forgotten within seconds of saying it. This was going to be easy. The formalities were typical for in-processing of the instruments used to place the high-performance neuro and orthopedic M&H implants currently in use at the facility, but it seemed he could use flattery and flirting to get faster results. Even given that his admin had submitted an itemized inventory the week before, Sheila had skipped several checks in the normal inspection process. Not good for quality, but he'd take the shortcuts he received. The equipment was all there and would be re-sterilized.

"Hey sunshine, where's a good place to hang out in this town? On a business trip, but wouldn't mind a little fun, little action. Where's a good place?"

"You've been having drug quality issues for how long? Well, I've been working locums here and there and... I'm with a hospital that's part of a chain now." It was late morning Monday, and one of Taryn's residency mentors was finishing her crash course on the realities of the drug shortages that many of her anesthesia colleagues had been experiencing for months.

"At least a year. Can't believe you hadn't noticed. Not like you to be so unobservant." Taryn was embarrassed to admit that she hadn't paid much attention to trends, issues, and the infrastructure of anesthesia practice for months. Too many life events, trips, and parties had taken priority. Being a pinch hitter with multiple groups was great for control, autonomy, and life, but not so much for continuity with specialty and practice specific issues. After dropping Cody at the airport that morning, she spent the balance of her day doing research before being on call. The call to her mentor from residency was confirming all that she found, and giving her additional issues to worry over.

"Taryn, it's the market, but docs and patients are the ones caught in the middle. Drug goes off patent, multiple companies can now manufacture generic versions of the drug with the companies that can make the drug most cheaply being the ones to generate the largest profit margins. If you can't cover costs and make a profit, why bother? Suppliers drop the product, which is now in shortage and subject to spiraling cost to purchasers. We still have to get the patients asleep, take care of them, *and* get the same results regardless of the drug shortages."

"There's got to be diversification in the market. Other companies..."

"There are no 'back up' or contingency drug manufacturing facilities when one goes down. There's only indefinite back order, and we have to suck it up and perform. The FDA does inspections, but pharma companies are all privately run; government's into assuring compliance with regulations not helping clinical facilities deal with product shortages."

After Taryn ended her reality check phone call to her mentor, her head was swimming with the possible implications of these facts and how they might relate to the speculations that she and Cody had made on Sunday. How could she dig deeper to figure out what was going on without arousing unwanted attention?

───────────

TARYN WAS WALKING MAXX AFTER LUNCH WHEN HER phone rang. It was a local number, but still early for any work responsibilities.

"Hey Taryn? Mike Downing. I've got a non-clinical day. Do you have time to meet for coffee?"

"Sure...just walking my dog before heading to work, but..."

"There's a place close to the hospital." He proceeded to give her the address to the coffee shop where she had met Shannon. "Meet me there in thirty?"

"Well...sure." Maxx and Taryn headed back to the condo,

and she tried not to worry or over-think as she got herself ready and dropped Maxx at daycare.

MICHAEL WAVED AT TARYN FROM HIS TABLE AT THE BACK of the shop. She waved back, joining him after she collected her drink.

"Hey Michael, what's up?"

"I'm fine, Taryn...question is, how are you? Are you settling in better at work? I see that you submitted a case for quality review. Everything seems to be done correctly; just wanted to hear from you what actually happened."

Taryn felt her pulse rate rise and her hands get clammy as she glanced over her shoulder at the press of customers in the café. She gave a low-voiced summation of the case in question. Michael nodded as she related the events surrounding the case, his face remaining blank. After she finished, he sipped his drink thoughtfully.

"Sounds like an appropriate response, and a legit instance of a medication problem. However, I'm going to ask you to let me handle this internally as well as address any issues with the pharmacy. I'm aware that it's a non-standard approach, but as a temp, you need to trust that I have both your interest and the department's as my primary concern."

"But what about other patients who might have the same issues? Do the rest of the docs in the department know what's going on? Is Harry..."

"Let me worry about taking this to Harry, and the rest of the group, hmm? We'll follow our facility protocol."

"How's it protocol to take this out of the quality assess-ment process, and *not* notify other docs who might use the same drug? The process is there to protect all of us...."

Without warning, Michael's bland demeanor changed. "Taryn, shut up and drop it." He leaned forward, nose-to-nose with Taryn, his physical menace reflecting his words. "If you want to have any type of longevity here, do yourself a favor, keep your goddam mouth shut and stay out of what doesn't concern you."

The loud rumble as he shoved the chair back punctuated his words. Without further discussion, he ended the meeting and shouldered his way through the line of customers waiting to order. Taryn was left speechless and stuck with disposing of his coffee and hers. Now how should she proceed? Was there anyone else at the hospital who could help her, or shared her concerns about the patients?

As she struggled with answers on how to deal with Michael Downing and his edicts, Taryn found an unexpected envelope with her name on it taped to the window of the surgery control office when she arrived for her call shift. She ripped it open with a frown; it was a new badge with instructions to return the old one to security.

"Glad I've run into you, Dr. Pirelli. Can we have a chat?" Harry motioned her into the empty operating room control desk and closed the door. "Any reason you were down in the main pharmacy on Friday?"

Taryn blinked. "Um...I had to complete some paperwork for controlled substance handling."

"That's not an usual area for folks in our department to be in. They could have sent your paperwork here to be completed; the trip there was unnecessary. It will be best moving forward if you restrict your movements to the operating room, intensive care, and related support areas. Oh, and the doctor's lounge is fine, of course. But, be aware that your movements within the hospital are logged and tracked. Further deviation from these rules and restrictions will result in your referral to administration for disciplinary action." Harry checked his watch then headed for the door.

"Disciplinary action? For what? Is this some new rule for everyone in the department?" Taryn called after him.

Harry paused with his hand on the door. "Do your job and stay in the peri-operative areas. What you do impacts our group. First and last warning."

Taryn struggled to regain her composure and place herself in a patient care mindset as people began to filter back into the control desk. Other than a few stilted greetings, the warmth and easy camaraderie of the previous week had vanished.

TARYN WAS DEEP IN THOUGHT WHEN SHE REACHED THE door to the operating room lounge just as it was opened by someone exiting. She automatically shifted right to avoid colliding, but found herself toe-to-toe with the person exiting. Her sheepish smile gave way to a frown.

"You?! FML! What the hell are *you* doing here?"

"Supposedly working, but looks like we're dancing... fancy meeting you here. What's up, Sugar?" Ski Sasquatch was as charming today as he had been disagreeable on Saturday. The verbally offensive address was unfortunately exactly the same.

"You know, you're marginally civil today, but just as big of an ass today as you were on Saturday," Taryn hissed. "Most people view being addressed as 'sugar' in the workplace as unwelcome familiarity. I'm with the majority; I'm working, and you're out of order. Your tone, word choice, and attitude are unacceptable."

"Ah, sorry...Doc...," He flicked a glance at her badge, "Pirelli...no insult intended...my bad...we're probably too casual at corporate in Denver; small team mentality still. Remembered you from Saturday, and kinda...anyway, it's Blake; I'm doing a site visit for one of my reps' accounts. No idea we were going to be work colleagues. Saturday's collision, same as today's, is all my bad. I was in a bad mood. Please accept my apologies for my rudeness."

Taryn relaxed and nodded stiffly, then he ruined his good PR when he quirked a smile and whispered, "But you're definitely just as hot as you were Saturday." Taryn counted to ten and choked off the insult begging to tumble out. This was work, even if he was being a jerk. Hopefully, she could avoid him.

Well...," she said, sneaking a look at his badge, "*Mr. Anthony*, I have neither time nor energy to pursue workplace relationships with the situationally nasty, so why don't we forget the past few minutes...and Saturday, and call it even. I'm having a tough day."

"Fair enough...Doc, fair enough. Take it easy, and good luck with your day!" Taryn got even more annoyed when the human bulldozer winked and gave her a lopsided smile as he moved aside. She really shouldn't be paying attention to the fact that the man had a great smile, shaking her head as she stopped into the locker room. More drama would not make her life better. Blake watched Taryn leave, then smiled as he sauntered to the OR Main desk.

"Stacy...any chance you can do me a favor?" The unit secretary looked up with a smile, and fluttering eyelashes.

"NICE WAKE-UP, DOC. CAN I HELP YOU GET THE PATIENT into recovery?" Taryn gave a shrug and a grudging, "Thanks," as Blake helped the circulating nurse push the bed of the portly patient into the recovery room.

Blake had been the orthopedic rep for her first case. Despite her negative bias against him, Blake had been appropriate, helpful, and professional. No inappropriate banter with the surgeon at the expense of the otherwise all-female OR team. Helpful when needed, including opening items for the scrub tech when the circulator had been busy. Taryn snuck a few glances at him chatting with the recovery room charge nurse as she finished charting. Maybe she'd just gotten off to a bad start with the man. Or, could it be that she was making excuses for everyone and everything in this town?

Her last case was general surgery, and no Blake, but with the same nursing team from the previous case. She rolled her eyes at the post anesthesia induction conversation, which centered on musing about Blake's marital status and personal life. The big draw was the Happy Hour that he and his company were apparently sponsoring at one of the local bars. Taryn saw it as either bribery or trolling. Likely the man played the game with every woman he met, in every city he travelled to. Luckily due to her being on call, she would be spared a command performance of what she had already witnessed. Taryn blocked out the conversation, focused on her patient, and strategies to survive the job posting in light of the reprimands she had received. Much as she wanted to disregard Charlie's insistence that Harris' disappearance and the current adverse drug reactions were related, her recent experiences seemed to tie both tightly together. So how would she handle things?

BLAKE WATCHED THE VERY HOT, BUT PRICKLY WOMAN from Saturday leave the operating room. The intriguing Dr. Pirelli had been as quiet in the OR as she had been fiery outside of it. He was biased toward the hot-tempered version, but getting a taste of that fire would take some extra time, investigation, and effort. Nothing he was doing in town would preclude some more off work diversions and a challenge. He returned his attention to whatever the head nurse was saying, giving a winning smile as he agreed with her.

"Absolutely. I'll follow all of your procedures for outside equipment and implants; no worries."

"Glad you understand...our protocol may be a bit different than what you have seen at other facilities."

"I'll save you a step and call central myself to make sure they're processing the trays as you've instructed." After getting the number, he gave the nurse another disarming smile and made the appropriate call.

After the nurse was off to the recovery room and out of sight, he slid over to the Stacy, the unit secretary's desktop, and logged in, using the logon gleaned after an ego stroking and info gathering session earlier. He inserted a USB drive and entered the command mode of the computer, glancing around to ensure the hall was still empty as his fingers flew over the keyboard, submitting data and code for the access he needed. The information he entered resulted in a briefly blank screen, then a scroll of information as the USB drive began to blink. He snapped off his mask before grabbing his briefcase and heading to the men's locker room to change.

The charge nurse returned from recovery and went out of the surgery suite without returning to the main desk where the blinking light of the still-active USB drive pulsed. When Blake returned from changing, he retrieved his now inactive USB drive, and with a few more keystrokes and commands, logged the computer to the off mode and erased the last few minutes from its history, hoping that he hadn't tripped any mainframe flags. He whistled as he left the OR, his mind on other topics and diversions when his phone rang.

"Yes Charlie." He pushed the down button on the elevator as he checked the time. "Absolutely... I can meet in fifteen. Which bar? Got it."

<hr>

"GLAD MY INFO CHECKED OUT, BUT I WAS UNDER THE impression that I'd have to go through Jenna and your protocol hoops to get another appointment with you." Blake took a seat and gave his drink order to the bartender. Charlie was only halfway through his own and shook his head on the offer of a second.

"I decided to handle things myself. Mind taking a look at this?" Charlie asked as he handed a folder to Blake. Blake thumbed through the pages, his expression stoic as he returned the documents to the folder. He mulled over the best way to frame his next statement, taking a sip after the bartender slid him his drink.

"Look, there's an explanation..."

"Really Blake - or whatever the fuck your name is. Which are you? PI, equipment rep...none of the above?"

"My *middle* name is Anthony. Blake's definitely the first."

"So name shuffling too. Given that the number you gave me tracks to a company called M&H Healthtech, and whoever is answering phones there is obviously in on whatever it is that you're doing, I'm guessing that there's more truth somewhere in that pile of shit you've been shoveling."

Blake swirled his drink before he selected his reply. "Like I said, I can explain, but I'd still rather keep this as quiet as possible. First, I'm not doing anything illegal. Gun's registered, and I *am* connected to M&H."

"If you're looking for discrete and confidential, this isn't the place." Charlie shook his head. "I still don't know if I trust a goddamn word you say, given everything you've lied about."

"And I was covering my ass; I've got no real reason to trust your version of the supposed facts, either. You live here; you could be part of the problem," snapped Blake.

Charlie pushed his glass around the table, remaining silent. Finally, he sighed and shrugged. "James Harris was a friend. I *did* get some info that I may be willing to share, but I sure as shit want to be sure about who I'm sharing it with. I need some truth."

Blake ran a hand through his hair before nodding. "Fair enough...and I need help...and someone here I can trust. You're not just a real estate agent. Truce?" Charlie nodded as he rose, throwing several bills on the table. "I'll meet you at my office," said Charlie curtly, then paused. "For the record, consider yourself lucky that I've mellowed in my old age." Charlie rapped his knuckles on the table as he left Blake wondering just who he'd managed to tangle with.

CHAPTER NINE

Blake

"I get that you and your friend, Steve, think you can manipulate things and get answers, but you're both in over your head. You need to wait until I've had my expert take a look at the journal and review what we have so far." Blake swore as he ran his hands through his hair and started pacing...again. They had ended up in Charlie's office for Blake's explanation, and for Charlie to peruse his data.

"And how long will it be before you get this so-called expert in to look at the journals?" Charlie looked at the journal and documents that Blake had brought, which were now spread over his desk. They represented the first hard evidence that James Harris had found something irregular going on at the hospital concerning pharmaceuticals. He heard the whole tale of Steve Harris and Blake's daring, but poorly thought out plan of Blake going undercover in the hospital.

"Expert's on the way." The entrance alarm chimed.

"Make that here." Charlie went to the outer office, coming back with Taryn in tow. She stopped in the doorway as a number of expressions chased across her face.

"*You!* Charlie, you know this cretin? He's Anthony, the new M&H equipment rep; why the hell is he here?"

"*Myers* is co-owner of M&H Healthtech. James Harris' brother is the other owner, and why Blake is here. Why don't you have a seat; I'll fill you in."

After getting the details of the plan and reasoning, along with Blake's full name, Blake *Anthony* Myers, Taryn crossed her arms and leaned against the office door, fuming. She rolled her eyes and shrugged as she looked at the second client seat next to Blake.

"Whatever...you deal with him," Taryn declared. "I see no reason to sit down since I'm not planning on being here long. What's such an emergency for me to see that it couldn't wait the night?"

"No need for company manners, Charlie; I'm not impressed with the good doctor here." Blake and Taryn began to argue as Charlie cursed under his breath, and the verbal jousting picked up steam.

"Both of you...shut it. She's the anesthesiology expert Blake, so deal." Charlie waved at the papers spread over his desk. "Who better to give an impression about what you have here than someone in the same field as James?"

Taryn rolled her eyes as she huffed. "This is about Harris? Again?"

Trying to keep the peace, Charlie responded, "This is about connections...look, just tell me what you think of the information here."

Taryn looked at Charlie then Blake, then muffled a curse before sliding into Charlie's chair to read the documents covering the desk. Irritation morphed into amazement as she read. "Where did you get these? Do you know what this looks like?"

"You tell us...I believe that's the missing link between what you told me about your last week at work and James," answered Charlie.

Blake concurred, "Steve and I've looked over all that stuff...other than names and dates, there's no deciphering it."

"That's because neither of you is an anesthesiologist...and why you're in over your head. This looks exactly like the info I've been recording about days, dates, and lot numbers. With what I see here, James has a two-week record of dates, drugs and issues, and a reference to a computer with more info. Where's the computer?"

She looked at Blake, who shrugged and grimaced. "No idea. He mailed us these records the week he disappeared. I got no leads on where he'd even hide a computer, and I've been looking a week."

Taryn rifled through the journal, finding pages of narrative in addition to the drug identifying data. She then leaned back as she speculated. "Finding that computer is gonna be key...as well as having a look at whatever gear James brought with him."

"Police sent the effects to the family some time ago." Blake shook his head. "We thought about that and combed through everything. Nothing there but clothes, ski gear... routine stuff, and nothing remarkable."

"Charlie, any chance I can look at the place James stayed?" Taryn asked.

"Does this mean you're in?"

"Why do you think you'd find something that everyone else missed?" Blake and Charlie spoke simultaneously, Blake shrugging. "I may be biased, but I can't see the doc here coming through on anything significant."

"You mean now you trust our 'hillbilly police force?' Make up your mind, Blake, they either know what they're doing, or they don't. And Taryn's here because she's got insider access and the knowledge of being an anesthesiologist, like James."

Taryn smirked as she cast a dismissive glance at Blake. "Just like my ex, I think he's too blinded by me being a woman to see things clearly...especially if I'm right. If I'm in this, I'm taking point. I've got the access and expertise..."

"I work at the hospital now, too."

"I've got the magic MD key, Sherlock. Despite the site restrictions, I'm in a better position, and have better manners, than Mr. Personality here."

"What site restrictions?" Charlie inquired.

Taryn filled Charlie and Blake in on the newest developments with her physical access at the hospital.

Blake nodded, "You've either pissed someone off or alerted someone who's trying to keep a lid on things."

"On what?

"There's the million-dollar question. Why don't you both meet me at the condo at 10?" Charlie scribbled an address on two scraps of paper and gave one to Taryn and one to Blake. Taryn looked at the paper, then Charlie before shrugging. "I'm not doing anything anyway...and I'd like to take a look at the place. See you tomorrow." She trudged out without looking at Blake, who silently tracked her progress.

"What is it with you two?" Charlie started gathering the documents and journals that Blake had brought, placing all of the information back into the briefcase that Blake brought them in.

"Long story...and a couple collisions. You wanna keep those documents or should I?" Charlie paused as he considered options. "I'll keep them...I've got a safe at home. We've done all we can here."

Blake nodded as they geared up, continuing to chat as they walked to the door of the office. After Charlie locked the door and set the alarm, the men parted to their respective vehicles, which were the last in the lot. A few minutes after they left, a car across the street, in the dark island between street lights, turned on its lights and drove away.

TARYN MULLED OVER THE DAY, ESPECIALLY HER unexpected meeting with Charlie and Blake, of all people. Against her will, she was being roped into the Harris situation, which admittedly appeared to tie together the issue with the abnormal drug reactions. Maxx shoved his nose into her shoulder from the backseat, distracting her from her thoughts, and making her even happier that she had been able to bring him on assignment with her. As she drove into the garage of the condo, she decided to save her problems for the next day and try to have a peaceful rest of her evening. Just as she and Maxx were settling in for the evening her pager went off, and she fumbled for her phone as she silenced it.

"Dr. Pirelli... I'll be right there."

Tuesday Morning

TARYN PULLED HER VEHICLE TO A STOP BEHIND Charlie's pickup, and what must have been Blake's rental SUV. She let Maxx out of the back seat, slipping his leash into her pocket as he ran to sniff the surroundings, and leave his mark. She called to him as she trudged to the front door of the condo James had rented and rang the bell.

"Little late aren't you, doc?"

Before Taryn could reply, Maxx ran up and did his usual 'sniff the human' character inspection of Blake, surprising her when he wagged his tail, gave Blake a head butt, and leaned into him.

Blake grinned, and obliged him with pats and a head rub. "Great dog...how old is he?" He stopped as he noticed Taryn's frown. "Surprised? I'm not as bad as you seem to think."

Before Taryn could reply, Charlie came to the door.

"Hi Charlie...I worked late last night...or this morning."

"Figures...Blake and I just went through the upstairs... totally clean."

Taryn looked around. The condo layout was similar to hers. "Mind if I check the garage? Is it off the kitchen like in my unit?"

"Yup."

Taryn pulled out the leash, and clipped it to Maxx's collar, and handed the end to Charlie, after giving Maxx a firm 'Stay'.

She turned on the light over the stairway that led down to the garage, surprised when both the light over the stairs and the garage light went out as she stepped on the last step, leaving only the light coming in through the windows of the garage door. Taryn fumbled for her phone to activate the flashlight function. She shined the light on the bulb over the stairs and in the main garage area. Both bulbs appeared to be intact. There hadn't been a pop to indicate that either bulb had blown. Besides, it was beyond belief that both bulbs would blow at the same time.

Taryn went back up the stairs, and both lights came back

on. She looked at the bottom stair, stepping cautiously on it again; both lights went off. She dashed back upstairs to open the door to the mudroom.

"Hey you two...come on down. Something's up with this light."

Charlie left Maxx in the mudroom before joining Blake on the stairs. "What...you scared of the dark?"

"Not hardly, but....," she walked back down the stairs, ready with the flashlight function on her phone when both garage lights went out as she stepped on the bottom step. Charlie swore, and fumbled for his phone to activate the flashlight function, as did Blake since the light streaming through the garage windows wasn't adequate for a detailed evaluation.

"I'm guessing this wasn't a special feature for this unit... and that no one came down the stairs during the police investigation." Blake peered closely at the bottom stair, as Charlie put in a call to the police.

"Pretty sure they just opened the garage door and the back door." Charlie put his phone on speaker as he answered Taryn; he was on hold.

"Back door?"

"This unit has a back door direct from the garage into the back yard...the original owner had it put in." Taryn gestured toward the steps with the laser pointer function of her phone.

"Someone installed a pressure switch on this step, that looks like the others. Look...there's a seam on the step and wires running up to the switch at the bottom of the stairs... which I'm assuming control both lights just like the switch up top?" Charlie looked at the wires leading from the wall side of the bottom step up to the light switch, then disconnected the call.

"Yes...the switches control the same lights...that's a lot of work and premeditation."

"And knowing exactly when to be here." Charlie nodded at Blake. Charlie retuned his focus to his call, which had finally connected.

"Police are coming. Don't disturb anything else." Charlie hit the garage opener, flooding the garage with the light.

Blake took some pictures of the steps as Taryn continued to explore the area between the stairs and the back door, finally crouching down to look at the last wooden support for the stairs. "Anyone know if James Harris was a smoker?"

"Not that I ever saw. And I don't allow smoking in any of the units."

Blake joined Taryn at the back of the stairs. "I've known James for years...he didn't smoke."

"This looks awfully like a cigarette butt." Taryn pointed to a white cylinder with blue metallic lines at one end, wedged between the floor and the inside of the last support for the stairs. Charlie joined them and shone a light under the space under the stairs; empty and bare. Blake stood up carefully, edging under the stairs. "Lot of room under here Charlie"

"I agree...don't touch anything under the stairs. Police are here." A cruiser pulled into the drive, and two men got out. Charlie walked to greet them. "Chris...Bruce...What's important enough to bring both of you out?"

"We just got the results of the second post mortem back."

"What second post? Blake and Taryn had joined them.

"Bruce this is Dr. Pirelli and Blake Myers...had you check him out last week. Taryn, Blake, this is Bruce Peterson; he's Chief here at the PD. Chris works Homicide."

Taryn and Blake shook hands with both officers.

"You have someone *local* do the redo post?" Taryn raised her eyebrows.

"FBI." Charlie shrugged. "Ex-military, but still got the contacts."

"Why another pathologist? Just duplicates the efforts." Blake inquired.

"Blake, loyalties matter; in this case those of a hospital-employed and loyal pathologist."

"FBI pathologist thinks that no way are all the hand small bone fractures consistent with a fall into a tree well. This wasn't a skiing accident. We're changing COD to 'Suspicious.' Trick will be keeping any new investigation quiet, so that everyone's guard is down."

"Like someone at the hospital." Taryn shook her head as all evidence pointed toward her deeper involvement in determining what had happened to Harris and why.

"And whoever else is involved." Blake was still convinced that the scope and complexity of problems pointed towards a larger conspiracy and involvement than just people at the hospital

"Charlie, mind if I try the condo key in this lock?" Taryn was hovering by the door into the back yard. The outside knob still showed smears of fingerprint dust, and the yellow crime scene tape still decorated the doorframe.

Charlie shook his head. "You can, but I key all the exterior locks in each unit with the same tumblers."

"Humor me." Charlie handed the condo keys to Taryn, who ducked under the crime scene tape, pulling the door closed as she stepped into the back yard. Charlie opened the door to her knock.

"Key doesn't work. Someone else has a key to this place."

"Easy enough to replace these type locks."

"Easy to pick, too." Both Blake and Charlie gave Taryn a

wide-eyed look, as she shrugged. "I have my odd non-doctor talents that I don't actually advertise. So now I'm convinced that Harris ties into whatever is going on at the hospital. What's next?"

"For you? Nothing. This is now an official investigation into a presumed murder. No amateur input needed." The chief and officer conferred with Charlie before leaving.

Taryn shook her head. "Nah, it's time for me to get started. First off, I gotta figure who's hospital employed among the docs."

"How exactly are you going to do that?" Blake's glance at Taryn was assessing as Charlie hid his smile. "You obviously haven't gotten very far into your investigation at the hospital." Blake pulled out his own keys, with a USB drive attached.

"Think again, Sugar." Taryn looked at Blake, incredulous that he had tried something so risky without backup or research into the situation. Recklessness would get him, and her, fired.

CHAPTER TEN

Tuesday Late Morning

"Hey...It's Taryn. Any way I could see what you got when you scanned the hospital comps? I'm having more trouble than I thought getting back in. Maybe meet later tonight? I know you're working now."

After Taryn had unexpected difficulty accessing the files in the hospital mainframe relevant to personnel and medical staff, she realized her need for the information surpassed her grudge against the man who might be able to help her. When she exhausted her go to options for access, she decided to swallow her pride and get help from Blake. Taryn stored her computer in her car, thanking the universe for her temporary reprieve from another Blake encounter. She took Maxx for a mid-afternoon walk to clear her head before dropping him at daycare and heading to work.

"IF YOU CAN'T GIVE ME A CLEAR JUSTIFICATION FOR THE name discrepancy, I'm afraid I'll have to revoke your credentials, and reconsider allowing your company to market and place their product in this facility. Of course, this will also mean that I'll be forced to forward a contract cancellation recommendation to corporate for other hospitals who maybe using your products." Wyatt Cook leaned back in his chair at the conference table in the administration suite, documents spread before him. Blake smiled slightly as he stood before Cook.

"Easy explanation, Wyatt..."

"Mr. Cook. Please enlighten me, Blake...and have a look at the information on the M&H website, which corroborates everything I've said about the name discrepancy." He spun a laptop around to face Blake, the biographical material about the company's owners displayed. "The M&H website lists a Blake Myers as head of research. No picture, but the bio fits you and what I've seen of your credentials. Steve Harris is the other co-owner...which would make him James Harris' brother, correct?"

"Historically, both my business partner and I do site and facility checks in person to assure that our customers are happy, and that our reps are performing as expected. I choose not to use a name associated with the company since it could result in less than candid information about both the reps and opinions about performance of our implants. Steve usually meets with hospital executive staff and business managers of the surgical groups. The admin team at M&H can verify this information, and document that this is standard procedure for our company."

As he spoke, Blake pulled out a business card, and scribbled the relevant contact information on the card, which he passed to Cook. Cook summoned his admin and gave her the card and instructions to confirm information.

"Steve is James Harris' brother, but this visit to your hospital has been on the books for over six months. It's a routine site check. I was definitely interested to make this visit, given current events, but it's not outside of our usual company practice."

After a few uneasy, silent minutes when both men checked their emails, Cook's admin confirmed everything that Blake said, including the longstanding nature of the M&H site visit, including emails documenting similar site visits at other facilities. Cook frowned as he read the documents and emails, then closed his laptop. Blake fought to keep his expression bland.

"Very well...but please observe all of our vendor protocols...and as a precaution, we've decided to restrict your mainframe access. You should be able to submit all information to our OR Front Desk crew for data entry by hospital personnel." Cook stood, smiling slightly as he stood to shake Blake's hand. "Any questions?"

"None at all. Thank you, Mr. Cook." Blake pulled out his phone to text Charlie and Steve as soon as he was on the elevator, unsure if he had broken even in the exchange.

AFTER BLAKE LEFT THE CONFERENCE ROOM, WYATT Cook flipped the com device on the table, which had been open during his conversation with Blake. "You heard him.... sounds like a plausible story to me."

"Maybe. The info checks out; still bothers me that his partner is Harris' brother...and that he just happened to show up for a site visit." The voice on the intercom was expressionless, but Cook could imagine the disdainful expression on his colleague's face. "I'll have to make up a reason to meet Anthony, or Myers actually, face-to-face. Something just doesn't feel right. " Cook hoped that he'd at least get some credit, and none of the blame, since he'd contacted his direct superior when he found something amiss.

"Hmph...well, I'll need you to keep me updated. As we discussed after your screw up with Harris - and maybe this latest gas passer, moving forward I need to have final approval of anyone new coming into the OR." Wyatt Cook's expression twisted in frustration, but he dutifully voiced acceptance of the edict from his immediate boss, hospital CFO Ken Raynor. After disconnecting the call, he patted his pockets for his cigarettes, then punched the button for his admin. "I'm leaving campus to meet my wife for lunch. I'll be back sometime after two."

TARYN DETOURED THROUGH THE HOSPITAL DR.'S LOUNGE for coffee before heading to check her emergency patient from the night before. Her last phone report was he was currently stable, but still in ICU.

"Dr. Pirelli...do you have a minute?"

Taryn sighed and gave a long blink as she failed at morphing her face into something more pleasant than resting bitch face for her favorite colleague. "What's up now?"

Downing strolled closer as he sipped his coffee, causing Taryn sudden unease when he ended up ending up significantly inside her comfortable work space bubble. "Another patient with a problem last night...you're making quite the impression. I hear it's another likely Q/A incident. Wondering what happened..."

Taryn shifted uneasily, truly seeing Downing for the first time. Despite having worked with him almost a week, she realized that the man had made absolutely no impression on her as a person, unlike everyone in the department. He was unremarkable and nondescript; turtleneck undershirt blending into his hospital scrubs, and mud-brown hair escaping from under his surgeon's cap. It wasn't until she looked at his mocking expression and roving eyes that she realized his bland exterior might camouflage his darker nature or emotions. She shivered despite the warmth of her parka and stepped back.

"What happened, if you had either checked with the surgeon, or bothered to look at the damn chart, was a patient with a kidney stone, who got septic despite antibiotics. All of that happened before he hit the hospital. Nothing that I could have predicted...or prevented. I made appropriate interventions; patient's alive and improving."

"Any reason you're so defensive?" Downing shifted to block her path to the door, making Taryn even more uneasy.

"Unless you have something to say that could help me understand your group's practice better, I'd like to follow up on my patient and do my job...excuse me." Taryn skirted her colleague, escaping before he could respond. She realized in the hall that she was breathing easily for the first time since the conversation began.

Downing watched her leave, smirking as he withdrew his mobile phone and made a call as he ambled out the door, and to the hospital exit.

After changing into scrubs in the OR locker room, Taryn began second guessing herself; maybe she *had* missed something? After reaching the intensive care floor, she activated the push-pad for the ICU, heading directly for the patient's bay rather than reviewing the chart. As she had anticipated, the patient was awake, off the ventilator with the breathing tube removed. He still had multiple medications hanging from his various IV poles, but was visibly improved than when she had dropped him off. She confirmed her visual review with objective data and the computer. Vital signs were good; the invasive monitors were still in use, but the overall trend was toward improvement.

The patient's nurse came to the station where she reviewed the cart. "You his anesthesiologist from last night? You did a good job...surgeon said so too. Things are looking up; I think he'll be booted out of Intensive Care soon."

Taryn felt relieved that not everything she did here was turning to crap as she continued to review the chart with the ICU nurse. She was on her way out of Surgical ICU when she was hailed.

"Dr. Pirelli. Mind if we talk for a minute?" A dark-haired man in a suit marched down the hall from the Medical Intensive Care Unit. A group of nurses who were chatting as they exited the elevator fell silent when they saw the man and no sooner slipped into the surgical intensive care unit where Taryn had just exited. One of them stretched her eyes at Taryn while pressing her lips together, while looking at the man out of the corner of her eyes.

It seemed to Taryn that everyone was taller than her, but this guy was imposing in both height and attitude. He snapped closed a folder of documents as he stared at her head to toe and crossed his arms. His silent, black-eyed gaze was unreadable and unnerving. Taryn buttoned her lab coat and put her back to the wall.

"We haven't met yet, but I reviewed and approved your intake paperwork. I'm Ken Raynor; part of the admin team." No handshakes, no cordiality, just assessment. "I know Harry gave you orientation to the unit and department, but I wanted to meet you and make sure that you were clear on all of our hospital protocols. I also understand you have an emergency case that you reported to quality assessment."

"Yes, but..."

"Please make sure that you respect the confidentiality of the process and avoid discussing the case with anyone outside of the committee. Your department liaison is Dr. Downing. Make sure all communication is directed exclusively through him. After he's had a chance to brief me on his findings, I'll call you in for a chat."

Without another word, the man brushed by Taryn and headed for the elevator.

"Everywhere else I've been, index cases are reviewed in committee, not privately. Are you over operations? Will Harry or Michael be there for..."

Raynor spun and walked close enough that Taryn backed up a few steps. "This isn't everywhere else, doctor. And I'm in finance. Your little patient misadventure has pushed our budget out of line. We'll ultimately get to the bottom of what happened, but you need to follow protocol. I don't care for you temp people — had problems with your lot before. If it turns out something is out of order with what you did, or if you don't follow our protocol, you're done." He turned on his heel and stepped on the elevator, leaving Taryn with more questions than answers.

WHEN SHE GOT TO THE OR, HARRY WAS WAITING FOR her at the main desk.

"You talk with Ken?"

"You knew he was looking for me?" Harry looked away before folding his arms.

"Never occurred to you to give me the heads up that there were questions or issues? Or was the first day speech just for show?" Harry searched for words, relief clear on his face when Sherry Winger came up, full of apologies.

"Taryn, we've been in a difficult situation here for the past six months. The group was put on probation, which will last another six months. Anything considered disruptive or not in line with the facility goals could result in our expulsion."

"What are they trying to hide? And why aren't you even running interference, Harry?"

"I'm sorry?" Harry's attempt to look confused wasn't even mildly credible.

"Admin...or whoever is behind the probation. What are they hiding, Sherry, or has nobody bothered to ask? Even if the hospital's paying me, the anesthesia group has to have a say in issues impacting anesthesia care."

"Better for all of us if we don't ask those types of questions."

"Not even if there are drug reactions and patient issues happening? Are you on the patient's side or admin's, Harry? It's clear you won't ever have my back."

"You're sounding an awful lot like James Harris."

"And we all know what happened to him." Taryn looked at Harry, anger clear on her face.

"Before you ask, I'll serve out my contract. But I'm not interested in returning. Who's running the schedule today?"

"Sherry is...so it seems we don't have anything left to discuss." Taryn watched as Harry returned to the OR desk and picked up the phone.

"Please don't judge us harshly, Taryn. You have no idea what is going on."

"I'm all ears; what is going on?" Sherry looked at the corner mirror/speaker across the hall and shook her head.

"Let's go to the board. I'll give you report."

TARYN JOINED THE OR GROUP AT HAPPY HOUR, AFTER Blake made it clear that attendance was his price for assistance with the computer access that had prevented Taryn from making progress in her hospital personnel research. She chose to observe her nemesis in action rather than attempt to join the fawning and largely unfamiliar circle of women around him. He might be the typical ass with an attitude, but that man was some primo eye candy! He had on a blue sweater that did amazing things to his eyes, but Taryn was more inclined to believe her initial observations of his character. She snuck a furtive glance in his direction before joining the conversation and group at her end of the table. As the server returned with her Pepsi, someone pulled a chair up beside her.

"Nice that you finally showed up...and came to your senses." Taryn turned to find Blake giving her the once over as he smiled and sat down. A few members of his fan club were slanting dirty looks in her direction, but she shrugged.

"It's a no brainer...and a command performance; not my choice."

Blake gave her a lopsided smile as he tsked and shook his head. "All work and no play..."

"Not looking for a playmate. I'm here...I've had a drink. When can you give me the USB drive?"

"Not now...and not here. Why don't you order something to eat; nothing out here's fresh. If you stay until this is over,

I'll have the chance to walk you to your car, and you get what you need."

Taryn's glare at Blake was met by a smirk; he had anticipated her objections and strategy. She shifted away from Blake, who was looking at her more closely that she would have liked. She decided to feign interest in her drink and the person to her left.

"If I didn't know better, I'd think you were avoiding me, Doc," Blake said as he got comfortable and stretched out his legs while draping a hand on the back of her chair.

Taryn scooted left out of reflex. "Whatever...and you would be wrong since you don't know jack about me."

"And there's the firecracker from Saturday...welcome back, Sugar," he said with a half-smile as he tossed back the rest of his drink.

"Why would I avoid you? Other than the fact that you're incurably rude, that is?"

"Just trying to be friendly...no idea why that would be a problem."

"Look, I've had a shit day..."

"How? You worked maybe two hours..."

"Not patient related...I had a couple meetings that headed south."

"Well now you're here; it's happy hour. Loosen up...tell me that you don't have someone waiting for you at home in..."

"Seattle....and I'm not feeling the inquisition dance."

"So, who were you skiing with on Saturday?"

"Saturday...who was I... Stalker, much? Not your biz, and I repeat, what's with the third degree? I didn't see you any more after you ran into me..."

Blake leaned closer to whisper, "Let's keep it real, Sugar; *you* ran into me...had to make nice at work, which *was* my bad. You just weren't looking on Saturday. We were on some of the same runs, at the same time. You're pretty good." Blake settled back in his chair wearing a half smile that reminded Taryn of Cody at his most devious.

"Blake! Got you a freshy!" Kylie, the scrub tech, was holding up a shot glass.

Taryn rolled her eyes. "Your harem is calling."

"Interesting comment from someone who claims to be uninterested. Hold that thought," said Blake as he left to claim his shot.

Taryn cursed her poor choice of words and jumped back into conversation with the group near her...until Blake and his arm returned to invade her space.

"Where were we? Ah...your ski buddy from Saturday. We're not working...mind if I call you Taryn?"

Taryn studied him and wondered why this assignment was turning into a a trip to crazy town...and whether Blake's determined efforts to get to know her socially were really making her nauseous...or if that funny feeling in her stomach was excitement butterflies. And how pissed with herself was she that she had to even figure that out?

***

Taryn looked at the time — 6:45 p.m. After successfully extracting the USB drive from Blake, obtained at an additional cost of a date later in the week, she headed to retrieve Maxx from daycare. Becky was on duty again.

"I know you said you'd be on call this week. We're happy to board him any time you can't pick him up."

"Good to know...he's company away from home, but sometimes I work late."

Taryn and Becky turned as the door chimed, and hospital CEO Wyatt Cook entered with a pair of yappy and fractious

Bichon Frise, while in the midst of a phone call. Both dogs went right up to Maxx, who woofed in greeting, as they went through the usual doggie hello of sniffing one another. Becky waved him over.

"Hi Mr. Cook; I'll take the pups, and we're set for grooming first thing in the morning."

As Wyatt continued to walk forward to hand-off his dogs to Becky, Maxx placed himself between Taryn and Cook, who was too absorbed in his call to notice the changing dynamic. As he walked closer, the deep rumble of a growl within Maxx's throat began to build.

Becky picked up on the undercurrent of tension, and moved to intercept Cook and his dogs before he came any closer, and grabbed the leashes

"I've got them; we should have them ready for you by four o'clock. Sound okay?"

"Yes fine," said Wyatt, who looked with a sniff at Maxx, and glanced at Taryn without recognition. "And make sure that they don't get dirty playing with any of the other dogs after their grooming."

He was instantly absorbed in his call again as he turned to leave, missing the full smile and bared teeth of Maxx. Taryn shook her head. Being rude and not a dog person may have been annoying, but it wasn't a crime...yet Maxx really didn't like Cook. She gave Becky a sheepish smile and shrug.

"People."

"Right? See you tomorrow." Becky smiled and waved as Taryn dismissed the incident, focusing on getting home to work on gaining access to the hospital personnel records.

AFTER LEAVING MAXX, SHE DOVE INTO HER WORK FOR

the evening. The mainframe organizational info she had courtesy of Blake helped her confirm that Michael Downing was the only hospital-employed member of the anesthesia department, as she expected. She also confirmed that the pathologist who had done the original post-mortem on James Harris was also a hospital employee. Since that meant he was in charge of the hospital laboratory, the news extended the possibility for hospital/admin control to that area and would have been a reason for James Harris not to trust any drug assay or abnormality report done at the facility.

As she pondered where she would go with this information, she pulled up the data from James Harris' journals that she uploaded in spreadsheet form to a cloud account she had established. After a few minutes, she opened her own spreadsheet that she had done on abnormal drug reactions and zeroed in on the drug lot and batch numbers for Propofol and one of the muscle relaxants she had used. Next, she decided to compare similar info from the abbreviated journal information that she had from James Harris. She stared wide-eyed when she saw some of the same drug lot information repeated in his entries. Highlighting the pertinent files, she realized that she had five patients with the same information that James had noticed. She grabbed the phone to call Blake.

"You reconsidering already?"

"Not a chance. That's not why I'm calling."

"You just wanted to hear my voice?"

Ignoring his quip, she asked, "What progress have you made finding James' computer? I need more info."

"On?'

"A hunch...that would fit in with what I've already

noticed on my patients and the files I have from James. There's something going on with at least two of the drugs on stock here. I need more info to confirm that it's not a coincidence, and then we need to sit down with Charlie and figure out why and what."

"Not following."

"Why are these drugs problematic, where are they coming from, and why are these anomalies centered here? None of my colleagues are reporting problems with anything, but shortages."

"Charlie has the original journals in his safe."

"Let's call tonight. I know it's late, but this is important."

"Okay, I'll bite, Sugar...let's give him a call."

"I told you, I'm not your Sugar."

"Hope springs eternal."

CHAPTER ELEVEN

Wednesday

"New deadbolts and cylinder door locks should be in by the time you get home. I'll get the keys to you." Charlie was personally supervising a full re-key of Taryn's condo after the discovery of the altered lock on the back door of James' condo.

"Thanks...you dropping it off at the OR desk? Charlie shook his head.

"Too much at stake...in person hand off's best. Having any luck with the pharmacy stuff?"

Taryn was continuing her work connecting the information she had gleaned from the main and satellite pharmacy with her drug utilization records. "Yes and no. There seems to be a discrepancy between the stock in the pharmacy satellite, and what I see of the records and tracking from main pharmacy. Take a look."

Charlie peered over her shoulder and shrugged. "Could be just a math error."

"No way. They're ordering almost three times as much Propofol as is being used in the OR from everything I see, and that's confirmed by the fact that I've been using drugs from some of the same lot numbers that James reported as defective. I've only glanced at the other anesthesia drugs, but same appears to be true."

"So?"

"There's no way that with the volume of drugs being ordered that A...someone hasn't noticed that there's a discrepancy between what's ordered and what's actually being used, and B...that they're still using the same drug lots as they were in November. Both can't be true."

"What you're proposing expands the number of people involved in whatever is going on. Logic says the least number of people who know what's going on is the safest and most likely."

"This has to involve at least two departmental categories...Pharmacy and Finance.

"Pharmacy I see...but it could be anyone in Admin, actually.

"Do you have any contacts there? I know you haven't worked at the hospital for years." Charlie considered the information on Taryn's computer screen, then pulled out his phone. "Let me make some calls and get back to you. And I'll bring the docs Blake brought with him from Denver."

"Great. There's gotta be clues in them that will help us find that computer."

"I agree, and since Blake and Steve couldn't figure them out, you're the only logical person who could."

"You telling our friend from Denver your conclusion might make my life easier."

"I'll think about it...but it might go over better coming from you."

"I'll respectfully disagree rather than saying 'Hell no'... and see you later."

Charlie chuckled as they disconnected.

DURING TARYN'S REVIEW OF THE INFORMATION SHE obtained from the main pharmacy over the weekend, she confirmed that the hospital had ordered unusually large amounts of both Propofol and a muscle relaxant, Rocuronium, for at least the last six months. From all of the pharmacy correspondence that she managed to access, it was clear that there was no official reference to the extra stock by anyone in pharmacy or in stores. Given the volume of excess stock, it was clear that it had to be stored at a site remote from the hospital. Looking at the delivery schedule, pharmacy delivery should have occurred on Monday. Where would be the most likely place the excess stock was stored?

After she dropped Maxx at daycare, Taryn remained focused on the problem of the location of excess stock, and how she would investigate where it was stored. Lost in thought, she slammed on the brakes when a panel truck made a sudden left turn in front of her, into a storage facility. Her SUV slid sideways, but came to a stop short of clipping the back end of the truck.

"What the hell?!"

Taryn blew her horn in frustration as she watched the gate to the storage facility rise, suddenly realizing that that the hospital logo and BRMC initials were displayed prominently on the sides and back of the truck. Before Taryn could get her vehicle turned around, the entrance gate closed, and she had to watch the truck roll down the central aisle, then turn left into the maze of storage buildings. As she resumed her drive into work, she placed a call to Charlie.

"What do you know about remote storage sites for hospital supplies?"

"What?"

"Hospital remote storage...where's it located?"

"Not sure if they have any. Why are you asking?"

"I just saw a truck with a hospital logo go into a mini storage lot."

The line was silent, then Charlie answered. "I may be able to have the answer by the time I get your keys and the journal to you. Why don't we plan on you dropping by the office rather than me coming to the hospital? More chance to chat that way."

"Sounds like a plan."

Taryn activated the push plate to the OR, stashing speculation on the storage facility issue in favor of dealing with the afternoon relief schedule and remaining surgery cases.

"Dr. Pirelli, could you call pharmacy? They've got some questions about some of your narcotic documentation from Monday night. Oh, and this is for you." The OR charge nurse handed Taryn the message and an envelope with her name scrawled on the front. The narcotics issue was important to correct, but not catastrophic. Most of the narcotics documentation was taken care of by an automated medication dispensing/return/wasting machine, which required two-person medication verification for each patient. She had done everything by the books the night before, so this could only be a technicality or mix-up. Taryn stuffed the envelope into her backpack and changed into scrubs before calling pharmacy.

"Pirelli here. What's the problem with my documentation?"

"Doc, it looks like you didn't return a vial of fentanyl on your last patient. We've got a count that's off in Central. The pharmacist who handles OR and ICU is on his way up to speak with you."

Taryn frowned, and inquired about the nursing schedule. The evening charge nurse who had confirmed her final medication returns for the evening would not be on duty until 6 p.m., so at least initially, she wouldn't be able to provide secondary confirmation for her narcotic accounting.

As promised, the critical care pharmacist entered the OR minutes later, report in hand, and accompanied Taryn to the main OR narcotic dispensing machine. The pharmacist printed the report from the satellite machine and compared it to the central report.

"Funny...the report here confirms that you returned the vial. We haven't refilled the machine today; let me do a manual count and check the return bin." While they were trying to figure out the issue, both OR nurses and anesthesiologists came and went, signing drugs in and out. After a few minutes of tension on Taryn's part, the pharmacist confirmed that everything had been returned properly.

"Sorry for the mix-up doc. Looks like just a glitch in central. Happens every now and again. Nothing for you to worry about..."

"What do you do if you can't resolve the discrepancy?" It was a huge issue for Taryn, since anesthesiologists had both the more regular access to controlled substances, and the highest rate of dependency of any docs in medicine. Narcotic addiction was a sad, but true occupational hazard in the stressful area of the OR, and in light of everything going on currently, Taryn was concerned.

A history of diversion or rehab counseling was one of those things that every doc applying for state medical license or hospital medical privileges had to disclose, but wasn't an automatic disqualifier for a job. There were tons of rules governing the post diversion process that she had no desire to learn about. Even without substance abuse or addiction issues; it was still important to keep her narcotic accountability and documentation record clean.

"Well we usually find the error and correct it in Central. At worst, we may have to do drug testing for anyone in contact with the drugs."

"What?"

"Drug testing; while we can't track the item if it's been stolen or lost, we can test for illicit use by the practitioners on record as a last resort to absolve them from implication."

She had a few more comments, but the gist of the conversation stuck with Taryn, and made her wonder how the discrepancy had occurred. As she struggled to determine who might have turned her in, Harry Lam entered the OR control desk office, the strained look on his face easing when he saw Taryn.

"There you are, Taryn...I'm running the board today." Harry shuffled through the list of afternoon cases, all of which were crossed off except one. "We've got one room going; that doc needs out ASAP. You get your pharmacy issue cleared up?" .

"She's good to go, Dr. Lam. Just a clerical error."

"Machines! Give me the old-fashioned daily narcotic box. Mike Downing's in that room; you'll be relieving him."

Taryn was polite, but wary of an unexpectedly cheery Harry, and of relieving her least favorite member of the group, but focused on the fact that she was there to do a job as assigned. She fixed a pleasant expression on her face before entering the OR to relieve Downing, who was waiting for her, arms crossed, and a hostile expression on the portion of his face not covered by his mask.

"Problems with your narcotic count, Pirelli? Looks like you can't stay out of trouble." Taryn froze as Downing spoke, automatically checking the surgical team, who were too engrossed with what they were doing to pay attention to events in the anesthesia area at the head of the operating room table.

"Michael, could you just give me the report on the patient." She signed into the electronic record, and focused on the patient rather than the recurrent human thorn in her side.

"So why are you doing locums work, exactly?"

It was easier to ignore Downing than cause a scene.

"How long do you think the surgeon has left on this case, Michael?" Taryn frowned at the profusion of unlabelled medical additive bags and pumps currently connected to the patient. "And what drips are you running? Does she need BP support?"

"What, you can't handle a complex case? Typical for your lot."

After a cutting glare that actually made Downing back up, Taryn just shrugged and shook her head. "Look, why don't you just go. I'll deal."

"You didn't answer my question."

Taryn silently scrolled through the medications listed in the record, causing Downing to leave after biting out a curse.

THERE WAS A DIZZYING ARRAY OF SYRINGES AND VIALS TO go with the forest of medical additive bags hanging on the IV poles. Taryn picked up one 10cc syringe of clear liquid with no label. She picked up another...also not labelled. When she found the same with the next syringe she picked up, she closed her eyes, then swept the whole collection of chaos into the needle box and picked up the anesthesia phone.

"Hi Shannon...please bring me another anesthesia drug tray and box of infusion IV bags."

AFTER TWENTY MINUTES OF CONCERTED WORK SORTING out the drug administration nightmare and discarding all of the unlabeled medications and drug infusions, the patient was stable, and Taryn had time to think about her recent narcotic documentation issue. Normally, such problems were confidential, but Michael Downing clearly knew about her narcotic discrepancy non-issue. What were the chances that the discrepancy had been engineered? Or maybe that was her paranoia in effect. She shook her head, determined to file further speculation for after her case. She took a more critical survey of her patient, who was apparently a trauma patient. The woman's bruised and battered face was so swollen as to be unrecognizable. The documentation itself was another annoying issue. Drug documentation, the condition of the workspace when she entered, chart notes...everything was just a bit off. Taryn frowned as she continued to review the patient data. There was something nagging about both the patient and the case. The silence in the room was unrelieved by the usual background OR music.

"She still okay? I stopped asking Dr. Downing since he snarled at me every time I did." The circulator nurse had left her area to chat with Taryn. Taryn did a double take when she realized that the woman was red-eyed and nervous.

"What on earth is wrong? Patient's fine...question is, are you?"

The woman smiled and shook her head. "It's one thing when the patient is a stranger...something else when it's someone you know. She's been pretty unstable in here."

Taryn frowned as she looked at the patient then the circulating nurse, who finally realized her confusion.

"That's Rhonda, one of the OR night nurses; you worked with her Monday. She went out for dinner after getting off from work last night...and they found her near the restaurant this morning. She'd been assaulted; took them until almost noon to get her stabilized enough to come to the OR for surgery. They still aren't sure if she's going to make it. Taryn froze, realizing that now two women in two weeks had been assaulted and were OR workers.

"Didn't Dr. Downing tell you who the patient was?" Taryn shook her head, speechless, as she looked at the patient and the electronic record.

"No..he..."

"I know you'll take good care of her doc...not like..." Taryn nodded automatically to the rest of what the circulator said, suddenly distracted by movement at the window to the main OR door. Michael Downing stood there, ripping off his mask, a faint smile on his face. As the back of her neck prickled in sudden apprehension, Taryn reviewed the patient status; everything was as stable as it appeared. When she looked at the window again, Downing had disappeared. The surgical nurse went to attend to requests from the field as Taryn's silenced text alert vibrated.

What do you think about takeout tonight? Charlie says

you're working on finding James' computer tonight. What do you want me to bring?

Taryn rolled her eyes...so much for her idea to work with Charlie on finding the computer rather than with Blake.

That would be great...I'll buzz when I'm leaving work. Charlie keeps throwing us together...kinda like throwing poo on a wall and wanting it to stick.

No Charlie involved; this one's all me.

Right.

What do I have to do to get on your good side?

How long do you have?

A smile emoji was all Taryn got back, and she shook her head as she checked the patient and surgical progress and reshuffled her plans for the evening. As she hung her back-pack from a cargo hook at the back of the anesthesia cart, Taryn remembered that she had stuffed the letter waiting for her at the OR desk into a pocket when she arrived for work. Other than her name, there was nothing remarkable about the white envelope, not even a return name or address. After another glance at the patient's vitals, Taryn opened the letter.

Please call me when you get off work.

Sherry

Now what?

CHAPTER TWELVE

Wednesday Evening

"Sherry, what's going on with Harry? And did you know that Michael Downing's patient today was one of our OR night nurses? She's in the ICU now...she's doing well... but what the hell is going on? And have you ever taken over a case from Michael?"

"Where are you, Taryn?"

"On my way to pick up Maxx...and why does that matter?"

"It matters because we're convinced...Harry and I...that James Harris did discover something going on with the drug supply at work."

"Why the hell did it take you people so long to see the obvious? And any reason that I'm having this chat with you and not Harry?

"Because he still wasn't convinced until you had that trumped up narcotic issue today...and because as department chair, he's under more scrutiny than I am. He...we don't think we've been getting all the information from Michael Downing..."

"About what?" Taryn was at Maxx's daycare by this time, and fully focused on everything that Sherry wasn't saying. "How long has Harry known that something was wrong?"

"Since he approved Michael Downing joining the group as the price for allowing the group to continue here."

"What?"

"It's a long story."

"I've got time."

Sherry's story was both disturbing and frustrating, as it showed the lengths that administration, headed by Ken Raynor, had gone to insure Michael Downing was accepted as a member of the group. The secondary price had been that all complaints and issues from the group relevant to OR issues had been filtered by Downing, rather than by usual protocols. The narcotic accountability had apparently been the last in a string of escalating events that Harry couldn't ignore. Taryn was still unclear on who submitted the narcotic complaint, but the nurse who verified her information was now a patient. Could someone in central pharmacy have manipulated the machine that distributed controlled substances? Sherry refused to answer her hesitant questions about case hand-off and organization issues similar to those she had that day. Taryn reflected on her previous observations of Downing's cases while she was on-call. Other than the obvious and growing personality conflict they seemed to have, her only observation after the case earlier was that his anesthetic management was haphazard...not unsafe, but not what one would expect from an experienced anesthesiologist. She filed it all under 'Check Later,' and concentrated on the relief of picking up Maxx, who gave her his usual enthusiastic greeting.

AFTER COLLECTING MAXX, TARYN HEADED FOR Charlie's office to pick up her new keys to the condo and the journals and documents that James Harris had mailed before his death. It was snowing again, and the short trip to Charlie's office took twice as long as normal. Taryn brought Maxx in so he could be comfortable while she and Charlie chatted. Charlie was alone in the office and packing up to leave. After greeting Charlie with a woof, Maxx settled down to gnaw the chew bone that Taryn tossed him.

"I was expecting you earlier...what happened?"

"Just an unexpected phone call, and insight into the anesthesia group." Taryn gave Charlie the summary of the conversation and growing issues with Michael Downing. "What did you find out from your contacts at the hospital?"

"Contact...Lydia Thompson, who's the COO on paper, but apparently has been kept out of the loop on most major decisions."

"What? Why?"

"Loyalty. Hers is to the community and Bend. Cook and Raynor are corporate climbers. They came within a year of each other and have since gradually moved her to the periphery of the decision-making. Lydia's more concerned with keeping a job than moving up the ladder with CHG."

"She's really okay with that?"

"More or less. She tries to keep an eye out for things at the corporate level that could impact the community, and intercedes when she can. Anyway, she confirmed that there's no off-site storage of hospital stock."

"So, what was that truck doing at the storage facility today? For everything I figure out, more questions evolve."

"Such as?

"Why Michael Downing decided to move here...there's something more than what Sherry told me."

"Sounds like you need some help.

"I'm putting Cody on Downing research. I'll do more digging myself after Blake and I try to find James' computer. Thanks, but no thanks for arranging that, BTW."

"What do you mean?" Charlie's wide-eyed expression made her huff in frustration.

"Charlie, you're a great guy, but you should give up the acting and stick to your day job." Charlie laughed as he put on his coat, and Maxx jumped up from where he had flopped at Taryn's feet.

"Guilty as charged. Come on...I'll walk you out."

Taryn texted Blake as she and Charlie left for their respective vehicles.

"I've got Cody working on history on Michael Downing. Getting into secure docs and people's background is what he does best. There's something missing from his records that I'm not seeing clearly."

Taryn rehashed her conversation with Charlie. "Have you been in the operating room with him yet? Any issues or unusual stuff you've noticed?" As she asked, she admitted that Blake made a great choice for takeout, and that she was starved.

"I've been rep on some of his cases...but didn't really pay

much attention, but I'm not a doc or an 'anesthesia expert.'" Taryn looked at Blake, his smirk and air quotes making a point that she decided to ignore. She shrugged, resolving to find other ways to get the information and impressions she needed. She and Blake were having more success with dinner than their review of James' journals for clues about the location of his computer.

"Other than the spreadsheets dealing with the defective medications, what else do you see in the journals?"

"As an anesthesiologist, case log type info like this is pretty standard." Taryn flipped to the back section of the journal, which contained stickers with redacted patient names, dates of service and medical record numbers. "James is noting the date of surgery, and anything unusual or remarkable about the case. That kind of information is two-thirds of the stuff here. The defective drug info is next." Taryn flipped to five pages in the middle of the journal. "This is the part that I can't really figure out. Any ideas?" She pushed the journal toward Blake, getting up to stretch and let Maxx out the back door to potty. Blake scanned the pages before grabbing a notepad.

"First thing is just to make a list of the different topics listed here."

Taryn rejoined him, looking over his shoulder to review the first of the five confusing pages, which contained a series of dates. "When did James start working here?"

"Steve thinks August."

"That fits, since the first of these dates is from mid-August. I think our best option is to print out or create calendar files and circle the listed dates." Taryn launched a calendar file on her laptop, marking the dates Blake read.

"First thing I see is that all of these dates are either on

Mondays or Thursdays. But I just saw the BRMC truck today...Wednesday...so those dates likely don't apply."

"Not necessarily. What if the events in question occur on the listed days, and today was a fluke?

"Possible...but what are the events?" Taryn flipped through the rest of the pages. "No other dates, places...nothing listed. I'll keep thinking about that and keep looking for anything pointing toward the computer location. The rest of the stuff here is just about local places for food, services...that kind of stuff. Not actually sure why he's got it written out, since James could have just as easily bookmarked and entered this stuff on his phone."

Blake rummaged in his backpack, before extracting a phone. "Brought the phone, but neither Steve nor I have tried to get in it. James always did a self-wipe trigger for two wrong access attempts. Not sure if it's numerical or pattern."

Taryn frowned as she looked at the list of coffee shops under the heading 'Keys'. "This is pretty clear that one of these places is associated with either keys or a place where James hid that computer."

Blake looked at the list and shook his head. "Saw that... already checked those places out. None of them have any kind of storage near or in the shop."

Taryn flipped to the third page, which had more lists, and the underlined title Blucifer with a sketch of a key labelled 'F94' by it. "What on earth is a Blucifer?"

Blake grinned as he leaned back in his chair. "You obviously have never been through DIA. Blucifer is the blue, fire-eyed, devil horse sculpture in the middle of the vehicle approach to the airport, with no way to see it up close. There's quite a story about both the sculpture and the artist."

Opening another window, Taryn did a Google search, pulling up all of the available information about the sculpture and its creator, who had apparently died after part of the sculpture fell on him, fatally injuring him. She frowned and shrugged. "Creepy, gruesome tale...that's a total non sequitur for anything."

"Except James lived on Blue Mustang Way in Denver... always made jokes about the stupid Blucifer statue...said it was the airport's guardian."

"What's on that last page?"

Blake turned to the fifth page of the seemingly irrelevant collection of information. "Just a list of hospital divisions...Pharmacy, Admin, Pathology, Anesthesia....no clue at all on what that..."

"Give me that." Taryn pulled the book over, recalling her chat with Charlie earlier. "This ties in with something Charlie and I were talking about...we discussed how many people would be needed to cover up a problem with problematic drugs or patients with unusual reactions. This is the complete list of what we guessed would be needed to hide or coverup reactions."

"Hospital issues...not our priority...we need the computer. It may give more clarification on that."

Taryn flipped back to the list of local businesses, doing a double take as sudden realization hit her. "Four of these places are underlined...two coffeeshops and two bars...see? Second bar is Mesteño Bar and Grill...isn't that just another word for wild horse...which is what mustangs are?"

Blake nodded, and grudgingly admitted to himself that Taryn had solved many of the outstanding issues that had stymied him. "Yeah...and Jimmy went there a lot according to his charge records. It's out near Bachelor. It's a local's hangout." Blake pulled up the file he had created for charge receipts.

"Looks like he went to all of the places, just Mesteño Bar

the most, Taryn checked the time. "Just nine thirty. I think we should visit."

"I already have...nobody had anything to say about Jimmy...nothing to see. No lockers or storage."

Taryn pulled up a page on her computer and flipped it around so Blake could see it. "Except the place is on a page with keys at the top and ties into James's home street in Denver. Ever hear of Key Cafés?"

"What?"

"Key Café's...secure places to drop off and exchange keys that gets around the key under the rock thing for visitors."

"You think one of these places may have one of these Key Café things?" Taryn scrolled through another page.

"All four of those places are Key Cafés. This is too much of a coincidence not to look at...My money's on Mesteño Bar and Grill... Maxx!" With a woof and doggie smile, Maxx came in from the great room and followed Taryn and Blake to the mudroom coatrack.

"You wanna drive, or should I?"

"My truck's outside...I'll drive."

"Good...that gives me time to download the app and sign up for the service."

"If there's an app, there must be a code or password you have to give to get the key."

"Pretty sure I know what that would be."

"If you're right, I owe you a coffee."

"I'll take a double-shot mocha...with peppermint."

"LOOKS LIKE WE'RE OUT OF LUCK ON GETTING THE computer tonight." Blake drove by Deschutes Storage, which had storage access hours only from 7-9 p.m.. Taryn dangled the key chain with two keys, retrieved from the Key Café at Mesteño Bar and Grill. The password to access the key were the address numbers of James's home in Denver. While they had been lucky enough that the storage facility had been identified by the attached promotional keychain, they would have to wait until the next day to confirm that the F94 written in the journal was the storage unit number. Maxx stuck his head between the seat from the backseat, and she rubbed his head as she mused over their options.

"If that is the unit number in the journal, the only thing I need from the office is the gate access code and directions."

"You did an awesome job tonight. I'm impressed." They pulled into the drive of Taryn's condo and parked. "I owe you an apology."

"Apology?"

Blake smirked as he tugged one of the braids that had escaped Taryn's updo. "When I met you at Charlie's, I didn't think you had the smarts to match the wrapping...especially after Saturday."

She frowned and pulled back before unlocking her door. "Well I was exactly right...you're an ass...and obviously only deal with idiot, airhead women. And you owe me another apology. Goodbye."

Before Blake could reply, Taryn had exited, and opened the back door for Maxx. "Maxx! Out!" He gave a woof and leaped out of the back seat and swarmed around Taryn's legs as she rounded the back of the SUV and headed for the walkway for Maxx's night-time walk.

Blake turned off the engine and climbed out of the vehicle. "Wait...that came out wrong." Taryn rolled her eyes and crossed her arms before facing Blake. Maxx woofed and ambled over to nudge Blake before pacing around them both. Taryn's expression was a mixture of scorn and impatience.

"Another pattern you have. If this a continuation of the current stupid, I think I'll pass."

Blake raised his hands in surrender. "I give...I'm not saying the right words....about anything. If you hadn't looked at the journal, we'd still be stuck on zero with finding out what James stumbled into...and what's going on now with the drugs in the OR. I'm sorry." Taryn looked down, and rubbed Maxx, then looked at Blake. "Apology accepted. I need to walk Maxx and turn in. Are you working in the morning? Wanna go with me to the storage?"

"Sorry...early case. Call me before you go, and after you leave?"

"Deal."

Taryn watched Blake drive away, then followed Maxx down the walk, watching as he sniffed, raised his leg, and reclaimed his territory. Lost in thought, she started when she realized that she was out without her walking stick at night...and that there was still no suspect in the string of assaults. Even though her condo was nowhere near where previous victims had been found, caution was better than regret. She shoved her hand in her coat pocket and fingered her keys, with their attached Mace canister. She also had one of Maxx's spare leashes in her pocket. She pulled out the leash, deciding that keeping Maxx close would be her best option. "Maxx...come!" She walked toward him to attach the leash just as he began growling at a clump of bushes about ten feet away. Taryn looked around; the street was empty for just after ten, and they were between the orange circle of light from the regularly spaced street lights. The closer she got to Maxx, the more he growled, finally backing up to shove his bulk between the snow-covered shrubbery and Taryn. She smelled cigarette smoke and what had to be a man-made fragrance, in the dead of winter, with temperatures well below freezing. Her neck prickled with foreboding as she began backing up, Maxx pushing her as he continued to face the clump of shrubbery and growl. Taryn decided against attaching his leash, finally reaching to grab Maxx's collar and urge him back with her.

"Come...let's go in." She had her keys in hand, and the safety of her Mace canister as she cursed both her decision to walk Maxx at night, and not having her convertible walking stick. When she reached the circle of light cast by the last streetlight before she reached the driveway of her condo, she finally turned around and hustled toward her front door. Maxx's growl subsided as they approached the condo, but he stopped twice to look back at the bushes and growl. When Taryn was inside her condo, she engaged both locks and breathed a sigh of relief. She dropped down to hug her dog before she took off her coat. When her breathing and heart rate finally dropped, she pulled her phone out of her coat pocket, hesitating before she called Blake. She paused, then in the same pocket to finger the key and tag she and Blake had just retrieved.

"Hey...I think someone was watching Maxx and me just now. We got halfway up the block, and he started growling at some underbrush...and I smelled cigarette smoke and some kind of...cologne."

"You okay? Do you need me to come back over?"

"We're fine...and happy Charlie got the locks changed yesterday."

"I'll call him...see if he can get his friend Bruce to run some extra patrols by your place." Blake hesitated before adding, "Changing your locks was smart...someone's been in my place...they had plenty of time while I was gone. Nothing's missing, but someone's too nosy for my taste."

Taryn shivered as she double-checked the front door locks and started on a circuit of the condo to check all the doors to the outside and flipped on the outside lights. "No way is this a coincidence."

"What the hell did James stumble into?"

CHAPTER THIRTEEN

Thursday

Taryn trudged back to her SUV from the office of Deschutes Storage with the map of the small, eight-row facility and access code in hand. Because of a truck blocking the main entrance to Row F, where James' storage unit was located, she took a circuitous route, winding up a few doors down from where the truck was being loaded. After opening the outer garage door with the external access key, she found space 94, which was actually located in a locker-like collection of 18x18 storage lockers. She had imagined finding any number of things behind the heavy-duty padlocked enclosure, only to find a computer and its power cord. It was almost anti-climactic. Taryn was shortly back in her car, waiting for the truck ahead of her to exit when she froze at the sight of the men who had been loading the truck rolling down the cargo door revealing the BRMC letters and logo. She dialed Charlie who was the only person who could help her, since Blake was working.

"Charlie I just got James' computer and am right behind a Bend Regional cargo truck leaving the storage space. Three guys are loading boxes."

"Jesus! Have they seen you?"

"No reason for them to suspect me. I'm gonna follow them and see where they go." Taryn looked at the time; she had almost two hours before she was due to report for call.

"Be careful...and give me the truck's license plate, and the direction they're headed." Taryn rattled off the info, counting to fifteen before following the truck to the exit gate.

"They're turning right; going back into the city."

"We'll follow them tag-team so they don't get suspicious. I'm driving back to the office from an appointment, and I'm close. I should be able to intercept you shortly if they don't make any more turns. Stay on the line."

Taryn maintained her following distance, becoming anxious when the truck turned into a strip mall after going a mile from the storage facility.

"They just turned into the strip mall off Cedar."

"Keep going; I'm behind you...there's a FedEx shipping outpost there. Why don't you head home? You have work, they've seen your vehicle, and I'd like to see where they go next. But first, one other update."

Taryn paused before disconnecting to hear Charlie out.

"Blake told me about his break-in, and we both decided that playing ignorant might get us further than letting whoever visited know we're onto them...but you need to be careful with your coming and going."

"I am...and thanks again for the new locks."

"Anytime." Charlie disconnected to follow up on the newest development, while Taryn used her remaining time before work researching the hospital credentialing information on Michael Downing that she had accessed.

The credentialing information looked much like what she had completed; standard inquiries about previous places of work, medical training and education, along with certificate documentation. As she was debating about the direction to go next, Cody called.

"I did a deep info dive on Downing. Sent everything to your email. Take a look; let me know if you need something more." Taryn opened up her email and downloaded the files that Cody had sent. All of the work and education information matched the documents she had reviewed, until she looked at the page with the ID badge and physical demographics from Downing's last hospital in Colorado.

"Are you sure you have the correct person? Who is this?"

"What do you mean?"

"Hair and eye color are different, and the records from Colorado say Downing is 5'6". And just with the headshot, he's a totally different body type. The Michael Downing here has to be at least six feet, and athletic."

The line was silent except for the clack of keys. "I'm re-checking everything...yup, the Colorado information is correct. Any way you can send me a picture of your guy?"

"On it now." The appropriate information was on its way. "I hate to generalize, but no one ever lies about height in favor of claiming to be shorter. And hair and eye color can be changed."

"Why would anyone go to the trouble of faking their identity for something as complex as medical credentialing... not to mention how could they do it from a training aspect for something like anesthesiology?"

"T-baby, there are shows and movies about people who make a living by being imposters, even of doctors."

"Well the question would be why?" Taryn thought back to everything that Sherry and Shannon had related about the drama surrounding Michael Downing's acceptance into the anesthesia group. She looked at the computer she had retrieved, and the journals and documents on her counter.

"This new Downing issue has to be tied to everything else. Whatever is on that computer will show us how it relates to everything else."

"I'll help any way I can on this end." After chatting with Cody for a few minutes, Taryn disconnected, and after checking the time, began packing up her things and Maxx for work. She placed the retrieved computer and journal in their own bag, which she stored in a hidden cargo space in her SUV. She was parking at Maxx's daycare when Charlie called.

"After the hospital truck left the strip mall, they went to cargo shipping at the airport. They ended up at the hospital."

"What?"

"They're moving whatever they had stored in that unit. I'm calling in a favor and getting someone in facilities to take a look at the truck. I got close enough to see a vehicle number." Taryn turned patted Maxx absently, trying to guess how this new angle fit into everything she had learned. "So, they're shipping something...probably drugs, and now Cody tells me Michael Downing may not be who we think he is."

"What?"

Taryn shared the latest with Charlie.

"I think it's time we get help on this. Let me tag a friend in Homeland Security in the Portland office, see what he can do. You think you and Blake can make some progress getting into that computer tonight?'

Taryn shrugged. "Maybe. Depends on call and having some luck."

"See what you two can do. What we do next depends on what James left us there." Taryn spun her keys as she thought. "What do you think about finding a way to get into that storage space?"

"It would be a crapshoot trying to find the exact space without getting into the office records at the storage facility, even knowing the row the unit was on. None of us needs extra attention or a B&E charge, so don't get creative. And watch your back at work."

TARYN'S TEXT ALERT WENT OFF WHEN SHE REACHED THE hospital.

You make it to that storage unit?

Yes...long story...we got it.

Thanks for the timely update. You're a hard woman to keep track of.

Taryn sighed, and opted for no response, and collected her things to go in, realizing after she got to her locker than she had run the work entry gauntlet without incident or new infraction. Harry was pacing in front of the assignment board; he was the daytime anesthesia coordinator. When Taryn reached the board, he flushed and cleared his throat as he avoided eye contact. Taryn nodded stiffly. "Hi; who'm I relieving, and what's on tap for tonight?" Harry handed her the On-Call pager.

"Quiet day; we got Michael out early. Ray's finishing the last case. Nothing's scheduled, so you should be out of here quickly."

"Great...I'll check Ray and be in the lounge doing chart work."

"Taryn...I...hell, I over-reacted earlier this week. I'm sorry. We aren't restricting your access...we actually can't... Check Ray, and join me for a coffee?"

Taryn looked at the hallway traffic mirror, which was likely doing double duty as a surveillance device and nodded. "Sure."

She completed her operating room rounds, exchanging silent stares with Blake who was the rep in the orthopedic surgery room that was the last to finish, then left the operating room suite for the small coffee café in the hospital admission lobby. She collected the coffee she ordered before joining Harry, who was dressed for the outdoors. She allowed him to break the awkward silence.

"Nothing's really changed for our group. We're still essentially on probation, and I'm limited in what I can do to help you, or even our group. You're correct; there is something going on with the common drugs we're using in the operating room. The problems are intermittent, but every time we send off a report, the testing comes back negative."

"Testing sent out through pharmacy?"

"Yes." Taryn nodded, reluctant to give Harry any potentially sensitive information. Harry crossed his arms as he leaned back. Taryn's text alert went off...Blake. "After the uproar before Harris disappeared, all I could see when you had similar complaints was you being an ongoing part of the problem."

"And now?"

"I'm not sure. But I'm sure that narcotic issue you had was bogus...just can't prove it. I do know the hospital hiring you directly, rather than through the group was a power play."

Taryn's text alert went off; Blake again.

"Addiction has never been an issue with me, but I'll do whatever it takes to clear my name."

"I know...I've made some calls. Everyone I called agrees

with what we have for your references. I'm sorry, and I'd like us to start over."

Taryn nodded. Despite the usual shoot the messenger assumption when one reported issues, she was glad that Harry took the time to get actual facts and references. She also was unsure of what sparked Harry's abrupt change in attitude, but needed to give the politically appropriate response.

"Well I guess that's all I can ask for."

She stood to leave, with a slight nod, the neutral expression on her face revealing nothing. "Apology accepted. I need to catch up with charting."

Harry rose and nodded then watched her leave, before extracting his phone to text before leaving through the main hospital entrance.

Why are you just getting back to me? I hear you're meeting Harry; why? And why the hell didn't you let me know before you went to the storage space?

Taryn was in the middle of a text argument with Blake, and still hadn't made it to the doctors' lounge to complete her charts.

No... I forgot...and Charlie was back-up, but he's not acting like my keeper.

I'm not your goddam keeper either. I don't want to lose another friend to whatever the fuck is happening in this hell-hole...by the time you whip out that glorified toothpick Charlie said he lent you, you've already let the wrong people too close. Just sayin...

Taryn gave a sheepish smile at truth.

Well okay...thanks...we still on tonight? I've got no cases.

Yes. 6 okay? I'm finishing up now.
Done.

As she walked to the hospital doctors' lounge, Taryn debated her options for locating the on-site general storage areas without being obvious or relying on people with questionable loyalty.

She was outside the lounge when she heard raised voices and smelled a mingled aroma of cigarette smoke and cologne. She glanced around the empty corridor. She referred to this time as the post 3 p.m. and pre-5:30 p.m. lull when most docs didn't make use of the lounge; there was no one around. She gave in to her instincts for caution, decided to do some surreptitious listening rather than doing her charting as planned.

"Are you sure we're in the clear? What about..."

"Shipments went out this afternoon. We're on trial delivery basis for the next two weeks, then we'll ramp up to full capacity."

"But what about..."

"Taking care of that."

"We good for space? We receive full delivery starting next week."

Three voices...all familiar... but not clear enough to identify...or speculate the connection to the odor that had agitated Maxx the previous night. Another twangy voice joined in. *Four people?*

"Junior, done tole you ...you worry too damn much..."

"Shut it! Not here."

"Whatever."

Taryn frowned, weighing her chances of getting close

enough to peer through the open door when her text alert went off. She swore silently as she slapped it off and raced for the intersecting corridor and the women's bathroom that lay a few feet away from the corner. She leaned her head on the door as she willed her breathing and heartbeat to settle. There was no chance that she would hear any footsteps on the carpeted floor, and none of the unseen men would dare come in the bathroom...would they?

She checked to see who had sent the text; Charlie inquiring about her availability for the next morning. She responded, then waited five minutes before slipping out to return to the operating room, failing to notice the mirror nestled in the top corner of the corridor.

"Here's trouble! Where's Maxx, Sugar? I'd counted on having a couple of work break walks with the two of you to clear my head."

Taryn shrugged. So, the current Blake forecast was chipper, cheery, and chummy. They should be due for a mood change within the hour. Blake took Taryn's coat and slung his arm around her shoulders as he ushered her into his great room.

"He's holding down the fort; decided I'd feel better about going back home if he'd been on patrol. Soooo...I'm guessing we're friends, or at least not adversaries now."

Blake sighed and looked away. "I'm just trying, again, to extract myself from a very large hole that I created with my mouth and some assumptions. I'm sorry."

Taryn nodded. "We can try at the friend thing."

Seemed like the day for apologies. For some reason, she was much more inclined to move on without suspicion with

Blake than with Harry...and tried to tell herself it was unrelated to the growing attraction that she felt towards Blake. "I took a chance on bringing a red for dinner, since I had no idea what you were cooking." She handed him the bottle she had purchased.

"Perfect! I've got chili cooking."

Taryn laughed at the national guy dinner fallback, second only to spaghetti.

Blake waved her toward his work center, while he fetched a corkscrew and glasses. Blake's work setup and the riot of papers on the coffee table told Taryn as much about his MO as the blues rock wailing in the background. She hoped she'd remembered her noise cancelling headphones. After settling at the short end of the table remote from the chaos of Blake's work-space, Taryn pulled two laptops from her backpack. She booted up James' laptop and lined up her notebook with a couple pens and her computer to the side. Blake returned with wineglasses and the open bottle and poured for Taryn before filling his glass.

"I'll need some clues before we try to access the laptop. Pretty sure James is the type who'd have an automatic wipe if there were too many failed access attempts."

Taryn nodded and sampled her wine. "Probably has the same on his phone. The fact that it's a MacBook is a huge break, since my brain works best in Mac. You know James best; my only commonality with him is we both happened to be anesthesiologists. What did he enjoy outside of work other than skiing? And did he have a password retention program on his smartphone?" Taryn started playing with her favorite pen and thinking aid.

"That would pre-suppose that Steve or I could get into his phone. Neither of us were willing to stumble around it for access."

"Hmm...most people, most guys actually, use dates, which is the reason they get hacked so easily. I may be wrong about that; it'd still be nice to be able access his phone to see if he had a password retention program."

Blake put down his glass before tasting the wine, his face twisted in disgust.. "Really? You're gonna generalize about men, pass codes, and dates?"

"Nothing personal; just an observation after what I saw with my ex, and the one time I managed to hack Cody's phone. Birthdays, especially girlfriend birthdays, seem to be an easy default. Was James more a numbers guy or into patterns?"

"How's that relevant?"

Taryn sighed and rolled her eyes rather than saying anything that would provoke more arguing. Nothing involving this man was going to be easy, even brainstorming. "I'm just wondering if he had a pattern or numeric passcode on his phone, and if there are hints about significant examples of either."

"I'm still trying to get why we're talking about his fucking phone and not his laptop."

"Are you always this obnoxious when someone's just trying to have a...never mind," Taryn shook her head, remembering how they met.

"Hey, I love blues, but is this problem-solving music for you?" Blake frowned.

"Yeah...is that gonna be another issue? In addition to dates and pass codes?" Now he was scowling at her. Storm clouds gathering, and thunder-snow eminent...music obviously would stay, and maybe she could figure out the pass code without getting access to the phone. And yet, Taryn realized, the man managed to be total eye candy even though he was being pissy with her. As soon as she had the musings, she realized that line of thought was not going to be conducive to much progress. She immediately came back to the task at hand. "Do you have any pics of Steve and James?"

"Actually, I do; it's one of the three of us the night before James left for Kilimanjaro. It was his first gig as an expedition doc, three years ago. He always said that trip changed his life." Blake opened his photo app, found the picture he had spoken of, and turned the screen towards Taryn, who smiled.

"Awesome pic...Date?" Taryn mentally perved on the picture of the three handsome men as she scribbled the numbers down and woke James' laptop. The lock screen pic was of a stunning, smiling, redhead in front of a canvas filled with riotous color. "Is this his girlfriend?" She sipped her wine and looked in vain for distinctive numbers or signs in the picture.

"Fiancée...Dianna; that was at her show in Denver. You want her birthdate, too?" Blake leaned back and draped both arms over the back of the sofa with a smile, focusing more on what Taryn was wearing and how she looked in it than in what she was saying.

Taryn hummed as she sipped her wine and debated the options. Pic of a fiancée on his screensaver, art show...expedition trip that had changed his life... "Did he meet Dianna before or after the trip? What was her birthdate and the date of her show?"

"Years before and her birthdate's June 3, 1979. The show was after he came back from Africa. You sure enough about this birthdate thing to bet on it? More wine?"

"When did they get engaged?"

"Christmas, last year. You didn't answer about the wager...or wine. And that's *three* dates; you said birthdate before. You changin' your mind...or are you afraid to put your money where your mouth is, Sugar?"

"I'm neither, and no...just thinking. More wine would be great with dinner, not before." Taryn twiddled her pen while looking at the picture. She sneaked a glance at Blake and wondered how his Henley undershirt looked without the flannel shirt over it. "You get many women you work with who let that 'sugar' nonsense stand? Pretty much in the same category as 'mansplaining."

"Never...and I would never mansplain."

"You lie...flagrantly. Okay, I'm in for twenty; I'll also want a music change, and loser cleans up after dinner... I'm going with the date of the Kilimanjaro trip, not the birthdate. James was an interesting man; I wish I could have met him."

"What's wrong with my goddamn music? And what's with the extra conditions? And yes... he was."

Taryn was only half listening to Blake as she held her breath and typed in the date James left for the Kilimanjaro expedition: 1- 29-2010. No luck...after thinking more, she then typed out January instead of just 1, then spun the computer around to face Blake. He looked at the screen, then her, before leaning back in his chair, with a half-smile.

"WIFI code's 'Downhill' ...I'll get your money.... pretty slick, Sugar. Just tell me why you added cleanup duty after dinner?"

"Cook never cleans up, so I would have been stuck. I also have a brother and know how much chaos men leave when they cook...one disaster clean-up at a time."

Blake roared with laughter at her perception and accuracy, becoming more interested in finding out what made this complex woman tick.

"THERE'S INFO ON OR DRUGS AND REACTIONS GOING

back to when James started working here. It's been going on for months. It's gonna take hours to get through what's here." Taryn entered the information into her existing spreadsheet on drug data between mouthfuls of chili. She was also up another $20 for winning another wager with Blake, as James' address was also the unlock code for his phone.

"Why'd he wait until December to make a stink?"

"In a word? Downing...who apparently is his own enigma." Taryn told Blake about the picture discrepancy dating to Downing's previous job.

"With what you overheard before you left work, it all fits with some type of op involving pharmaceuticals...so big bucks involved."

"This is bigger than just Bend...and why Charlie told me he's tagging his friend in Portland. You able to join us tomorrow?"

"No cases tomorrow, so yes. We talking a phone or in-person meeting?"

"Not sure. I just have to be at the hospital for call at three."

"Wouldn't dream of missing it."

CHAPTER FOURTEEN

Friday

Taryn scrolled though the file list on James's computer as she half-listened to the ongoing debate between Blake and Charlie. They had just ended an hour-long phone conference with Charlie's friend, Cy Foster, who was Division Chief in the Portland Office of the Department of Homeland Security, DHS. Cy was convinced that the scant information they had fit with a cold case involving a drug counterfeiting scheme that DHS had been attempting to track down for over five years. There had been similar reports of defective drugs in use at a Chicago hospital, but an extensive DHS investigation had not produced further leads or suspects. Both the individual reporting the problems and the physical evidence had disappeared shortly after the initial report had been filed, and there had been no recurrences... until now. Taryn's chance discovery of the hospital truck moving stock meant that the operation might have resurfaced in Bend. The bits of conversation that Taryn had overheard the day before were consistent with this possibility. Taryn was convinced that the counterfeiting scheme was about to go to live. She just needed to find the proof to prevent the enactment of a process that might put the national and international pharmaceutical market at risk from defective product. The problem was that no one could agree just how the she and Blake would get the information that DHS needed in order to act.

"If the only samples we have of defective drugs are those that James sent, it sounds like we just need to send in more samples. Taryn can do that; problem solved."

"Nope. That just shuts the program down here, and just like Chicago, everything gets packed up and moved somewhere else. We delay the inevitable." Blake had come to Taryn's condo for the conference and turned to look as she rejoined the Face-Time call with Charlie. "From what I understand, we need proof of involvement of the organizers here, along with connections to the company manufacturing the drugs, and proof that they are moving product outside of Bend."

"We need more drug usage data."

"I've sent you a copy of a file I found on James' computer. It's similar to a list I've been working with. He documents the hospital departments that he guessed were aware of the issues with the defective drugs." Charlie pulled up the file while Blake shared Taryn's computer.

"I'd suggest adding Facilities to the list of Admin, Pharmacy, Pathology, and Anesthesia departments. Someone in all five of those areas would have to be involved to hide evidence that there were defective drugs being used and moved."

"Not following you."

"With the stuff I've already gotten from the files I

accessed in pharmacy, I can prove they're ordering amounts of Propofol above what's needed according to usage in the OR and ICUs."

"Why's that significant?"

"If you can't maximize profit by having drugs under patent that you can charge premium prices for, you have to make up for it by making profit by moving volume. Propofol's the most used drug in any operating room outside of oxygen. Think of the number of operating rooms in hospitals and surgery centers across the country. If they're trying to launch a counterfeiting scheme, makes sense that they start with moving a drug that's used frequently to maximize their profit."

"So, who in pharmacy orders drugs?"

"Not pharmacy. We need the person authorizing the purchases, which has got to be either Cook or Raynor...or both."

"Admin, then..."

"And the company manufacturing the product."

"I'm still not following."

"Blake, most of the operating room drug stock here is made by one company, Eagle Pharmaceuticals. The information James collected confirms what I've found. I just sent you what I've compiled from both sets of records."

"I have it...so you think if we identify the manufacturing company, we could also find the factory where the counterfeit product is produced?"

"Absolutely. Even though there are FDA satellite offices overseas to insure internationally sourced drugs are manufactured to U.S. standards, there's no way that they can 100% guarantee that foreign run companies adhere to those standards outside of times when they are under direct inspection. Production variances can happen even in U.S. based companies. When you factor in a tendency or opportunity to take production shortcuts in foreign-based facilities, you have even more potential to cut costs for increased profits."

"Why the hell would anyone take that kind of chance? Why not manufacture the drugs according to standards, and just make the profit you can based on maximizing volume of product you move, undercutting the competition on price and quality?"

Taryn shook her head. "Spoken like someone who's in R&D rather than involved in practice. The U.S. is the largest pharmaceutical sales market in the world. Look at TV ads; how many people do you know who either take a pill, want to take a pill, or think they need to take a pill? With the potential for profit, I guess I'm surprised this hasn't happened sooner."

"She's spot on, Blake. My question is how the two of you are going to manage to stay under the radar while you get the info you need on who in the hospital is involved. Especially since they are likely the same people who killed James."

"Not a clue, but we'll do what we need to do."

"Yes, but we're talking about a drug counterfeiting plan preparing to go national; let's think beyond Bend. The organizational superstructure could potentially involve someone high up in FDA, not to mention Customs, since they inspect and certify drugs made internationally before they can be inspected by FDA and imported. We need access to whoever is behind this operation, not just peripheral operatives. Cy and DHS have the juice to make that happen."

"But I think, and Cy agrees, that after one expensive fail, the folks here who are involved are high up in the organization and committed to success. They can't afford for this to head south like it did in Chicago."

"Who do you suspect?"

Taryn shook her head and shrugged. "There are too many possibilities. We first have to connect individuals in all of the departments on the list to definitive activities. It's time consuming, but likely to be most successful."

"Why don't we start with getting proof of who's ordering the excess Propofol? There's got to be a purchase order for that."

"That would give us the admin, pharmacy, and facilities connection."

"Knowing the vehicle number of the truck Taryn saw at the storage facility should lead us to the facilities person who was driving the vehicle."

"I've identified some possible hospital contacts who can help us, and who aren't likely involved in the scheme."

"Closer to home...who in the anesthesia department do you think is involved?"

Taryn thought back to her meeting with Harry, and encounters with Michael Downing. "Toss-up between Harry and Downing, but given the info that the Colorado version of Michael Downing is not the same as the Bend version, he gets my vote. We still need to find out why and how he came to be here."

Charlie shook his head. "Hard to believe that someone could fake being an anesthesiologist, but that's what it seems like is happening."

"What better time to swap people than when people change jobs and states? Anyone bold enough to pull it off is intelligent and has tons of backup. And Downing's always bothered me on a subliminal level; maybe this is why."

"Sugar, I'm not suggesting you don't know your stuff...but who can help with computer access? I can be your physical OR backup, and basic computer stuff, but hacking isn't my forte." Taryn blinked in surprise at Blake's candor.

"Cody's always my first call for that."

"I can get you an assist from Cy and his DHS team in Portland."

"Let me look at what I know from my access of the pharmacy, and I'll let you know what I need help with."

Charlie agreed, then ended the call. Taryn tilted her head to regard Blake as she rubbed Maxx's side as he slumbered at her feet. "Sugar?"

Blake shrugged then gave her a sheepish smile. "Dr. Sugar?"

"You call me that at work, and I won't be responsible for the consequences."

"Promise or threat?"

"You know, somehow, you're growing on me...maybe like a mushroom."

AFTER BLAKE WENT TO WORK FOR HIS AFTERNOON CASE, Taryn spent her remaining time before going on-call pouring over the information she had managed to gather about the organization of the hospital pharmacy and how non-controlled substance product and usage were tracked. She managed to infiltrate the hospital email, and was tracking the stock orders and invoices, finding nothing but expected purchases and orders for Propofol and the other drugs of interest. She was able to access the records for the previous year, and the purchases lined up perfectly with usage, making it clear that there had been a change in records handling. After over an hour of not finding the results she expected, she sighed, then began to pack up the laptops and prepare for her call shift. Her cell rang as she finalized her work prep...Charlie.

"Not sure if you had thought of this, but what do you think of backing up the information on James' computer and journal?"

"Already done... I uploaded the info to a secure account after we spoke this morning and was planning on dropping everything by your office so you could secure the laptop and journals, maybe send them to DHS."

"Good idea. Any new brainstorms?"

Taryn paged through James' journal for any evidence that she might have overlooked. "I didn't find the orders and invoices I expected to see in pharmacy records. I've actually decided that I'm overlooking the obvious. Where would you hide paper docs and invoices if you were trying to hide what you were doing?"

"Paper? Really?"

"Electronic footprints and files would be the first place someone would think to look for this kind of stuff. What if the powers that be in charge of this tangle decided to use paper...which you can get rid of as fast as you can operate a shredder."

"I only see that for internal issues. There have to be electronic records for an operation this massive."

"Means we have to figure a way to get access to the original files, which have gotta be on the comps or records of the people over the local op."

"Which leads us back to someone in admin. Unlikely that person or persons would bring their electronics to work."

"We need to access their personal comps or networks."

"Do you have a plan or is this just speculation. And we need likely suspects."

"I need to talk to Cody on the how...then I'll get back to you."

After ending the call with Charlie, Taryn hustled to get

Maxx to daycare and herself to work on time, with time out to drop their only real evidence at Charlie's office.

"DR. PIRELLI? WOULD YOU MIND STOPPING BY THE Med-Staff office before reporting for work today?"

"Sure." Taryn frowned before ending the call and checking the time. She should still be able to make it in to the operating room on time since the Medical Staff office was around the corner from the hospital doctors' lounge. She entered the office, finding hospital security, a lab technician and the Nursing Director instead of the staff secretary.

"Dr. Pirelli, I'm here on behalf of operations and Med Staff. We got an anonymous tip that you were experiencing conduct and performance issues consistent with substance abuse. Coupled with some recent drug accountability issues, we feel that it's necessary for you to have a blood and urine narcotics and toxicology screen before you can assume your call duties tonight. Can you leave your things here and accompany the technician to the lab?"

"What?" Taryn initially panicked, then considered her options. "You mean go with someone who could potentially falsify results with some pre-drawn blood and urine samples so you can railroad me out of here? Not a chance." The small knot of people glanced among themselves uneasily at Taryn's refusal, making her realize that she had both options and leverage. She pulled out her cell and called Charlie, being careful not to call him by name.

"Hi...it's Taryn. I'm in the Med-Staff office with some people who want to do some drug and urine tox screens since I'm apparently under suspicion for being intoxicated while on duty. Any way you can help me out?" Taryn nodded as

Charlie outlined a quick workable solution, then disconnected the call, and shrugged out of her coat, and dropped her backpack by one of the chairs in the waiting area, before smiling at the Nursing Director. "I'm happy to give you all of the samples you request, as long as I have the option to get the samples verified by an outside lab, to protect both my confidentially and my practice." The staff in the office were uneasy, and clearly unprepared for a counterproposal, but regrouped and agreed to Taryn's logical and workable proposal. Taryn relaxed, and pulled out her phone to answer the day's texts and emails as she waited.

THEY WERE STILL WAITING FOR THE OUTSIDE LAB courier when Harry Lam, breathless and white-faced, burst into the office.

"What do you mean you're detaining Dr. Pirelli because she has a drug issue? Wasn't the pharmacy discrepancy solved?" Taryn smiled, as at ease as Harry Lam was confused, and the collection of hospital officials were nervous.

"Apparently not...or this is something else. It seems someone has a concern that I'm impaired, and need to be drug tested." The initial bravado of the people who had confronted Taryn had devolved into a nervous shifting of feet and whispers. Harry focused on the uneasy cluster of people trying to disappear.

"Unacceptable...and not according to protocol. I'm Dr. Pirelli's direct supervisor, even if she is temporary. Any complaint should have been directed to and executed by me, and I have no knowledge of any such problems. Who lodged the complaints? On what data are they based?" There was more mumbling, before the Nursing Director answered.

"It's confidential, when this type of complaint is lodged, Dr. Lam, as I'm sure you know." Harry looked from the Nursing Director to an unusually calm Taryn in frustration. "Taryn...I don't know what to do. The complaints about substance abuse are always confidential."

Taryn smiled and shrugged. "Thanks Harry...and I have no problem getting drug tested...but I'd like to ask that the test be repeated by an independent lab."

"What?" Harry looked from Taryn to the Nursing Director, who was now red-faced.

"I'd like a duplicate test done by a lab apart from the hospital."

There was a knock on the door before it was opened by an officer from Bend Police Department. "We got here as fast as we could Dr. Pirelli. Seems they want you drug tested for something here at the hospital, and you need a backup test done by an outside lab? We'd be happy to transport the samples to the secondary lab the PD uses to confirm our results. Will that meet your criteria? And those of the hospital?"

"Absolutely. That okay with you two?" Both the Nursing Director and the hospital security officer nodded reluctantly, clearly at a loss for rebuttal. Taryn smiled and rose, leaving both her backpack and coat behind.

"If there's protocol to ensure test integrity and evidence chain, we can do the blood draw here, and then the urine tox. You do have enough sampling containers for duplicates?" Taryn smiled at the pale, sweaty hospital lab tech, who nodded after a quick glance at the nursing director.

"Great...let's get this done, so I can get back to work.

THE SAMPLES WERE SENT OFF TO THE LABS AND TARYN was in the elevator headed for the OR, with Harry at her side stammering an apology, which Taryn accepted with a shrug. "Harry, given the way everything's been going here, I'd have to say I'm not surprised. It's not your doing, or fault. There's something abnormal here, even if I haven't figured out exactly what. The biggest question is what are you going to do to help me?"

"What?" Even as he said it, Harry closed his eyes in anticipation of Taryn's next response.

"This isn't an accident, it's a pattern. Someone wants me out of the way as much as they wanted James Harris gone." The elevator door opened, and Harry followed Taryn out and through the automatic door to the surgical suite.

"You're right; again." Harry sighed.

"How long will it take to get the drug test back?" Operating Room staff going by made a pointed effort not to meet Taryn's gaze or greet her. Great....somehow *everyone* seemed to know about her 'confidential' issues.

"Everything was sent STAT...should have results in less than fifteen minutes from the time it was entered."

"Great...I'll just wait in the lounge." Taryn waved, and grabbed the remote before flopping into the couch in front of the TV. Call me when I'm cleared to go to work."

WHAT THE FUCK DO YOU MEAN SHE GOT A BACKUP TOX *screening? You're being paid to make things happen, not cause more problems. Even if we're still on schedule, this is an issue.*

As Taryn waited for her drug screen results, she texted and emailed Charlie and Blake with a recent event update.

Nothing succeeds like success. If I'm being accused of substance abuse, I think we've pissed off the right people. Thanks for the help with the secondary lab, Charlie.

Help and a rescue this time, but what about next time?

Why on earth do you look at pissing people off as a victory?

If they're this desperate to get rid of me, we must be close to figuring out who's involved.

CHAPTER FIFTEEN

Saturday

The phone rang early, short-circuiting Taryn's plan to sleep in after her night on call, and the barely averted disaster of the drug test. She fumbled for the phone, expecting to have to chew out either Charlie or Blake for waking her early for more endless debate on how to proceed with the investigation.

"Hey Taryn! It's Trina...you didn't tell me you had a pharma distributer in Bend. BMC Industries saved the day and our OR schedule last week."

"Ah...what?" Trina was a friend and former residency classmate who was in a private practice group outside of St. Louis.

"Our usual supplier was out of Propofol; it was backordered or some nonsense. Of course, none of our alternate suppliers could help us. One of our pharmacists happened to know someone who had a contact who knew an independent distributer in Bend, and poof...problem solved."

Taryn bolted out of bed, wide awake, searching for paper and something to write with, while formulating questions to avoid giving out too much information. "Hey...good for you... and what's the name of that company again? And any chance you could give me the name of the pharmacist?" She wrote down the information from her former residency buddy as she organized her thoughts. "Can you also send us a bottle of Propofol from that shipment? Maybe even the packing invoice?"

"Sure."

Taryn rattled off Charlie's office address before she disconnected from Trina and realized that targeting the ordering invoices and authorizations from the hospital pharmacy had jumped a couple places higher on the priority list. Before she could plan further, her phone rang again.

"Sweetie? Your mom's in the hospital. They just got her transferred from ER."

"What's happening? I thought they had her on a different drug regimen."

"Which ended up not working."

Taryn was silent as she replayed all of the drug-related patient events she had dealt with over the previous two weeks and debated the odds.

"Can I talk to her? What are her docs saying?"

"She just went to sleep...and they're hoping to have her out within a couple days."

Taryn sighed as she watched Maxx rise from his pillow at the foot of her bed, doing doggie yoga before ambling over for a head rub. Logically, she knew that her mother was in the best possible place, but she felt even more protective for her than she did with her patients who had drug reactions.

"I feel badly that I couldn't be there as planned."

"And it would have happened even with you here. She's fine. I just called to keep you in the loop."

After more conversation, Taryn disconnected the call, and rose to dig out her workout gear, deciding that a run would be the only thing that would settle her down enough to work.

"Maxx! Let's go."

"Getting computer access to introduce the back-door program to access Pharmacy and Admin emails won't be a problem as long as I get some help on data analysis." Taryn worked on her laptop as she chatted with Cody, fully committed to executing her plan to gain access to the pharmacy invoices and Purchase Orders.

"From the info you sent on the hospital mainframe, the security sweeps on the network are timed. Piece of cake to introduce malware to gain access then obtain the info we want and self-terminate before the next sweep. We should have all the data we need by tomorrow morning, if you can get the package in sometime before ten tonight."

"I always have charts to complete. I'll do it then."

"Public access computer would be best. I can do a few tricks so they can't track the introduction back to your login credentials or IP address, but finding a high traffic computer is the best intro route."

"Doctor's lounge it is..."

"And I'll find and alter the security cams in that area."

"Crap! I forgot you could do that!"

"What'd you do?"

"There was a corridor traffic mirror tied into the camera Thursday when I went into work."

"Too late to fix it now; just have to hope for the best. Where's your research buddy, Blake?"

"He's hitting the office at the storage facility today. We've gotta get into that hospital storage space."

"He renting a space?"

"Yup. Best way to get operational info. He should be back here with the scoop any minute." The doorbell rang and Maxx ran to the door, barking. "Right on time...he's here...I'll give you a buzz when I'm on my way into the hospital.

Taryn disconnected then followed Maxx. Blake was at the door, backpack slung over his shoulder, carrying a coffee caddy, wearing morning scruffy sexy in a way that even rivaled Cody. Taryn realized her stock objections to Blake were collapsing with each new day. "Double shot mocha with peppermint, right?" Maxx swarmed excitedly around Taryn and Blake as Taryn went on tiptoe to give Blake an unexpected peck on the cheek, before grabbing her cup and closing the door behind him.

"Yes...you're making some style points. What did you find out about Deschutes storage?"

ALTHOUGH TARYN WAS CHAGRINNED TO FIND OUT THAT Blake had charmed his way past the woman on duty at the office that morning, she tried to focus on the positives rather than obsessing and speculating about his process.

"A shared exterior door key for all the space on a given row means that we can at least get into the first level of security. The space James rented is in the same row where we saw the hospital truck. Wonder who's on the books as renting that space? Wanna bet it's the BMC space, too?" Blake was combing business filings to find if the BMC Corp that shipped the Propofol had also filed as a legitimate business.

"Once we decide when we're doing it, getting in is not gonna be a problem. Never found a lock that I can't pick."

Blake looked up from his work on the business filings, incredulous. "Where'd you learn how to pick locks?"

"You say that like it's something far afield. Lots of people can pick locks"

"Not any docs I know, so I'd say it's sketchy."

"Hey, everyone has a hidden talent.... or two. And people in medicine are far from monolithic."

"And you're just full of surprises." Blake spun his laptop so that Taryn could see the screen. "I've got the business filing info on BMC...tracks to a PO Box. They're less than a year in business according to this. No associated owner."

"Looks like an attended postal center; there's a street address in addition to a box number. They still have to present a government ID of some sort to rent a box. We'll hopefully get one name."

"Assuming they aren't using a fake ID. Think Charlie's friends at DHS can get us the rest of the registration info?"

"I'm counting on it. No way should either of us take a chance on walking in there. Speaking of which, what's the security cam system like at the storage facility? How are we gonna get around it?"

"There's a new and mysterious malfunction...I unplugged the cable to their external storage drive. Pretty low tech."

Taryn narrowed her eyes at Blake as she realized the likely extent of Blake's distraction of the attendant in the storage office. "I'm starting to take back the points I gave you for bringing my mocha. You're an operator."

"And you're jealous, Sugar." Taryn's immediate, but subtle blush told Blake that he had effectively assessed her likely response to his provocation, and his smug smile let Taryn know that in some small way, she had just been played.

"You know, I think it's time for me... and you to leave."

Blake laughed at the abrupt change in plans. "You really are jealous."

"Nope, just need to get to the hospital and get this portal established."

Blake got an unholy light in his eyes as he stood and shrugged into his coat. "Okay, you get a bye...why don't we resume this over dinner?"

"Ah....well..."

"You're not wimping out on me, are you?"

Taryn realized that she had been cornered...again and frowned. "Dinner it is."

"Let's shoot for 6."

TARYN WAS STILL FUMING OVER HER UNCHARACTERISTIC reaction to Blake as she drove to the hospital. It was typical Saturday afternoon light, after most of the staff with patients in the hospital had done morning rounds. Eager to minimize her time there, Taryn parked in the visitor parking lot and entered through the main entrance rather than her usual path from doctor's parking. Lost in thought, she almost missed the window labelled Outpatient Pharmacy, located just past the hospital gift shop. There was a short line of customers in front of the service window, and Taryn shivered when she realized that the last name of the on-duty pharmacist was the same as her friend Trina had given. After shaking her head, Taryn continued to the thankfully empty doctor's lounge, where she completed her chart work. After introducing the back-door package Cody constructed, Taryn headed back to her vehicle, texting Trina to act on her latest hunch.

Any chance you could ask your pharmacist how he came to know his pharmacy contact here in Bend?

Already did... he and Jason apparently go way back to pharmacy school in Chicago.

Taryn thanked her, and called Charlie as she started her SUV, and began the drive home. "How likely do you think it is that that manufacturing company, Eagle, is into making oral as well as IV medications?"

"Unknown. But that would be another way to increase their coverage area, and potential profit."

"Did they have an outpatient pharmacy at the hospital when you worked here?"

"They did, but were planning on closing it because of declining profits."

"Well it's still here, but I'm betting with a new in-concept and operation. And another possible revenue center." Taryn was pulling into her condo garage and checking the time; only a few hours until she would meet Blake for dinner.

"We've been concentrating so much on the operating room and what you and James found that we hadn't considered a retail pharmacy could be an option."

"It's a plausible area the operators of the scheme could expand into, but we've got way too much on our plate just to prove the IV stuff."

"I agree. What are you up to tonight?"

"Just strategic planning and dinner with Blake... I need a break."

"Nice to see you two managing to get on."

"And your point would be?"

Charlie chuckled. "Just fun watching two control freak type A's battle for supremacy. Collaboration isn't a dirty word."

"But being a nosy matchmaker is." Taryn huffed in frustration, ignoring Charlie's chuckle as she disconnected the call, then texted her dad.

Can you send me pics of Mom's most recent prescription bottles.

Sure. Why?

Humor me. I'll explain later.

As Taryn waited for Blake to pick her up for dinner, she stared at one of the five hodgepodge pages where James had written numerous, cryptic passages, only half of which had been deciphered. Her father's texted pictures confirmed that her mother's meds had been distributed by Eagle Pharmaceuticals, which gave another dimension to the counterfeiting scheme. The priority was still to determine what was going on at the hospital, although she had put Cody to work on a background check for the pharmacist, Jason Hunter, and was awaiting the results after her introduction of the back-door program into the hospital computer system. Everything at this point hinged on getting a break in connecting the pharmacy to administration. Maxx ran to the door, barking seconds before the doorbell rang. Blake was there with a huge bouquet of tropical flowers and a lopsided grin.

"What...why?"

"You gonna let me in?"

Taryn looked from the flowers to Blake, who tousled Maxx's ears before giving her the flowers.

"Somehow, these seemed to suit you. You have a vase?" He shrugged out of his coat, and walked towards the kitchen.

Taryn eyed the flowers warily then trailed Blake to the kitchen. Blake was making himself at home, peering in her refrigerator. "Not sure if I should put these in water or check them for incendiary devices."

Blake looked back at her and gave a crooked smile. "You always this cynical? Mind if I grab a beer?"

"Sure..and cynicism's SOP when dealing with someone who uses gender charm to get his way...or distract people. That *is* how you were planning on working things tonite?" Blake's guilty expression gave her the answer she needed.

"I thought I was just doing something nice."

"Kinda overkill and a sure sign of advance plotting to come up with flowers like these in the dead of winter. I've seen both my brother and Cody in action. Operators do what they do."

Despite her sharp words, Taryn enjoyed the way the sight and smell of the flowers brightened up the afternoon, and the issues facing them. She also appreciated that Blake had made a plan and taken the time to cheer her up. Another brick fell from her wall of opposition to Blake.

"And I do like the flowers...thanks." She went on tiptoe to plant a gentle kiss on Blake's lips, surprised when he deepened the kiss, and held her close.

"Pretty flowers for a pretty and wicked smart lady...you're habit forming." Blake's smile made Taryn blush. She covered her embarrassment by focusing on Maxx.

"Maxx! Let's go potty." Maxx gave a woof, then trotted out the kitchen door to the backyard to do his duty.

"Nice...Maxx is your camouflage. You bringing him with us?"

Taryn whirled, frowning and about to respond in kind when she saw Blake's smile.

"Gotcha, Sugar."

Taryn looked at him, then yanked the door open. "Maxx...come!" She gave him a bone then shrugged into her coat as the dog trotted under the table to flop down and enjoy his treat. "I think we should go by the storage tonight rather than wait for tomorrow."

"There's a topic change...Because?"

"I don't think we'd be likely to run into anyone there. And even though it's 4:30, it's dark..."

"Why the sudden decision?"

"I looked at the journal and thought about when we saw the hospital truck at the storage. I think Mondays are delivery to the space days, and Thursdays are shipping days." Taryn walked toward the door leading to the garage and her truck.

"And?" Blake grabbed the door before she could open it.

"Maybe inventory on Sunday? Or at least activity then."

Blake nodded. "Good idea. And a good reason for me to drive."

Taryn scowled. "I don't follow."

"You and your car are higher profile than I am."

"But you disabled the security cam. Who's going to see?"

"Why take the chance? They aren't exactly fond of me at work, but you've actively pissed folks off...by your own admission."

Taryn replayed her past two weeks and nodded. "Fine...so what's the plan?"

"I was thinking you should get in the back seat; on the floor actually when we get there. Stay hidden until we get through the gate, then you're on for access. We're both wearing dark clothing; ditch your parka before you leave the car, and we're good to go."

Taryn nodded in agreement as she and Blake exited through the front door, checking to assure it was locked before proceeding to Blake's truck. It had just begun to snow. "After we're done, we can continue our little chat about your jealous side from this morning." Taryn swore under her breath.

"Can't we just drop that, and deal with moving forward with getting pharmacy info?"

"Cody can screen the raw data, and we can do follow up with whatever he gets. I'm not letting go of the fact that you seem to be mighty interested in my recreational habits."

"Nah...just don't look forward to being part of the game."

Blake laughed as Taryn slid into the back seat and closed her door, then shook his head as he rounded to the driver's side mumbling, "Woman always has a comeback."

"Onward, Jeeves." Taryn grinned and waved. "I think you're kinda my chauffeur.

Blake rolled his eyes and flicked a glance at her in the review mirror before backing out. "So where are your tools for this lock picking B & E you say you're gonna pull." Blake gave a lopsided grin and got the expected response as he started the drive to the storage facility.

"Why do I get the impression you doubt my skills? I've got my toolkit in my pocket."

"Let's just say I'll believe you can do this after I see it."

"You care to put money where your mouth is?"

"Sugar, I do think you'll be able to get in...eventually."

"How much you in for?"

Blake gave a grin as he flicked on satellite radio. "Winner's choice."

Taryn opened, then closed her mouth as she looked at him warily. "As in?"

"You all in, or chicken?"

"And you're annoying. I'll take the bet and get in within five minutes of touching the lock."

"Done...let's do it...blanket's on the back seat for when we get close."

CHAPTER SIXTEEN

Deschutes Storage

"Clock's ticking, Sugar. How much longer you gonna take?"

"As long as I need, and you aren't helping matters." Taryn was having trouble with the second, target lock in the storage bay. The storage office had been closed, so Blake didn't get the opportunity to confirm that the security cams were still offline. They decided to proceed anyway. After using the gate access code, Blake parked his truck before the row assigned for his storage unit. He and Taryn took the long route to the row where the hospital storage space was located. They gained access with the external key for the bays on that row and found only two of four storage spaces occupied in the bay where Taryn had seen the truck parked.

Taryn accessed the first lock easily, only to find the space filled with household items. Her confidence in her skills started to slide when she failed to access the second lock as quickly. She stood up and shrugged her shoulders to relieve the tension before crouching to resume her attack on the lock.

"I usually don't have this kinda trouble. I'm not sure..." Before defeat kicked in, there was a click and Taryn smiled in triumph. "In!" She removed the lock and opened the door as Blake shone a light into the large space that was partially filled with boxes.

"I don't see any labels." They both entered, and pulled the door partially closed.

"And you won't. Taryn surveyed the collection of boxes. "My guess is that they have these boxes arranged in some order based on content...and have a list of what's in each group of boxes. No way that anything commercially shipped will have labels advertising that controlled or hypnotic agents are in the box. Too obvious."

Blake nodded. "Hah...makes sense. What's the plan?"

"First, take some pics of how everything looks now; then we have a reference point for what it needs to look like when we leave."

"That works."

After Blake had taken a series of pictures of the interior, Taryn went to one of the boxes stacked at the back of the space and pulled out a screwdriver.

"Let's see what we've got." Taryn snapped more pictures of the area around the box she intended to open before actually slicing the tape along the box edges. After shifting the packing material aside, she found boxes with the familiar blue and white Propofol color scheme. She extracted a box, carefully ran her screwdriver under the flap to open it, then removed two bottles of Propofol.

"No way anyone will detect that these bottles are gone just by weight. They won't know anything's wrong until the box is delivered." As Taryn stashed the bottles in a pocket,

Blake extracted a device from his own pocket and donned a pair of latex gloves. He crouched down, positioning the device in a shadow created by the corrugated siding. He attached it to the wall, a foot from the floor in an area slightly in front of the first row of boxes. Even with the light from the bay, the device was not easily seen.

"What are you doing?" Taryn looked over his shoulder with a frown. "I thought the idea was to leave things as they were?"

"We are...this is a motion activated cam. Wouldn't you like to know when someone comes in this space again?" Blake rose, then launched the app on his phone, before waving his hand in front of the camera; the phone chimed an alert.

"Yeah...but I also don't want them tracing it back to us. Hey, that thing doesn't even have an activation light." Taryn crouched to look at the camera. "Charlie hook you up?"

"Yup... only works with ambient light, so no visual details. No wires, no problems."

"How long's the battery last?"

"A month...maybe."

"Maybe we'll get lucky...and hopefully not caught."

"Wonder what's up with this?" Blake had walked to an area in the space with chairs and what looked like an OR Mayo stand. Taryn came over for a closer look, noting that all of the items were pushed to one side with a space cleared between them and the boxes.

"Not sure, but I don't like taking more time to speculate while we're here.

"Agreed. Let's get that box resealed." Blake pulled out the bottle of glue and tape from his pocket and helped Taryn reseal the internal box, replace the packing material, then tape the external box shut. They stacked another box on top to hide what they had done.

"Let's hope no one looks too carefully at each box."

Taryn and Blake exited after comparing the space and box arrangement to the picture they had taken upon entering. They closed the door and lock, then walked back to Blake's car. Taryn slipped into the back seat and slid onto the floor, again hiding under the blanket before Blake drove to the gate.

"Shit! This isn't looking good."

"What's up?"

"Someone's in the office."

"That sucks. Wasn't it closed earlier?"

"It was. There's a repair truck with ladders and gear, but no logo in the front lot. Wonder what's up?" As soon as the gate opened, Blake eased through, and drove away.

"Security cam repair? Anyone coming out of the office?"

"No...and if they're working on the security cams, I hope like hell they haven't fixed them...or at least didn't catch us. He rechecked his review mirror as he turned onto the street. No one emerged, and he breathed a sigh of relief as he headed toward the restaurant. "We're out of view of the office, and no one's behind us. I think we're in the clear."

Taryn emerged from concealment under the blanket. "What do you think the chances are that they got the security cams back up?"

"Unknown. If they figured out it was a power issue, they may have gotten them online quickly. I disconnected a com cable in addition to the power cord. Hopefully, they didn't start trouble-shooting the problem until we were done in the space." Both he and Taryn had on dark-colored clothing, and they had taken the precaution of disabling the motion-activated lights close to the areas they accessed.

"Was there a camera in the office itself? I'm thinking they may have a record of you coming into the office earlier," Taryn mused.

"There was a cam, but without access to their comp system, we aren't gonna be able to erase those records. All we can do at this point is hope we got lucky, and that they don't ID our entrance to storage. And speaking of luck, you took a lot longer than five minutes getting though that lock, Sugar."

"Yeah, I know. What do I owe you?"

"I'm thinking of a worthy payback...I'll get back to you."

"That's what I'm worried about."

"How did you and Steve meet up?" Taryn stirred her coffee; she needed info.

"College. He went on to get his MBA; I ended up starting the research that formed the foundation for the M&H implants. When I realized the potential for what I had, I left grad school, got Steve to help hook me up with the right funding, and developed the first M&H implant. Ten years later, here we are."

Taryn and Blake were having their first totally personal conversation after having enjoyed dinner. Over its course, Taryn found herself more interested in the man despite her initial reservations, and her focus on the drug issues at the hospital dissipated.

"Now that's a story. Huge, life changing commercial and professional success. Guessing you never bothered with the rest of grad school?"

"Actually, I did...a few years ago. I have a problem leaving things be once I decide to pursue a course of action. And in that vein..." He gave Taryn a half smile before twining one of her braids around his finger. "I've kinda got an idea about settling our bet."

"Pretty sure I can follow where this is headed." Given her

suspicions, Taryn had a jolt of panic when she realized she had no idea how she would respond; the butterflies in her stomach were dancing again. When her phone rang with Cody's ringtone, she answered on the second ring breathing a sigh of relief. She needed more delay time to think of what to do about Blake.

"You two still at dinner? It's showtime."

"Thanks Cody. We're on it." Taryn disconnected and forgot what she had intended to say when she looked at Blake.

"To be continued?" he questioned.

Taryn nodded. "The back door is open; let's see what we can find about our friends at the hospital." Blake gave a wry smile as he signaled their waiter for the check. "Not in line with my plans for tonight, but let's go with it."

As they prepared to leave, a voice interrupted. "Taryn... Blake...hope you're enjoying your...night out." Taryn turned to see Michael Downing approach their table as Blake finished paying their tab.

"Hi Michael...ah, how are...?"

"We're just leaving." Blake stood, grim faced, and helped Taryn into her coat before addressing Downing directly. "Excuse us?"

Michael gave a smile, which didn't reach his eyes. "Looks like you've both been making yourselves right at home. Didn't realize you were...friends."

"We are now." Blake answered.

Taryn looked in confusion first at Blake, then Michael Downing. "Something up with you two?"

"Goodbye Taryn." Michael watched them leave, then continued on to his table.

Taryn and Blake waited until they were in his vehicle before addressing the obvious.

"Okay was that some kind of male posturing bullshit that I just don't understand?"

"If we're lucky, it was...I'm not so sure that the wrong people don't know about our little stroll through the storage facility." Taryn was silent as Blake turned out of the parking lot.

"You think *Downing* is someone to worry about, and not just a low level operative?"

"Until we find out the reason for the discrepancy between the Colorado records and these, absolutely. And he just failed my sniff test."

"Okay, so one suspect person, in a critical area, but I don't believe he's a key operator in this, or involved with James' death. And, even if we turned up on the storage security footage, what exactly do they know? Or see?"

"Hopefully nothing...including that box we opened. Or things just might get a bit more interesting."

Maxx met Taryn and Blake at the front door, then raced first to the door off the great room, then to the one in the kitchen, barking excitedly. As they removed coats and boots, Blake watched Maxx's excited pacing and barking as he raced past Taryn, who was headed for the treat jar.

"He's wound up. Did you let him out to potty before we left for the storage?"

"Of course! He probably just heard an animal out there. Maxx! Go potty!" Before Taryn could get the door fully opened, Maxx shouldered through and ran out, barking. She shook her head as she shut the door. "Not sure what's running around out there this time of year...maybe raccoons?"

"Don't they hibernate?"

"I have no idea...but I want to get on with looking at what Cody's back door got us." Taryn fired up her laptop as Blake looked over her shoulder and paced. After a few minutes, Taryn flicked a glance at him. "If all you're gonna do is pace and hover, make yourself useful, get Maxx in and dry him off."

"Yes, Boss."

"Wiseass."

Blake smirked, then opened the door and gave a piercing whistle before calling for Maxx, who took his time before eventually bounding up the steps and into the kitchen. Blake dried him off with a towel before giving him a treat. Maxx crunched down the treat, gulped some water, then resumed his pacing circuit between the great room and the kitchen.

"He's acting strangely. I wonder what has him so stirred up?" Taryn looked up with a frown. "Well, come here and let's focus."

"You don't want me to hover; now you want me to look. Do we really have to do this? Can't I just look at the information?" Blake shook his head, then dropped down onto a barstool next to Taryn at their makeshift work center. "Next time, I'm bringing my own laptop."

Taryn scowled at him before she pulled out her tablet and deposited it in front of Blake.

"Here...use this...can't have you not being able to lend a hand."

"You're fun to annoy, know that?"

Taryn gave him a withering glance as he turned on the laptop.

"Screen share?"

"Yes. I've pulled the pharmacy PO's going back historically for the past year." Taryn accessed the files on her laptop.

"Starting 6 months ago, they started purchasing twice the amount of propofol than previously. When I pull the files from the last six months usage, it shows that nothing has changed as far as the amount of Propofol used here at the hospital. So now we have confirmation that there is an excess amount of Propofol floating around. If we can find out who authorized it to be ordered, and who is taking it from the hospital to the storage space, we should have an idea of who is involved."

"Didn't Charlie say he was working on getting the name of the driver of that truck you saw on Thursday?"

"Yup. I'm leaving all of that to him. But the critical thing is getting all the info we need from pharmacy files, and whatever else we can find before the security sweep terminates the access package that Cody inserted." Taryn leaned back in her chair, her expression intent.

"I'm surprised you're able to swing any of this. I thought the hospital operations stuff is all HIPAA protected."

"Getting slick at unauthorized access has been an acquired skill...but I always like knowing how things work... and don't work. Patient related data and communications is private, both classified and HIPAA protected. I don't go through that door if I want to keep my job, let alone my career." Taryn stretched then walked over to Maxx's treat container to toss him another treat, trying to reason her way into the next step.

"But yeah, operational info isn't necessarily that way. You know, we have our own company specific files and communications that we keep separate from patient files on implants we place, surgeons, that kind of data. All the patient related stuff is held in a separate, and differently secured manner and...."

"That's it!" Taryn sank into her chair and accessed the

computer organizational schematic file that Blake had duped shortly after beginning work at the hospital. She pulled up the file, then spun the screen to show it to Blake. "This shows that there's a parallel information stream at the hospital, with HIPAA compliant and non- HIPAA compliant limbs. There's email access through both as well as the hospital operational stuff separated from patient related stuff. Cody's back door let us into the pharmacy info, but there's a second security tier of information that I bet contains access to the emails, which could contain operational info like invoices and ordering from vendors."

"Unless the corporate chain is in on this thing, and the stock is coming through corporate..."

"Which we have no way to prove anyway." Taryn shook her head. "That's something that Charlie's friend in DHS will have to work on...if we can get connections to the operatives here."

"Which still leaves us trying to sort those emails."

"That's a lot of data to sift, unless we target the computers from admin. That's where the invoice authorization is coming from."

"I need help...this is Cody level stuff." Taryn dialed her roommate and put him on FaceTime. "Code, back door's working great...but I need access to emails."

"Hmm...I'm assuming they use SMTP protocol..." As he and Taryn launched into a litany of compu-geek speak, Blake leaned back in his chair with a smile that grew wider and wider. After another ten minutes, Taryn and Cody disconnected, and Taryn twisted her braids into a loose knot, and began working on her laptop.

"Guessing you figured..."

"Shhh! Working!" Taryn worked feverishly as she glanced at the clock. "We've only got 'til nine to get in and get what we need copied...and it's 8:48...this is my first time doing this level of a hack."

"Would this be another one of your little hidden, unexpected talents, Sugar?"

Taryn gave a faint smile as she glanced at Blake. "Talk later...work now."

"This'll be good."

After the flurry of activity to get all of the information from the hospital non-patient related server before Cody's back door access was inactivated by the security sweep, Taryn ejected the USB drive and closed her laptop with a sigh.

"Done...and I took the liberty to duplicate the emails and send everything to a cloud account we started. Just sent Charlie an update. I think I'm done for tonight. I'll sort through everything tomorrow and see what we have."

Blake nodded, then gave a lopsided smile. "Does this mean we can talk about dessert?"

"Excuse me?"

"You still owe me for losing that bet on getting that lock open."

"Seriously? I pull the amateur hack of the year, and you're still yammering about me not making time getting into that lock?"

"Bet's a bet, Sugar. I've decided I'll take dessert." Blake leaned closer and wound one of Taryn's braids around his finger as his smile grew. Taryn gave him a wary look.

"Why didn't we just get takeout dessert at the restaurant?"

"Sugar, I really don't think you're getting my meaning." Blake tipped Taryn's chin up as he gave her a gentle kiss.

As they pulled apart, awareness and a myriad of other expressions chased across Taryn's face, and her eyes narrowed. "Your girlfriend know you're this much of an operator when she's not on the scene?"

"I never mentioned anything 'bout a girlfriend...just some uncomplicated fun." He had a lopsided smile as he rose and bracketed her barstool with an arm on either side.

"I'm feeling like I've been worked into a corner on this."

"How? We made a bet. You lost."

Taryn frowned and thought about how Blake had worked his way around the attendant at the storage facility. "I lost... but I'm pretty sure you're not my type." It was the lamest, and only defense Taryn could think of as she realized how quickly her resistance to Blake was caving.

"Fun's everyone's type. I'm all about a little fun tonight... no strings... no agenda. Thought you were hot as hell from that first day I saw you... turns out I get seriously turned on by whip smart women." As Blake closed in for another kiss. "And I *do* like these braids..." he reached out and undid the knot Taryn had twisted just minutes before. He wrapped one hand in the braids now cascading about Taryn's head and gently pulled her closer. "Yes or no?"

Taryn met him halfway and tunneled her hands through his hair. A questioning kiss turned devouring, as Taryn melted, and surrendered to the attraction and chemistry that had been building since their collision a week before. "Yes... to everything."

She got a death grip on Blake's shoulders while he grabbed her ass and lifted her out of the chair. Lips fused, tongues dueled, and he walked her backwards until she bumped into something.

She was panting and grabbing for his shirt, focused on getting her hands on his skin as he boosted her onto the kitchen table, never breaking their kiss as he pushed her backwards and swept one hand out to clear the table as she lifted his shirt off. The crash of breaking glass startled her, but he turned her face back toward him and nipped a line up her throat to her ear.

"Ignore the noise...do you want this, Sugar? Because I want you...anyway I can get you."

Taryn was starting on the button of his jeans now. "Yes, and yes! Stop talking; get these off."

In between kisses, he yanked her sweater off and tossed it away as she continued to fumble with his button fly.

"Impatient, demanding...sexy, brilliant creature...let me..." He pushed her hands away, then undid his buttons and grabbed a condom out of a pocket. Taryn wriggled out of the last of her clothes as Blake kicked away his jeans, then positioned one of her legs around his waist. After some mutual fumbling, Taryn reached for his ass while Blake tightened his grip on her legs.

"I want ...ummm...please, just...oh, fuck..." She wrapped the other leg around his waist as he began to move. Taryn matched his movements. Both gave into the lust that had been underlying their encounters during the week.

"Yeah...just like that......I gotcha, Sugar."

Taryn could only think of how Blake's every movement ratcheted her hunger higher until she lost all ability to think at all.

CHAPTER SEVENTEEN

Sunday Morning

"Yes...back from vacation last night. Cayman's of course, darling. Villa Bonita...our place on Seven Mile beach... what? Of course, we got the yacht...went out on it...finally... much too much business...not nearly enough fun... I needed another week, but Wyatt has some stupid command performance community event that I couldn't care less about, and..." The chattering was bursting Taryn's bubble of sulking and self-doubt as she got her pedicure and brooded about her hookup with Blake the night before. Looking to the right, she frowned at the person delivering the vapid phone conversation.

"Girl...no use this polish...not that...too many people here have that shade on." Her pedicure neighbor with the loud, affected voice had extracted a bottle of nail polish from her purse, which she was waving at her nail tech with an annoyed expression and dramatically rolled eyes. "Look...I'll have to call you back...I must make sure this girl puts on the correct polish. You *know* how the nail shops are in this backwater. Hey...you...how much longer are you going to be? It's just a polish change! And you still need to fix my nail!"

Taryn's nail tech, Anne, glanced at her co-worker as the woman clicked off her call, and called another tech to begin the nail repair, which of course was on the hand the woman had been holding the phone with. She returned her smile as she shrugged and resumed her work. Taryn looked at the name tag of the other nail tech, then at the customer now berating poor Lynn for what she perceived as slow service. The woman appeared to be in her early-to-mid thirties, in full makeup, early on a weekend. Blonde, blue eyed, with forehead skin already showing the impossibly taught appearance that only Botox injections give. When she finished her petulant complaints, she pulled a magazine from her purse before allowing the second technician to begin work on her nail. Taryn replayed her end of the conversation and opted for snooping as distraction rather than rehashing the entertainment portion of the previous evening.

"Hi! I thought I was the only weirdo who liked to get my nails done first thing on a Sunday morning. I was told that this was the best salon in town. Are you a regular?"

"Not by any stretch, but it will have to suffice," sniffed the woman. "I had a bit of an emergency with some broken tips and decided to get a polish change on my toes while I got the repairs."

"Well, I'm just in town from Seattle; looking forward to some primo skiing this week. Have you heard how the skiing's been?"

"I wouldn't know." The blonde had a bored expression and insincere smile. "I've been at my villa in the Caymans for the past ten days. I find the weather here too extreme; Aspen is much more to my liking." She gave an affected flip to her hair and began to page through the magazine with her free hand as she said, "My husband, Wyatt, understands that I have to escape this god-forsaken Eastern Oregon winter weather." Taryn blinked in surprise and congratulated herself on her good luck.

"Oh, wow...Cayman Islands....so jealous! Skiing's great, but the Caribbean this time of year's the best. Where'd you stay? What did you do? Was there good diving?"

The woman, Brianne, as she had introduced herself to be, preened then gave a dismissive glance at Taryn, who was eminently forgettable in one of Cody's ratty University of Wyoming hoodies paired with leggings. "My husband and I have a home there...one of our vacation homes. Surely you've heard of him; Wyatt Cook; he runs the hospital here."

———————

"Slow down T...and how the hell do you know this woman was Cook's wife? What happened to low profile, taking it slow? Haven't you done enough hacking of the comps at the hospital?"

On FaceTime, Cody was in his version of the 'Batcave' with multiple laptops, monitors, AR displays, and a DJ quality sound system blasting rap in the background. Taryn was in the process of adding her newly gleaned information to the shared cloud account and trying to determine how to corroborate the information to enhance the investigation. They were currently stuck on trying to confirm Michael Downing was who he claimed to be, or better still, disproving it.

"I've heard gossip about Brianne all week... her annual winter Caymans trip to Wyatt's villa...and now the yacht. They apparently use the hospital holiday party as their annual brag-fest. I got her to talk about everything from where she grew up to international properties. Did I mention she's a raving bitch? Totally mean to her nail tech and snotty to me; anyway, I got the name of their place in the Cayman's, name of this new yacht, name of their bank...Cayman's Internationale..."

"How the hell did you get her to talk about her bank? Don't you think that's pushing nail salon conversation with a stranger a little too far?

"She wasn't talking to *me*...I was listening in when she took a couple calls."

"Too much of a good thing if you ask me, but I'll get to work on it."

"Great...I'm gonna tag Charlie...I got some ideas of stuff we might be able to dig up on Raynor and Cook."

"Why?"

"Admin involvement angle after getting the pharmacy stuff. You do any work on the emails?"

"You know you're kind of a shit boss...I got woken up early by my crazy roommate. I'm just about to head back to bed...for the rest of us peons, it's Sunday." Taryn noticed Cody's bleary-eyed appearance for the first time.

"Slacker...I hope you weren't up late losing at poker. Not bailing your ass out again. And I need results by three." Taryn disconnected, then got to work with her latest idea... who exactly were Raynor and Cook, and what did they do when they weren't at work?

———

Taryn got Charlie to tap his Portland DHS contact for Raynor and Cook's income tax records. Less than an hour after making the request, she pored through the last four years of data. Finding the U.S. real estate holdings for each of the administrators was easy. Then, comparing their properties, sale prices, and IRS stated income revealed tell-tale flags that the real estate holdings outstripped Cook's stated income. Even if she added in income or properties that Brianne Cook may have brought into the marriage four years before, combined with creative mortgaging, the holdings far exceeded possible property purchase based on income claimed on their W-2. Predictably, the Cayman's property was not listed. Her success in real estate forensics 101 was negated by not finding any information on Raynor, except that there was a K-Raynor trust where presumably all holdings were sheltered.

As she considered her next move, her text alert chimed. She rolled her eyes...Blake. Her gaze flicked automatically to the crumpled paper she had lobbed near the trash. After several rereads of the note since she found it on her nightstand that morning, she had the content memorized, but was no closer to opting into a course of action.

Morning Sugar,

Didn't want to wake you. Last night totally worked for me.
Give me a buzz if you want company
later. I could be persuaded to join you for a dessert run.
B

She sighed, unsure of the best way to handle what was probably an epic mistake in the making if this continued. A complex problem relating to work or snooping she could handle. But an entanglement with Blake pushed too many buttons out of bounds.

Maxx's excited barking at the sound of the doorbell broke

her musing. Taryn frowned as she followed her dog to the door; she wasn't expecting anyone. She looked through the window, then paused before opening the door to Blake, who had his backpack slung over one shoulder.

"Afternoon, Sugar, thought you might need some help with data sorting...Hiya, Maxx." After ruffling Maxx's fur, Blake entered, strolling past a speechless Taryn, who closed the door as he started to shed his outwear.

"I uh...hadn't decided whether..."

"I took your silence as an invitation...What are we doing besides getting into emails? And I brought cheesecake. You want coffee, too?" He extracted two packages before heading for the caddy holding the cups.

"We? Cheesecake?"

"We...as in the team...what's this Charlie tells me about you running into Cook's wife this morning?"

"You decided you could invite yourself over? *And* called Charlie to check on me?" Taryn trailed after Blake as he headed toward their usual work center at the kitchen bar, unsure of how she felt. Angry? Stalked? Flattered?

"I came to help the team...don't tell me you're getting all torqued about dessert last night? You want cream in your coffee? Usual place was closed." Taryn gaped, then blushed before mumbling and stumbling over to her workspace and dropping onto a barstool.

"Ah...yeah...cream and sugar...I, ah, ran into Brianne Cook this morning...and Cody has an idea about going after their bank records."

"Bank records? Dial him up...let's get moving."

Taryn struggled for a response, realizing Blake was grinning at her. "You *were* gonna call me to help you...right? Asking for help's not a fatal flaw, even for compu-anesthesia geniuses."

"I'm not sure that's a thing... and, you didn't give me a chance before you showed up on my doorstep.

"You mean, I didn't give you the chance to chicken out. I think I'm onto your game now."

"Why do I think you've been talking to Cody?

"Sugar, you're an open book. Let's call Cody for the plan."

"Why would we call *Cody* for the plan?"

"Do you know how to hack a bank?

"Well, I...

"Just as I thought."

Taryn huffed then conceded the point. "Fine... Since when are you and Cody tight?

"Guy code...could tell you...but then I'd have to kill you."

Taryn scowled. "What bleeding guy code is that?"

"Focus Sugar; we need to find how the Cooks are able to afford their Cayman's place..."

"Don't Sugar me...and I'm the reason we have this info."

"Spa time saves the world...again...any chance you think that whole episode was a setup?"

"You *have* been talking to Cody!"

"What are the odds of you being in the right place at the right time to just happen on Brianne Cook?"

"I'm lucky like that."

"It could also work horribly against us if we get exposed."

Taryn debated the options, then shrugged. "I vote we accept it as providence and move forward. If Cody can't handle getting us access to the information we need, he'll let us know, and we'll think of another way. I think we should sort through the emails for purchase orders for pharmacy stock while he gets a plan for getting us into the bank...which I wanna watch."

"Planning on some Bonnie and Clyde action to go with that lock picking thing you have going on?"

"You'd make a lousy Clyde...who got shot, by the way."

"Technicality...and I wasn't volunteering until you drafted me."

Taryn opened her mouth to reply before seeing Blake's smirk, then took a most convenient exit.

"Maxx! Let's go!" Maxx tore off for the front door barking, with Taryn breathing a sigh of relief as she followed to gear up for outside.

"You mind some company?"

Taryn turned, too intent on her thoughts to realize that Blake had followed her. She sighed and rolled her eyes. "You're not gonna let me off the hook, are you?

"Not a chance."

"WHY'S FINDING OUT ABOUT INTERNATIONAL properties so tough?" Taryn and Blake decided to halt hostilities in favor of the truce that walking Maxx presented.

They were on their way back to Taryn's condo. "If they're legit, they're easy, since they'll appear in some fashion on U.S. records, particularly tax records. If any international properties they have were purchased to hide or launder assets, or in anticipation of having to escape U.S. jurisdiction, not so much. Charlie started a dig on Raynor and his stuff and has run into a blank wall with everything being hidden in a KM Associates Trust, which is untraceable to the primary owner."

"Same as what I got. I realize he's the logical second administrator...but we still have no idea who else may be involved."

"Which is why you need to be careful. Teasing aside, I'm not up to losing another friend." Taryn nodded, looking up at Blake, who playfully tugged one of the braids escaping her hat.

"Let's get back to unravelling this thing."

"Deal."

After coats and outdoor gear for people were shed and doggie paws dried, Blake followed Taryn back to her workstation, and listened in while she started a Skype call with Cody. "Okay, walk me through this bank hack...starting with how you think you're gonna get anywhere with just knowing the name of the Cooks' bank. I thought you needed account and routing numbers along with luck, and brass balls." Maxx nudged Taryn for attention so she decided to oblige him with a good brushing while she got the details of Cody's plan.

"First off, this is an op that's just as much about skills as it is nerve. I don't know anything about the Cook's account...I just know in general how secure orgs work their security. Geographic distance is irrelevant in cyberspace. The only thing that matters is making sure what you are doing fits into the timeframe of activity in the place you are working to infiltrate. And, you need some idea of the systems that the place may be using," Cody continued to work on his laptops while he explained the process to Taryn and Blake, all the while keeping track of the scrolling data on his monitors as he worked four keyboards simultaneously. Even Taryn only understood half of what he said.

"The Cayman Islands are politically a British Overseas Territory. They're also an important international financial center. Several hundred banks are registered there in spite of it being a country of only 100 square miles in size. Finding out the name of the Cook's bank is huge...and the break we needed," said Cody, favoring Taryn with a grin and glance at Blake. "Entirely possible it's all a setup, so I'm covering my ass and leaving some dead ends for anyone slick enough to follow my back trail. With the bank name, I can find the associated Swift number. Now I need to work some of my sources and sub-routines and see if we can finagle an account number. Details are NTK for your overly credentialed profession; no Bueno for you to be associated with bank hacking and infiltration." Taryn prepared an automatic objection even as she knew that Cody was correct.

"I'll pass on that info too...outta my wheel box...that's Taryn's thing."

Taryn blinked in surprised, as she'd been out maneuvered; she had planned to extract the details from Blake later.

"I agree it's not great if she's involved too deeply, but it should be her decision."

Taryn reluctantly shrugged her assent. "Okay...no details...but generally, what are you gonna do?"

"Once I've got a handle on the bank, and how it operates, I'll get access to their account records. At one point, you had to ride activity waves correlating with the time zone the bank was in. These days, ops at most offshore banks are pretty much 24/7...slight dip on weekends.... Today, I'm getting an idea of the way the bank is structured, how and when they run maintenance and how I can best get remote records access." Cody continued to work as they talked. "As soon as I get a feel for the flows, I'll slip my traffic into their logs when they're at peak flow. I'll get our info, then ghost out. No messy electronic trail or fingers; no one tracing my back-trail and finding my IP address. Charlie's Portland friends hooked me up to next level stealth. I'm goddam He-Man, Master of the Cyber-Fucking Universe!"

Taryn rolled her eyes in a combination of envy and disgust. "Never gonna hear the end of this."

Cody leaned back in his chair with feet crossed and propped them on the desktop as he sipped his coffee, regarding Blake and Taryn with a half-smile. "What's up with you two?

WHILE BLAKE WORKED THROUGH THE MOUND OF EMAILS Cody had netted, Taryn worked on getting more information about Brianne Cook's father, Thomas McNeil, who just happened to be head of an L.A.-based shipping company, McNeil Shipping. Going on the premise that nothing involving the timing and sequence of events was accidental, she relied on general access records until she knew what details she needed to dig for. Relying on L.A. area newspapers, she found a marriage announcement for Brianne and Wyatt Cook in Tarzana, California, July 2009. She also found that five years previously, McNeil had transitioned from being a modestly successful, 40-year-old family-run company to moving more volume at the combined L.A.-Long Beach port. Although the financials of the privately held company were confidential, the profits likely reflected this fact. Taryn frowned, then used her skills to access the L.A. Port Authority shipping records for McNeil during the previous summer. She scrolled through the list of companies for which McNeil provided transport.

"I've got something to focus your search. Our very own Eagle Pharmaceuticals is one of McNeil Shipping's best customers."

"Not an accident. Are they truly a manufacturer or just a distributer?" Taryn looked at Blake.

"Maybe both. If they're into manufacturing also, that

could lead to a factory location. I need to find out where the local Eagle shipment was headed."

"This has almost been too easy." Maxx woofed for punctuation, then wagged his tail as he stood in front of the kitchen door.

"You're paranoid."

Taryn rose to open the kitchen door, pausing as something caught her eye as Maxx tore into the backyard. The outside keyplate for the door looked to be bent. "Someone's been trying to get in this door."

Blake rolled his eyes as he rose to inspect the door. "Now who's paranoid?"

But his expression froze as he looked at the frame side keyplate and the doorframe. "Someone's been at the deadbolt casing." He crouched down to look at the mixed slush of snow, ice and sawdust on the back stoop. "Can't tell if this is left over from when Charlie got those locks changed or not."

As Blake looked at the space around the door, Taryn grabbed her snow boots and walked down a step and looked at Maxx, who stood barking at the back gate. It was difficult to say for sure since Maxx had run through the backyard, but Taryn thought she saw foot prints interspersed with his paw prints. As she scanned the yard, Blake swore softly.

"I'm gonna circle around and come up the alley to that back gate."

"You think you see footprints in the yard, too?"

"Yeah. Hang tight." Blake went through the house to circle around the condo and came up to the back gate via the lane, while Taryn called Charlie to confirm that he hadn't used the back gate to access the back door when he changed the locks. She was hanging up when she heard Blake swear as he approached the back gate.

"Goddammit...I'm calling the PD. And get Charlie

back...someone's busted the fucking catch on the back gate, and been here long enough to take a smoke break."

"Same brand as before?"

"Looks like."

Taryn called for Maxx as he paced on the inside of the fence, giving him a hug and ruffling his fur. "If only you could talk...you've been letting us know something was up back here." He gave a woof and doggie grin as he nudged her.

CHAPTER EIGHTEEN

Monday Morning

"**A**nthony! Mind if we have a chat? I'm reviewing your company's RFP." Blake was in the basement retrieving his cart of implants. Intent on moving his supplies onto the elevator and to the OR, he was surprised to see Raynor so far outside of his usual environment.

"Sure Ken. It'll be a tight squeeze with the equipment, but I always have time for business. What can I do for you?"

Raynor engaged the emergency stop button after the doors closed, then crossed his ankles and leaned against the wall of the elevator. "So, you're R&D chief and part owner of M&H. You're not here just to check your reps or push product."

"It's a scheduled marketing and client survey trip as I..."

"Cut the shit, *Myers*...which is your real name, isn't it? What the fuck are you up to besides misguided fact finding on Dr. Harris? Dead is dead; police report's filed." Blake struggled to keep a lid on his temper and the hostility he felt toward Raynor.

"Not getting your point, especially since this a repeat of what I already told Cook...who already knows my full name. Steve and I are co-owners at M&H. Steve's also Jimmy's brother. It's a scheduled site visit and semi-anonymous quality eval *and* I'm helping a friend."

"Why do I think that's just a load of horse shit?"

"Your opinions and perspectives are your issue. What would you do if you had a friend who was found dead and no clues?"

"I'd believe the goddamn police report that said it was an accident; ski death due to misadventure. End of story."

"Glad you aren't my friend."

"What I am is the person who will approve your RFP... provided I think it's worth passing on to corporate. Seems there are facilities in our network you'd like to supply; you should consider that."

"Yes, we have other pending contracts. I still found that James ended up dead after skiing under circumstances he would never have done...voluntarily." The two men stared at each other as a tic beat in Blake's clenched jaw. Ken sneered as he folded his arms and stepped towards Blake.

"Just what we need... a behavior and assessment expert.

"James was the expert — in winter survival and avalanche recognition."

"That's irrelevant. I don't buy your motives."

"Your option to believe the facts or not."

Ken smirked as he handed Blake some grainy, but recognizable pictures of he and Taryn leaving the restaurant from the previous evening. "Seems you're spending quite a bit of free time with Dr. Pirelli. Convenient how she appears the same time you do and starts raising hell. Person might think she was in on whatever you're doing...."

"Dr. Pirelli, and I are social, as I've been with several other hospital staff. But if you aren't outta my grille like yesterday, we're gonna have other issues."

"Is that a threat Myers? Sounds like one...and I'd hate to press charges and involve your company."

"Consider it a personal promise, Ken." A flush crept up Raynor's neck as he struggled in vain to maintain his bravado while he flipped the elevator switch back on.

"Still hard to believe that she knew nothing about either you or Harris before her arrival here. Maybe both of you are due for some disciplinary action and activity restriction." He waited for a response from Blake that never came. "As long as she continues to perform her job appropriately, we have nothing to be concerned about...do we? Wouldn't want the lovely Dr. Pirelli to have any issues, would we?"

Blake struggle to contain his temper. "She's just another doc at the hospital where I'm working...nothing more." Blake bared his teeth to approximate a smile as he shifted closer to Raynor. "And I've found nothing to counter the police and coroner report on Cause of Death. That good enough?" Blake's text alert chimed, breaking the rising aggression. "Looks like they're ready for me in the OR. Mind if I get going and do my job?"

Ken Raynor gave a smile that didn't reach his eyes, as he flipped the elevator switch to ON, and the remainder of the ride proceeded in silence until the elevator door opened on the surgical floor. Predictably, people were waiting. An orderly and nurse wheeled an ICU patient toward them. As Blake pushed his supplies off the elevator, Raynor murmured a final rejoinder for his ears only. "Keep control of that bitch, or someone will be happy to do it for you."

Blake seethed, but held his temper as he continued to exit with his cart as the orderly prepared to assist the nurse pushing the ICU-bound patient onto the elevator. Ken Raynor was smiling and solicitous. "I've got the door. Have a good rest of your day...*Anthony*. And do take care." The door closed after the patient was loaded, and the elevator continued to the third floor. Blake pushed the OR suite push plate, then swore as he looked at his watch. He would be done with advisory support of his first case in an hour-forty-five tops. That would mean he could give Taryn an hour advance warning about his encounter with Raynor before she started work.

———

TARYN PAUSED IN HER FUTILE CANVASSING OF THE emails hacked from the hospital to tear into the just delivered FedEx package with the Propofol. As she expected, the label indicated the bottle had been distributed and manufactured by Eagle Pharmaceuticals. She both wrote down the drug lot number information and took a picture of the label as she called Charlie, and considered her next options to prove a connection between the administrators at Bend and Eagle.

"Propofol package is here. From what I have, lot and batch numbers match what we found in the storage space. How hard would it be for your DHS contacts to look for the manufacturing site on the other end and do the drug potency assays?"

"Next to impossible without knowing something about Eagle and how it's set up. International pharmaceutical manufacturing's exploded since costs started rising for factories here. We'll start with the potency assay."

"We still need info on Eagle since they are the distributer for 90% of what's used in the OR."

"Separate problem that'll have to wait unless we get compelling information otherwise."

"Every time we solve one problem, another one emerges. I tapped out on screening emails for invoice orders."

"So you'll have to make the supply and order connection through Eagle."

"That mean's getting into their mainframe."

"I don't need IT skills to know that's a really bad idea for you."

"There's a way, and I don't make a habit of getting caught." Taryn frowned as she realized the validity of Charlie's words. "But you're right. This is Cody-level stuff; he'll have some ideas.

"Call Cody, but my vote is we leave the rest of this to Cy and his team; they're the experts. Give them time to assay the bottles. Drop them at the office on your way to work, and I'll get them packaged and shipped. After we get results from Cy and the DHS lab, we'll know our direction. Taryn nodded, but was eager to keep working on her current Eagle leads.

"I'm moving forward on seeing what I can find out about Eagle...but I'll be careful."

"Have at it."

Taryn disconnected, and checked the time. She had less than an hour until she had to be at work for her noon case.

TARYN USED THE OFFICIAL EAGLE PHARMACEUTICALS website for the backbone of her research, finding that Eagle was a medium sized pharma company in an expansion phase after years of unremarkable profits and growth. It had been

founded by Richard Larkin in the early 2000s after he retired
as a senior director in the drug approval division in the FDA.
The company's profitability increased dramatically with the
ascension of Christopher Stephens as president in
2007/2008. She was currently reviewing emails from
Charlie confirming both the unremarkable, by-the-book
nature of Larkin's FDA career, and the fact that Christopher
Stephens had also been in the FDA drug approval division.
After reviewing more non-descript official material, Taryn
decided to hit public social media posts concerning Eagle.

Her first finds were of remarkable events at the company
with one of the biggest being a splashy announcement of
Christopher Stephens being installed as company president
in early 2007. She toggled back to the Eagle company
website, which still listed Richard Larkin as company CEO.
She frowned as she reviewed this timeline and compared it
with the one for Brianne and Wyatt Cook, and their
marriage. There appeared to be a collection of events that
were nexus events that served as catalyst to everything
currently occurring.

Determined to dig further into each event, Taryn applied
some of the information and ID search tricks she learned
from Cody to document facts on the McNeil and Eagle
websites. Unlike the hospital corporation that owned Bend
Regional, both companies were privately held, and not
subject to the information disclosure standards that CHG
Corp was bound by.

She worked with an eye on the clock. She had only
minutes before she had to report for work to get the information that would guide Cody's confirmation of what she had
learned. She sent him two files labelled Eagle and McNeil
Shipping via email, and promised to explain en-route to
work. After gathering Maxx and her work gear, and piling

into her SUV, she called Cody as she cursed the increasingly heavy snowfall that slowed her progress.

"You working from home?"

"Yup. Got your email. What are you after on Stephens?"

"I think it's mighty odd that Larkin suddenly became sick about five months before Stephens...his nephew...became President." Taryn's text alert went off. It was Blake. She silenced it.

"You got proof of that?"

"Second file in the Eagle folder. Stephens has a PharmD. There could be a chemical reason for Larkin's sickness and..."

"If he has a PharmD, he could be the technical backbone of Eagle's growth. *If* he's connected with our boys here in admin and..." Taryn's second line chirped for attention; Blake again. She sent it to voicemail with a frown.

"I accessed Port of L.A. records for our timeframe and did cross checks. Turns out McNeil shipping started carrying Eagle products about the time both companies started expanding." There was quiet except for the clacking of the keyboards as Cody ran checks on the data that Taryn had sent.

"I'm looking at the Eagle company newsletters. Pictures and information document the visible change in leadership around 2006/2007."

"Social media posts of Eagle employees confirm Larkin's health issues. No way that's a coincidence. I say we dig more into Stephens."

"What's your end game?"

"I've found files of what looks like some narrative journaling that James did. He laid out his suspicions and process, including copies and notations about the official complaints he filed with the Portland FDA office. My crash course on the FDA gave me background. You get me the facts I listed, and I think I'll have motivation, process, and the people involved here for the drug issue...and maybe what happened to James Harris."

"How quick do you need confirmation for all this?"

"I'm headed for work now. Maybe in four hours?"

"You ask for the improbable on impossibly short notice."

"Cyber He-Man isn't a whiner."

"Low blow."

"But effective. Later." Taryn had barely disconnected when Blake called again. She stabbed the accept button as she pulled into a parking spot only to come face to face with Blake. "What. Do. You. Want?"

BLAKE'S WARNING TO TARYN ABOUT HIS EARLY MORNING encounter with Raynor didn't impress her as much as he thought it should. The ensuing argument between the two of them was inevitable, and consumed the extra time she had allotted to stop for coffee before reporting to work.

"So now I should ghost myself from the job I'm due to report for in..." Taryn checked the time on the clock in her SUV. "In ten minutes. Thanks for chewing up my time yammering at me so I didn't have time for coffee. I'm caffeine deficient...and working with your oh-so-timely advance warning."

"That you ignored! By email, text, and call. What the..."

"I was busy..."

"No one's too busy to watch their back. Bad fucking move, Sugar. What are you thinking?"

Taryn huffed as she turned off the engine and unbuckled her belt before exiting and grabbing her backpack off the driver's side backseat, then trudged up the newly shoveled walk to the hospital entrance. "I'm working the regular day shift when plenty of people are around. Not much they can pull on me with a whole crowd of OR folk here." Taryn dropped her voice to a whisper. "Not like you can do anything to help me anyway. Aren't you on a case? What about not drawing attention to ourselves?"

"Given the pics Raynor showed me, that's too fucking late."

Taryn halted, undecided about taking the elevator or stairs to the OR, and trying to cover options considering the information Blake had shared.

"Company and crowds are your friends until we figure this mess out."

"We as in?" The elevator opened; Taryn stepped in to join the other riders.

"You, me, and the only people you seem to listen to: Cody and Charlie."

Taryn hit the end button, imagining accurately the swearing that accompanied her actions on Blake's end of the conversation. She shook her head; Blake's over-reaction and protectiveness would get her nowhere. She exited the elevator when the doors opened on the second floor. She had just activated the push plate to enter the surgical suite, when she was hailed by the OR nursing director.

"Dr. Pirelli, there's an issue with your computer login. Can you please check with IT before you start in the OR today?"

Harry was on vacation this week and Sherry was the call anesthesiologist for the rest of the week; she wouldn't be in until 3. Downing was the charge anesthesiologist in the OR, leaving Taryn without a sure ally in the OR other than Shannon at a very critical time.

BLAKE LOOKED AT THE 'CALL ENDED' MESSAGE ON HIS phone, then shoved it into his pocket with a curse. Wrapping up his records work for his case, he realized he had no valid reason to return to the OR to see how Taryn was faring.

After turning in the implant usage information to the clerks in Central Processing, he took the stairs to the exit level and called Charlie as warning bells within his intuition began an insistent chiming.

CHAPTER NINETEEN

"Dr. Pirelli thanks for coming. Would you mind signing into this terminal so we can verify your login credentials?" The warmth and welcome she had felt from the IT educator two weeks ago had vanished; today it was all business and protocol. Taryn dropped into the chair and logged in as requested, wondering what the issue could be. The educator checked the screen then made a few entries, before turning to leave.

"Thanks. Please wait here." While she waited for an explanation, Taryn opted for action over speculation. She began to reorganize her action item to-be-addressed list; Downing info, Stephens info, Eagle info, Financial records... She looked up when the door opened, and a man entered with Lydia Thompson, the COO and administrator who welcomed her to the hospital when she arrived from Seattle. The two of them took seats across from her.

"Doctor, I'm Kyle Evans, IT. I believe you know Ms. Thompson. I'll get to the point; it seems that your login credentials were used to access patient information this

morning at a number of work station and access points within the facility. Are you sure that you haven't shared your login credentials with anyone? I'd like to remind you that you signed a health information confidentiality agreement when you began working with us. Disclosing your login is a violation of our protocol, and potentially puts patient privacy at risk. Can you explain how or why there were so many logins this morning with your credentials?" Taryn straightened, and tried to recall any times when she might have left a computer without logging out.

"I haven't shared my login info. There's got to be a mistake."

"Afraid not. Your login just now matched those from several sites in the hospital this morning as well as several from yesterday." Taryn was presented with a list of times and stations, along with the Medical Record numbers of patient charts that had been accessed. "Physician Services provided me with a patient log of the patients that you've taken care of during your time here. As you can see," he presented two lists, side by side, which highlighted common data. "There's very little crossover on these lists, so you've accessed a number of charts of patients that you were not involved with. Why?"

Taryn stared at the list of patients she knew, and the long list of patients that she was clueless about. She needed a Cody lifeline in the worst way. He would have been able to figure out a how and why for the extraneous logins.

"Dr. Pirelli, I understand that you're new to our system and hospital, but this is a serious matter. If we can't get to the bottom of what's happening, we could be forced to take disciplinary measures up to and including termination of your contract with us. Can you tell us anything that might verify your location this morning?" Lydia was apologetic, but going

by the book on this one. Short of giving Kyle a list of her cell phone activity and hoping that tower triangulation could be done to verify her location, Charlie was the only person who could verify that she hadn't been in the hospital. The last thing she would need is anyone at the hospital knowing her call and contact list.

"Do you only need someone to verify my physical location?"

"Physical and virtual. Were you online anywhere at any point this morning?" The warning bells for trouble rang in Taryn's head, along with nagging worries that her computer activity for the morning had been tracked.

"I could do an abbreviated browsing and IP address history if I had your computer. We could look at times and IP addresses. If your login information was in active use at that time in the hospital, we would have some evidence that you weren't using a computer in the facility. We didn't give you a remote access client to the system since we don't allow remote computer access by docs with temporary privileges, so I know you couldn't access the hospital system from home. It's easy enough to talk to the staff here to see if anyone saw you. We can also check your parking and hospital entry badge history with security." Lydia nodded in agreement, while Taryn was relieved that no one had detected her backdoor entry into the hospital mainframe.

"You haven't lost your hospital badge, have you? No one else in residence in the condo with you?"

"I'm here alone except for my dog. I last used my badge to enter a few minutes ago. My roommate from Seattle last visited me a week ago."

"Let's check your laptop IP history; that will solve the issue. I'm sure you'd like to clear this up so you can get to the OR." Kyle was logical and professional; Taryn was stuck. If

she refused, not only would it look suspicious, but she might be terminated from the assignment. If she agreed, Kyle would have a record of the all sites she had visited including her info gathering from the Eagle Pharmaceuticals website. Who exactly did Kyle report to...or owe? Taryn managed to hide her distress as she thought of options and fallbacks, then remembered the security upgrade that Charlie had done at the condo.

"Kyle, Lydia...I need to make a couple calls that should help clarify this. I shouldn't be long."

TARYN FINISHED WITH IT IN LESS THAN 20 MINUTES showing that she'd been home and not logging in all over the hospital. After slipping outside to make a call to Cody to explain her dilemma, he confirmed her assumptions about a way to document her computer activity without surrendering her computer. She connected with Charlie, who was able to access her condo WiFi remotely. Through methods unclear and unimportant, he generated a list with the tagging information needed to confirm her location without the websites she had visited. The security upgrade Charlie scored from his DHS buddies was the bottom line for the how. She was cleared for the login concerns, got her login credentials changed, but received no apology from Kyle for the embarrassment of having to undergo the location and security checks.

After she changed into scrubs, she focused on her cases for the rest of the day rather than an assessment of what led to her problems. But before she went to meet her patient, Michael Downing opened the door to her OR.

"What were you doing logging into so many patients that

you hadn't taken care of?" Against protocol and past the surgical red line for street clothes and personal liquids, he wore a lab coat over his scrubs and held a to-go coffee cup. Taryn flicked a glance toward him, but continued with her case prep. How had he known the details of her IT issues?

"I guess I didn't log out somewhere, and someone got my credentials. It happens."

"Always trouble with you, Pirelli."

"Excuse me, Dr. Downing...we're opening the room now."

"I've got a mask for you, Dr. Pirelli." The scrub tech for Taryn's OR pushed past Downing, putting her own mask in place and waving a second one for Taryn, which she tied into place.

By the time she turned to reply to Downing, he had vanished. She shook her head and tried to decide why the conversation had disturbed her so.

"DR. PIRELLI, DESPITE THE FACT THAT YOU HAD SOME documentation to back up your issues with IT today, I'm quite concerned with how often you're at the bottom of some disturbance in the OR." After she finished her afternoon cases, Taryn had been summoned to admin, where she was now being questioned in Ken Raynor's office.

"Lydia was there but..." Ken threw his pen on the open file on his desk and leaned forward in his chair.

"I'm not Lydia. And I'm not satisfied with your performance here. I'm not even sure it's worth discussing or having your disruptive influence here any longer." As Taryn struggled for an appropriate response, Raynor focused past her, then stood. "We'll continue this discussion when I return."

As Raynor swept out of the office, Taryn also realized the

unforeseen opportunity she had been handed...or was it a setup? She glanced over her shoulder; the office door was cracked, and the murmur of conversation droned on in the reception area. Since she was already potentially getting fired, what harm would more snooping do? Recalling the security cams throughout the patient care areas, she looked for any obvious camera locations near the ceiling before beginning a visual survey of the office rather than attempting a physical search.

It was a typical office, with associated conference area, guest chairs, one of which she was seated in...filing cabinets, water dispenser, and nothing remarkable within sight. As she huffed in frustration and turned to face forward, Taryn realized that an open briefcase rested on the conference table. She shot a glance back to the partially open door before rechecking for less obvious sites where a security camera might be located. The only location where a camera might be secreted was in a collection of books and bookends topping the credenza behind Raynor's desk. After taking a deep breath, she rose to walk to the water dispenser, which was located near the door. She scanned the open briefcase as she passed by it, noting a laptop, file folders, and a computer access card emblazoned with an eagle attached to a Bend Regional lanyard. She considered her options as she filled a cup with water. Before she could return to her seat, Raynor brushed past her on his way to his desk.

"Where were we, Dr.?"

"How the hell did you end up in Raynor's office in the first place?" Blake ran both hands through his hair as he paced and tried in vain to contain his anger as Taryn replayed her afternoon. He opted for a visit after getting her text summary of her day.

"Why do you think my issues were because of your issues?" Blake counted to ten and resisted the urge to say anything to further inflame the situation or anger Taryn.

"You lack the ruthless gene. Brains aren't gonna save you from issues with these folks. Why can't you let me help you?" Taryn shook her head in frustration.

"I told you; I'll call you if I need help. Back off 'til I do. It didn't seem to matter with Raynor that I'd done nothing wrong."

"He's eventually gonna make you sorry you weren't more careful. What is it with you and not accepting advice or help?"

"Right now, I can take care of myself. And they need me more than they need your company, frankly."

"Famous last words." Blake frowned at her insistent determination as he recognized the potential danger her attitude and actions might generate. "I get that you feel on the edge of solving the whys...I just don't want you blindsided in the process...like James."

"I see everything happening as a distraction from the main event; who is behind those defective drugs, and what's their endgame. Another death would be messy and distracting." Taryn paced as she replayed her meeting with Raynor. "We've gotta focus on getting that access card."

"Good luck with that...for either of us." Taryn got a faraway look as she flopped onto the corner of the great room sofa not occupied by Maxx.

"Seeing the card...gave me an idea...just need Cody to call and tell me if it's possible." Right on cue, the FaceTime alert on Taryn's phone rang. Blake retrieved the phone from the breakfast bar where Taryn had left her gear, then sighed before pacing to consider possible options out of their dilemma.

"Hey how's Erika getting on with her toy?"

AFTER BLAKE LEFT, TARYN REVIEWED THE FILES THAT Cody had sent her and found...nothing new on Downing or on the hospital's pharmacy. Although she'd expected nothing new on pharmaceutical ordering without access to Eagle files and invoices, the blank wall on Downing was worrisome, and pointed to another person and situation who were not as they had been presented. As she struggled to reconcile the lack of information and the afternoon's events, her text message alert went off. Harry.

I heard about today. Headed home; should be there by morning. I'll call when I get there.

Taryn tried to call, but got voicemail. Wasn't Harry on vacation with his family? She heaved a sigh then called Maxx, grabbing the walking staff Charlie had given her as she geared up to go outside to clear her head and walk Maxx before returning to follow their remaining clues to what appeared to be a series of dead ends.

"YOU AND TARYN HAVING RUN-INS WITH RAYNOR THE same day says you both need to be out of this situation." Blake had left during Taryn's chat with Cody, but stopped by Charlie's office on his way home. His main focus was his contention that Taryn was in over her head with whatever was happening at the hospital.

"Damn straight...but she's not gonna be willing to step back unless...actually until Cody gets her to."

"He's here?"

"Picking him up tomorrow morning. He's bringing some device Taryn thinks may help with getting into Raynor and Cook's private networks. It's 100% the wrong thing for her to get wound up in." Charlie snorted and tossed a stack of pictures on his desk.

"Good luck with that. This is what I'm dealing with." Blake frowned as he looked at the pictures, then gave Charlie a blank look.

"Those are of my kids in Portland, time stamped last week. All of us are under surveillance." Charlie selected another picture of an auto accident where the vehicle was barely recognizable. Block letters took up the top of the picture: CHOOSE CAREFULLY. "This is a picture of my wife's car after the accident that killed her...ten years ago." Charlie got up to pace near the window of his office before completing his thoughts. "Worst fucking day of my life...until now. That they've pulled that in means this ties into my work on the SEAL teams. He turned to look at Blake. "Getting access to whatever Raynor and Cook may be running on their networks is the least of our worries."

"How the hell is you wife's accident connected?"

"I can't tell you enough of the story for it to make sense. End result is it's time the professionals took over. I've called Cy." Charlie scrubbed his hands through his hair before crossing his arms. "You need to talk to Taryn. You two are done."

IT WAS DARK BY THE TIME TARYN AND MAXX WERE

winding down their walk. Despite her personal protections and blustering at Blake's concern for her safety, Taryn felt the back of her neck prickling. The growing darkness and having put the day's events in perspective were increasing her anxiety. Every time she turned around, she found nothing untoward; no one lurking in the bushes, no cars parked in unexpected areas, but something felt very wrong. Maxx was off leash, and unconcerned except his periodic sniffing for recent news. As she made the final turn into the condo complex, Taryn saw a large SUV making its way up the road, which led toward downtown. She clipped Maxx's leash on and extended the staff to its full length before continuing towards her condo. She heard the crunch of snow and ice as the vehicle turned onto her street, and she realized that she would never make it to the front door before it drew even with her location. She blinked when the SUV passed her and turned into her drive as she recognized it, and Blake stepped out after parking.

"What do you think about some company tonight, Sugar?" Maxx woofed, and Taryn automatically let him off leash; he gave Blake an affectionate bump when he reached him. Taryn took some deep breaths to calm herself, finally realizing that her needless panic over an SUV she had seen several times was a reflection of her growing anxiety.

"Company tonight would be good. This is freaking me out." Blake gave her a hug.

"You're fine...I've got you."

CHAPTER TWENTY

Tuesday Early morning
Bend Airport

Blake parked his SUV at the curb before exiting to greet Cody with a handshake/chest bump. "Thanks for coming man...we're meeting Charlie in ten."

Cody threw his bag in the back seat and slammed the front door as Blake drove off continuing to say, "Taryn tried to explain how this thing works, but I'm stuck on why I've never heard of a program or app that clones a laptop."

"You haven't heard of it because it's in development; T and I happen to be investors and part of the feasibility team."

"You mean guinea pigs."

"Whatever; Erika's tried it on our laptops; it works. We had no clue that she was in and cloning our machines. You get close enough, you can clone the drive of the computer in question, then work backwards from that clone on a host computer and break the laptop security; instant IP address without a messy footprint or package left on the target machine. Plenty of time to analyze the comp security and get the info we need to hack the comp, and home network.

"You talk to Charlie about what you need?"

"Yup. He's convinced his friend Jake can in and get it done. Plus, none of this will be connected in any way to T."

"Great...let's do it."

They met Charlie and his associate, Jake Houston, who was ex-military and hospital facilities director facilities, at a coffee shop near the airport. Cody gave him a crash course in operating Erika's cloning device. After Jake was prepped and off to work, the three men had some time to talk strategy.

"We on for step two this evening?"

"Absolutely. T agreed to make herself scarce for the actual op?"

"Grumbled, but yes. She's doing dinner with Shannon and her husband, Jonas. Cody and I will do some pub time, for a cover."

"I'm sure we'll get Cook's comp... not so much with Raynor."

"Why not Raynor?"

"I've had no luck digging for info on him ...and I can trace down anything and anyone. Same issue with Downing. I think their stuff's been professionally wiped. No one leaves that small of a footprint unless it's orchestrated."

"I'll see if Cy has had any luck."

"Technically, we only need access to one comp. And sometimes slick has a bit of arrogance just beneath the surface. Raynor's both, and he'll make a mistake at some point." With Cody's confidence, Blake began to feel a lessening of the tension that had gripped him since his encounter with Raynor.

"I've got a case at 8:00. I'll tag you after."

"Cy's team launches their op tomorrow morning

provided we get what they need. Stay safe and lay low 'til tonight." Charlie departed for his car as Blake and Cody returned to Blake's SUV. During the drive to Taryn's condo, Cody recapped his last discussion with Taryn, summarizing with the update from the access to the Cook's bank in the Caymans.

"Should have what we need by the time you're done. You'll be on point with data analysis." Blake pulled into the driveway and activated the garage door opener. Taryn had already left for work. He swore when he realized that he got distracted after picking up Cody and hadn't gotten a text from her confirming that she got there safely.

"How'd you two end up as roommates?" Cody smirked as he exited the vehicle, then opened the back door to grab his gear. "Nice you have that opener...how'd that go down?"

"Fuck you."

"Talk to T...she'll have my ass if I talk, man."

"Your point is what?"

Bend Regional

TARYN RAN TO THE ET TRAUMA ALERT AS SHE CHECKED the time; just before seven would mean that all of the day shift people were likely still enroute. Downing, as the anesthesia coordinator, should have responded to the alert, but had not yet arrived. Taryn was already in scrubs in the OR since she had arrived early to prep for a complicated 7:30 case. As she followed the stream of people entering through the staff door of the ER, the elevator door from the rooftop heliport opened, and the trauma team pushed a gurney into the nearest trauma bay. As the Emergency Room doc received the report and the ER trauma team descended on the patient, Taryn slid into the plastic emergency apron and clear visor before taking her place at the head of the table. There was the usual controlled chaos of the patient being connected to the ER monitors, disconnected from the transport monitors, and IV lines sorted out. Good IV access, no obvious external bleeding except for cuts and scrapes; vitals were relatively stable on the man, late forties, who was drifting in and out of consciousness. He had apparently been in a rollover MVA near a mountain pass and was in cervical immobilization in addition to being on a back board. Taryn frowned as she looked at the bloodstained clothing being cut away and discarded as the man was covered with a warming blanket, and triage continued their report. She brushed shattered windshield glass shards from the man's hair before she removed his oxygen mask to assess his responsiveness and airway, freezing when she saw past the blood and bruising; it was Harry. One of his eyes was swollen shut, and he began to struggle in his restraints as he blinked his one workable eye and tried to focus.

"Is he stable enough for sedation? Need to clear the C-spine and get him to the scanner." As the triage team debated the advisability of sedation, Taryn leaned closer. Harry was mumbling something, and apparently still unable to see.

"Harry...you're fine...you're here in Bend. It's Taryn." Harry blinked, then calmed as he appeared to focus on Taryn while trying to speak. She slid his mask to one side and leaned in to hear what he was saying.

He rasped, "Semi...boxed me in...no room..." before he broke off in a wracking cough that sprayed fine droplets of blood over everyone near. Taryn wiped her visor, then looked toward the ER team leader who was waving the X-ray tech forward.

"Log roll him to get that plate under then shoot a lateral so we can clear his neck. How soon before they're ready for us in CT? And someone get a chest tube tray." The radiology tech and other members of the team scrambled to get answers and supplies. Taryn squeezed Harry's shoulder before replacing the oxygen mask and moving clear for the x-ray.

"I'm stepping away for the films...I'll be back." She looked at the monitors. His oxygen sats were still in the 90s, but the new bleeding was an ominous sign.

"What's the case? How long's it been here? I'm anesthesia charge...who's running things? Taryn heard Michael Downing, who had just arrived. She ducked out of his line of sight, and rechecked Harry. He had been log rolled, and the x-ray plate placed underneath him. With the sudden new movement, he roused and began to moan and thrash to the extent that he could with head immobilization, and all limbs secured to safeguard the IVs that had been placed. As she waited for completion of the series of x-rays, she realized that in between moans and coughing, Harry was still trying to speak. She scooted closer despite the warning from the x-ray technician.

"No...no...not him...no." Taryn scanned the room; she was the only one who had been close enough to hear Harry. The only people whose faces were visible from Harry's perspective were conferencing at the entrance to the trauma bay: the ER doc, Michael Downing, and the trauma surgeon. Downing was in street clothes. He looked around before turning up the collar of his coat, then refocused on his conversation with the ER doc. Taryn slipped away to a safe distance until the series of x-rays was completed, then returned to the head of the table.

"Harry, I'm here." She crouched by his head; her return

had quieted him. "You're gonna be fine...the team will take good care..."

"No...only you..." He began coughing again, and the light spray of blood turned into a steady stream. Taryn grabbed the suction device; his airway was slowly being compromised. The noise level in the bay ratcheted up as alarms began to go off. Harry's brief period of hemodynamic stability was evaporating. Taryn passed off the suction device before opening the airway cart. She connected the ambu bag to wall oxygen and prepped an endotracheal tube and laryngoscope blade as she got the attention of one of the ER nurses.

"I need someone on an IV to push drugs; get respiratory over here to bag. Not gonna lose this airway. And get a ventilator."

"No...wait ...only you...promise...sent you something...explain...." Harry coughed uncontrollably; his soft, raspy voice almost inaudible amidst the growing noise in the room. He was now requiring almost constant suctioning as he bled more. Taryn filed Harry's words for later as she flicked a glance to the door of the bay where the ER doc was looking at the new x-ray. The cause of the abrupt change in Harry was a collapsed lung, pneumothorax on the right side; the trauma surgeon was being gowned and gloved for the chest tube placement. Michael Downing was shrugging out of his coat, but halted when he saw Taryn. She thought she glimpsed a flash of color above his shirt collar before her view was obscured by the arrival of staff she had requested. The sat monitor rang alarms as oxygen saturation levels descended through the 80s. The respiratory therapist began to assist Harry's respirations with the ambu. His eyelids flickered, and his struggles ceased as he lost consciousness.

"Let's move... give him 12 milligrams of etomidate, 100 mics of fentanyl, and 140mg of sux...20cc flush. You... hold cricoid." As the alarms continued to go off, and Taryn's airway team followed her directions, the trauma surgeon placed the chest tube and the ER doc continued efforts to stabilize Harry before his trip to the OR. Taryn focused on the airway, and doing what she did best, resolving to stay with Harry until he was out of danger.

"HOLD ON, BLAKE BEFORE YOU GO TO YOUR ROOM." A security officer came out of the OR control desk to join the charge nurse. Blake was pushing his supplies down the operating room main hallway on his way to his assigned room and case.

"What's up?"

"I just..." The charge nurse looked at the email she had printed out. "I've been informed that your access at the hospital has been revoked. Security just came with the verbal to back up the email." Blake walked over to check the document. The email was from Cook and had been cc'd to Raynor. "I don't know what's wrong...and I'm sorry, but I don't have time to investigate. The schedule's in chaos; there's a trauma in the ER that's come up, and I have to get another rep and implant company to work the case you were on."

"What trauma?" Blake's thoughts shifted from himself to Taryn...who had still not responded to his page.

"Rollover MVA airlifted in a few minutes ago. Dr. Pirelli's with him in CT, then they're headed here." Blake was relieved, and anxious at the same time as he realized that Taryn would be without backup other than Shannon in the OR. As he thought of her, Shannon rounded the corner from the back hall.

"Room's set for the trauma...I'm on my way to blood

bank." She nodded as she passed Blake, walking close enough to whisper the assurance he needed. "I'll look out for her."

"Security will escort you out Blake. This is effective immediately. It's..."

"Politics...no worries."

"May I have your badge, Mr. Anthony?" The security officer confiscated Blake's badge before motioning toward the OR exit. He began to push his supply cart toward the exit, halting when the OR suite door opened to a swell of noise and alarms, and the trauma team, with Taryn at the head of the bed. As they rushed the gurney towards the waiting operating room, Blake watched the team go by; Taryn was too focused on her patient to see him. When they vanished around the corner, he resumed pushing his supplies to the elevator, escorted by the security guard.

"Any idea what happened?"

"Need to know Mr. Anthony...and you are now officially not one who needs to know."

———

BLAKE DROVE TO TARYN'S CONDO AFTER UNLOADING HIS supplies into his own garage. Maxx greeted him at the door of the mudroom, followed by Cody, attached to a coffee cup.

"Thought you had work."

"Got fired. Leaves plenty of time for other shit." Blake grinned as he ruffled Maxx's ears, then began to peel out of his outerwear.

"So much for under the radar. What the fuck did you do?" Blake flipped him off as he brushed past to Cody's work station at the kitchen bar.

"Exist." Bake shrugged as he took a seat. "Matter of time after the that chat with Raynor. What's doin?"

"Fire up your laptop. I'm getting results from Cayman's Internationale Bank. I need data backup."

"This the stuff Taryn stumbled on Sunday? You sure it's not a trap?"

"Not likely...I've uploaded info to the shared account." Blake booted up his laptop and accessed the files. Cody flicked a glance at the data streaming across the screens of his laptops before leaning back in his chair. "I need a second opinion. If you're here, who's backing T?"

Blake swore as he scrubbed a hand over his face. "Harry came in as a trauma...Shannon's the only one there."

"Motherfuck... when's Charlie's friend getting here?"

"Not damn soon enough." Cody swore as he got up to refill his coffee cup. Blake declined his offer to fill a cup for him.

"Not feeling this...too much is changing, too fast. How long before we hear from Jake?"

Midmorning, Bend Regional

"WHO THE HELL ARE YOU, AND WHAT ARE YOU DOING IN my office?" Ken Raynor snatched the earbuds out of Jake's ears, and yanked his iPod out of his coverall pocket before tossing them on his desk. Jake turned off the vacuum, and adopted a contrite, confused air.

"Housekeeping...you're on my morning assignment list."

"I've never seen you here; you can't have clearance for this area...Kat!" His admin came to the door. "Call the house-keeping day super. You! Stay put and keep your damn hands where I can see them." He surveyed the office; nothing was missing or out of place.

"Mr. Raynor, Isaac's on line one." Ken grabbed the office phone after giving Jake another withering glance.

"Isaac, who the hell is this clown..." he snatched Jake's badge from the pocket where he had it clipped. "Jake Houston... what the fuck's he doing here? Where are the regulars?" He stalked behind his desk to sit, flipping the badge to join the iPod. He glared at Jake, who had his hands shoved in his pockets, looking at the ground as he smacked a wad of gum. Ken sneered, then returned his attention to his conversation.

"Not sure he could even read any of what's out anyway... but in the future, you need to notify me in advance if there's a change in personnel." He slammed the phone down as he picked up the iPod and badge and threw it at Jake. "Here's your stuff...and mind your goddam business when you're cleaning up here, or you'll be looking for another job. Follow the rules, or your ass is done in this town."

"Yessir." Jake schooled his face into a suitably subdued expression, as he finished vacuuming, emptying the trash, then went to the next office in the suite.

"Charlie, I'm done in admin; haven't met Raynor before now, but he's a fucking tool. Snatched the device, and almost gave me a heart attack figuring how I'd get it back. Pretty sure I got a hit in Cook's office. You want me to drop the device at your office over lunch?"

"Thanks, no. I'm sending my secretary to retrieve it. Blue parka with a hood... emergency entrance."

"Good enough. No laptop in Raynor's, but he had a computer control card that I copied. I'll give your admin the card with the dupe. Maybe it's something that'll help. Let me know if I you need anything else." Charlie thanked him and disconnected, then turned to Blake and Cody, who had been listening on speaker.

"I think we got our first break of the day."

TARYN WATCHED AS THE INTENSIVE CARE NURSE pulled the first set of labs since Harry had been admitted to the Unit. True to her promise, she stayed with him the whole case, and hand-picked the crew of nurses who would be taking care of him in the ICU, working to remember all of the people he had remarked on during her time there. In addition to the collapsed lung, he had orthopedic as well as internal injuries that were addressed during surgery. Harry's wife was unreachable by phone, and neighbors reported that the whole family had left town over the weekend. Taryn's danger alarms started chiming low level, but Harry was confirmed by the authorities to be a solo rider in the car. In an over-abundance of caution, she agreed with the trauma surgeon that they should give Harry a few hours of recovery before attempting to remove the endotracheal tube. That would also give her time to track down Harry's family. It was not going to be possible to exclude Downing from his care and room without reason, or next of kin authority.

"He still doing OK?" Taryn turned to see Shannon at the door of the ICU room pushing a cart with the transport monitors and oxygen they had used to get Harry from the operating room to the unit.

"Yeah...just trying to figure how to keep him that way." Shannon stepped closer.

"Jonas is working on it...we have him covered." Taryn looked at Shannon as she reviewed the lab results the ICU nurse had just brought to the room; everything was within acceptable limits.

"How is..."

"We'll talk over dinner." Taryn frowned, as she looked at Shannon who pushed her cart towards the exit, realizing that she was being called from the central desk area. She hustled over to grab the phone as she looked at her blood-splattered scrubs; she should change before she went on with her day.

"Pirelli! Get your ass down here and start your next case."

"I'm finishing up with Harry..."

"Which is not your goddamn job unless you're an intensivist now. Get down here and do as you're told for once." The line clicked off before Taryn could respond. She realized her text alert had been going off since she was in the ER; she grabbed her phone from where she had clipped it at the small of her back.

I got permanently escorted off the premises. M&H contract is cancelled; it's a shit storm. Shannon's your only back up. Stay safe until you get out of there.

She rose and trudged toward the ICU exit, contemplating a call to Marsha to cancel the assignment as she headed to the OR.

"WE'VE CONFIRMED ACCOUNT NUMBERS, BALANCES, AND transaction activity for the past six months. The Cooks have around 6 million liquid in this account and have made several transfers to another account that tracks to a Swiss account. No details yet, but none of this matches the IRS info Charlie got us."

Blake and Cody were analyzing the information gleaned

from Cody's hack of the Cook's Caymans' bank. Although the information suggested that Cook had a source of income separate from his salary, there was no concrete proof of regular deposits or wires. Recent deposits had been made in the bank in cash. As he and Cody prepared to consider other options to research, Blake's phone chimed.

"Shit...we don't need this."

"What's up?"

"I left a surveillance device on that storage space we traced to BMC. Someone's in there...either they're onto us, or they have a shipment."

"I though those were on Wednesdays?"

"Exactly...we need eyes on what's happening." Blake dialed Charlie.

"Any way you can get over to that storage unit? Something's going down."

"This is a bad time for any of us to be visible. Let me get the PD to swing by instead. How'd you get in last time?"

"Taryn and her magic fingers...which are stamping out anesthesia chaos right now."

"Thought you were supposed to be working?"

"Got escorted out, and my company contract is cancelled. I'm helping Cody with analysis on that Cayman's account."

"Keep at it...Cy's due to call any minute with an update."

"Anything would be better than what's going down now."

CHAPTER TWENTY-ONE

Taryn's day continued in the same hectic vein in which it started. She had received brief updates from Cody and Blake on generalities, but was more intent on surviving her day considering neither Harry nor Sherry were a buffer and Michael Downing was in charge. In a true gift, she hadn't gotten in trouble for anything with admin, and Downing ignored her. After her workday was done, she returned to the Intensive Care Unit to assure that Harry was stable after removal of the endotracheal tube. She had just enough time to get to Shannon and Jonas' home for dinner, and catch up with Cody and Blake during the drive.

"What's up with the device? Did you figure a way to get it in?" She had both Cody and Blake on speaker.

"Done and done...your brainstorm is paying off. Working on access now."

"Everyone's talking about Blake's access and contract getting revoked; is he OK?"

"I'm fine, Sugar...question is, are you?"

"I'm still trying to decide. Might be time for me to bail on this place."

"No snap decisions for now... let's talk later."

"What's next?" Cody smirked then looked over his shoulder at Blake.

"Mesteño Bar and Grill first...then we'll see." Taryn blinked as she recalled the visit she and Blake had made the previous week.

"Don't know if that's good or bad."

"It's next on the list." As Cody disconnected, Taryn she arrived at the Barnes' residence. As she swung in to park, she realized that she hadn't checked her private email, or communicated with her parents. She frowned but decided to send them a text rather than call, then scrolled through her emails before finding one from Harry with a subject line: Colorado. It only aroused more questions.

Downing issues track to Centennial. Talk to Jonas.

She hesitated, then forwarded the email to Charlie and Cody before exiting her car and trudging up the walk to Shannon's home where a chorus of barks and shouts preceded Shannon opening the door. Her welcoming hug and smile slipped into place like a security blanket, and the tension Taryn had felt melted away.

"Jonas is on his way...so happy you could come for dinner!" Shannon hung up Taryn's coat, and shooed children and dogs into the basement before ushering her into the kitchen. The smells made Taryn's mouth water and remember that she hadn't eaten since breakfast. "No one has any word about why Blake got fired...and I'm wondering why I'm just hearing about you two having dinner a few nights back."

"Well...it's a long story."

"We've got time." Shannon poured two glasses of wine

and pulled over an appetizer tray, motioning for Taryn to sit at the kitchen table. "Jonas skied with him last week... everyone in the OR has a different story about him. He's always been polite with me, but I know smoking hot badass trouble when I see it...and when it's focused on my new best friend. What gives?"

"Umm, yeah, he's hot... and popular. Not really sure if he's my type, but we're talking."

"Not your type? I may be married, but fine-ass man-candy's everyone's type! You sure you don't have some visual or hormonal issue?" Taryn paced, still twisting in the wind about what to say.

"You remember the asshole I ran into on the day you met Cody and me at Bachelor?"

"Of course! Didn't know if we'd be hunting him and pushing him down the mountain later, but you never brought him up again.

"Well... that was Blake. We just sorta... kept colliding. It's been...complicated."

"Now *that* is poetic justice and karma!!" Taryn winced as Shannon peppered her with questions and details she had no answers for, and no desire to delve into further.

"Collisions and chemistry...excellent! Sounds like fate... what do you think about him?" Taryn gave Shannon a deer in the headlights look.

"I still don't know... fate can be a double-edged disaster. He's also too much like my ex for comfort...and we're always going head to head."

"Hmmm the ex who was also a heart surgeon? There's a beta male for you...NOT."

"Alpha sucks when it's permanently attached to a temper and attitude."

"Say's the non-beta female control freak...anesthesiologist? Really? Have you looked at yourself?"

"Daily verbal battles and chaos are no way to live."

"Men with drive aren't any easier to contain than you are, my friend. Look how trouble found you here!" Taryn was silent, then shrugged before pacing to look out the kitchen window, seeing only her reflection in the darkness.

"Life isn't about constantly being at threat level orange." She realized she had described her time in Bend perfectly.

"What exactly do you get by opting for the easy button?" Taryn thought about her most recent dating disaster, and the past two weeks in Bend. Before she could compose her thoughts to reply, the door from the garage opened as Jonas came in, starting round two of dog and child chaos, saving Taryn from something she had no rational explanation for. Jonas made his way through the thong of children and dogs, greeting each on the way, to greet Shannon with a hug and kiss.

"Hi babe...glad to see you made it here, Taryn. Harry's looking good...they should be set to transfer him out of here sometime late tonight." Taryn gaped, torn between friendship and HIPAA confidence.... about something that Jonas, who wasn't a relative of Harry's, seemed to know a lot about. She remembered the cryptic email she had received from Harry.

"He sent me an email that I didn't get until this morning."

"I'll explain everything over a beer."

"AFTER ALL THE PRESSURE TO TAKE DOWNING INTO THE department, Harry decided to do some digging into his history in Colorado. Although there were rumors of him having complaints filed by staff about inappropriate touching, nothing came through on either his staff application or recommendations here. Raynor was apparently critical in arranging some deal for him to be confirmed here." Jonas finished his beer as he and Taryn chatted, and Shannon directed final dinner and table prep to her children.

"Cody mentioned something like that but didn't find any proof either."

"Harry kept digging and got his family out of the country yesterday after he got the results."

"What? How?"

"When you started having issues with Downing, Harry decided he needed more specifics on his last place of work in Colorado. He was on his way back here with details to run by the chief about next steps when he had this accident. He also wasn't about to let you get into trouble and have another death on his conscious."

"He said a semi ran him off the road...but how are you involved?"

"Simple enough to change POA papers; did it after he got his family out. He suspected there was going to be trouble if he dug into Downing's past, so he wanted his family clear. They're out of the country for awhile. He made me promise to get some information to you." Jonas withdrew a USB drive from his pocket and handed it to Taryn. Shannon came over to Jonas and Taryn; the children were already seated.

"Ok...no more talking work...it's dinnertime." Taryn and Jonas rose to head to the table.

"No idea what's on this, but Harry said you'd know what to do with it." Taryn nodded.

"I do...and I want to talk to Harry." Jonas shook his head as he took his seat.

"He's being transferred to Portland. He's safe."

Seconds after Taryn had walked to the door of the Barnes' home, a Jeep Wrangler, headlights out, had pulled in to park several car lengths back from her vehicle. Jonas Barnes drove up and pulled his vehicle into the drive and garage about five minutes later. After another ten minutes, the Jeep Wrangler started its engine and slowly drove away, not activating headlights until it passed the home and disappeared into the night.

"This looks to be the best spot. I'll try to find the correct network, then we'll get to work figuring out the password." Cody and Blake were settled in the great room of a friend of Charlie's who was on vacation. They'd given Charlie the green light to use the place for the evening. The home was situated on the next street over from Cook's neighborhood.

"You using a password cracker?"

"Nah...got my own system for that, but we need to find... Got it! WCook1 is the lamest network name, but I guess if you aren't expecting company...let's hit it." Blake watched, and took direction as Cody did the heavy lifting, getting the external drive set to store the data once Cody was able to access Cook's computer. Charlie's intel had Cook leaving the hospital. They now needed Cook on premises and the computer activated to have a chance at getting what they needed. Blake's text alert sounded.

"Charlie had some of his PD buddies confirm that Cook is headed home. Show time." They waited another ten minutes, then Cody got to work using the IP address and the information they had obtained via the cloning program.

"He's on his comp. Let's do this." Cody initiated the data transfer process and they were done within minutes to then head over to the next stop on their pub crawl alibi. After another stop designed for maximum visibility and memorable sighting, they planned to return to Taryn's condo and start data analysis. The duped Eagle mainframe access card was also waiting with the only dilemma being using it at a time least likely to arouse suspicion based on the local time in Kansas City.

Blake backed his SUV out of the garage, then closed the door before driving toward their last stop for the night. True to form, it was snowing again. Cody frowned as he checked his phone.

"Nothing from T or Charlie. Not sure if that's bad or good news." Blake glanced at Cody. "You teach her how to pick locks?"

"Nah...think her dad did." Blake blinked incredulously.

"Do I even wanna know more?"

"Not my story to tell, my man." Cody stretched before slouching against the door. "I'm feeling lucky...hundred says I can dust you in a game of pool." Blake smiled wryly as he thought of the raucous late-night pool games he had engaged in with Steve and James over the years. Never again. Maybe it was time to say goodbye with something that had been a happy pastime with what appeared to be a new member of his circle.

"You're on."

"I still have questions about Harry, but it sounds like he's at least gonna be safe."

Taryn, Shannon and Jonas had retreated to the great room with after-dinner drinks while Shannon's teens dealt with kitchen cleanup.

"That he will. I'll get my laptop. I'm as eager as you are to see what's on that drive. I downloaded the files to the drive without opening them." As Jonas went to grab his laptop, Taryn's phone went off; she frowned. Caller ID said the hospital, but she wasn't on call or even high in the callback line-up.

"I hope this isn't trouble." Shannon gave her a questioning look.

"Hi operator, it's Dr. Pirelli. Put me through to the nursing supervisor, please." As she spoke, Shannon frowned and tilted her head. She knew the call line-up as well as Taryn did. This was either an emergency or a huge slip up. "Are you the night sup? I'm not on for callback, and I've had wine with dinner." The nursing director gave Taryn a terse message and disconnected before she had time to answer.

"Shannon, Jonas, I have to go. There was an accident on 97 about a mile outside the city. Multiple victims expected; hospital's activated the disaster protocol. It's all hands."

As Taryn moved to gather her outdoor gear, she heard Shannon's cell and land line go off as well. She looked at Taryn as she answered the phone; it was the hospital operator. It looked like they were *both* headed in. Jonas tossed his laptop on the sofa, then headed to gear up.

"Maybe I should drive you two in...it was snowing pretty hard when I pulled up." Taryn shook her head.

"I'll be fine driving...Shannon will be company, and she can call you when we're done. I'll call Cody or Blake to get me if it's too heavy when I finish. We should be fine."

"THAT'S THREE GAMES NOW, ASS-WIPE. I THINK I'VE been had." Blake tossed another hundred on the table then racked his cue stick to the jeers of a group of men at the bar. Cody smirked as he grabbed the money, then sauntered to the bar to collect another handful of bills and a series of back slaps from the noisy group he and Blake had joined at the bar. Blake glared at Cody as he finished the dregs of his whiskey.

"This smells like a setup. What did you say you do for a living other than sucking down my spending change?"

"No hustle...just some friendly games of pool with some side bets between friends. There was no discussion about my skill level at pool. You can afford it, Mr. Genius Biotech Whiz."

"Fuck you, Cody."

"Not my roll, my man." Cody checked his watch, then added quietly. "I think we've put on enough of a show here. Let's get back to T's place and get to work." Blake nodded and the two donned their coats and sauntered towards the door after saying their goodbyes at the bar. Blake pulled his phone out of his pocket when he realized it was vibrating.

"I forgot I'd left this on silent," he said checking the screen. "Shit! Taryn's had an accident." He showed Cody the face of the phone as they ran for the door. The caller ID blocked text had a picture of Taryn's vehicle off the side of the road in a ditch with the message: *Your very pretty woman is in a bit of trouble. You should guard her more carefully.* Cody swore as they jumped into Blake's truck, dialing Charlie as he launched his tracking program on his phone.

"Can you get an address to give to Charlie on that app?"

"Working on it."

"Taryn's been in an accident. This is where Blake and I

are headed." Cody rattled off the address. "No other details."
Blake took off, tires spinning as he exited the parking lot.

"That's a mile short of the hospital."

"What the hell is she doing there and not at Shannon's?"
Blake looked at Cody who shrugged

"She didn't contact either of us, so I'm betting she's
caught up in something, too. All we can do is get there as fast
as we can."

"I'll meet you there." Charlie clicked off, and Cody
concentrated on navigating.

"Left at the intersection." The truck fishtailed right, then
straightened out as he and Blake sped towards Taryn and her
vehicle.

"Wonder who the fuck sent that text?"

"No idea, but this whole situation has taken another giant
step to the FUBAR zone. T's not the best snow and ice
driver. I'm just hoping she's OK."

CHAPTER TWENTY-TWO

"We're going in circles. That's the same fucking truck we passed a few minutes ago."

"We're on a divided highway with no U-turns possible and snow build-up; we had to go the long way around." Blake ground his teeth and checked the speedometer before edging up his speed, gambling that he wouldn't find a patch of ice; snow tires without studs meant plus minus traction for his high-profile SUV.

"How. Much. Further?"

"Half mile; less than ten minutes." Cody grabbed Blake's phone to examine the text and picture that started the current chain of events. He made a few maneuvers, then unlocked the phone and forwarded the information to his phone and Charlie's. "No emergency vehicles in the pic... wonder how long after the accident it was taken?" Blake frowned as he glanced over

"How the hell did you bypass my passcode?" Blake mentally cursed himself for not checking more closely on

Taryn's status earlier as he coaxed a bit more speed from the truck.

"Know how, my man."

"Shit...she answering your texts?"

"Negative." Blake swore in a steady stream, as his phone rang. He pushed the accept button on the car Bluetooth.

"Myers."

"Blake, it's Charlie...I'm with the officer in charge... Taryn's OK. I got the pic from your phone...we'll talk later." Blake gave a sigh of relief as the call disconnected and the truck rounded the corner to a sea of flashing lights and emergency vehicles. Taryn's truck was nosed into a mountain of snow that had been plowed off the road. When they got as close as they could, they parked, and ran toward the ambulance.

Taryn held an ice bag to her head as she spoke with an EMT. Shannon was talking to the policeman who had apparently been first on the scene. Blake quickly pushed to Taryn's side, Cody trailing close behind. Blake crouched down as he reached for her shoulders, relief battling with frustration. She gingerly lowered the icepack, giving him a glimpse at the growing lump on her forehead.

"God*damn* it Taryn, what were you thinking? You were supposed to stay put with Shannon and Jonas...where the fuck were you going? Are you OK? What happened?"

"Take a breath and stopping bitching at me.... you ever engage your brain before you start blabbing? How the hell is this is my fault?" Taryn scowled, and acted on reflex as she pitched the icepack at Blake, then winced.

"Ouch! Now you made my head hurt worse! Don't you have something else to do?"

"You still didn't answer my question... Do you bother doing risk assessment outside of work?"

"Why the hell are you still riding my ass? Shannon, tell him..." Taryn looked for support, but narrowed her eyes when she saw Shannon standing with Cody, who smirked and draped an arm around Shannon's shoulder as she glanced at him before smiling at Taryn and Blake.

"Isn't this how they met?"

"Pretty much...took me a while to sort it out and get to the bottom of it, but, yup."

"Nice."

"Not helping, Cody." Blake and Taryn echoed each other. Taryn glared at Cody and Shannon in turn.

"I'm *hurt* here!" The paramedics attending Taryn coughed discreetly to cover their laughs as they edged away, leaving her with Blake. Taryn realized how badly her head was pounding...and started to re-apply the icepack, but realized that her hands were empty. As she winced, Blake gently placed the icepack on her forehead. He took a deep breath and nudged Taryn over so he could sit beside her.

"Assumptions...again. Sorry...Why were you two driving around?"

"Emergency call-back to the hospital for mass trauma; all available staff. We spun out taking that turn and ended up in the snowbank. I couldn't correct." Shannon nodded and stepped closer.

"Not sure how we ended up in the ditch except the vehicle didn't respond." Jonas arrived, embracing his wife after working his way through the collection of emergency personnel that now surrounded the scene. Shannon filled him in as Blake and Cody interrupted for details. As they talked, the paramedic who had initially examined Taryn returned.

"Dr. Pirelli and Shannon are both okay. Dr. Pirelli got the worst of it with that bump on her head. It would be best if she got formally examined at the hospital, but she's signed the paperwork not to go." Taryn shrugged.

"No need as I didn't pass out; I'm going home."

"Overruled; you're going to get checked out ...let's go." Taryn frowned as Blake beckoned for her to rise, appalled as Cody sided with him.

"I agree with him, T." After a cutting look at Cody, Taryn shook her head, wincing at her increasing headache.

"Nope...neither one of you is my keeper...and I actually *do* have the magic M and D letters that mean I *can* make that decision. Of all the stupid..." Charlie walked up to Cody whispering something before drawing him away. Cody gave Taryn a grin and admonition before joining Charlie.

"I'm outta here...behave and play nice, you two."

After Blake countered every argument Taryn gave him, with Shannon and Jonas chiming in to support him, Taryn relented and agreed to go to the hospital ER for a full exam, but not in the ambulance.

"Where's Cody?" Shannon and Jonas stopped as they turned to leave.

"With Charlie. We'll track him down. Any message?"

Taryn craned her neck searching for Charlie and Cody, but was diverted when Blake drew her to stand.

"If you don't start walking, I'm carrying you."

"What is your issue? My head hurts, not my feet. I need my keys and purse and...."

"Fuck this." Blake scooped a still protesting Taryn up and strode to his SUV, depositing her in the front seat. "Sorry to pre-empt your whining, but let's get this done." He rummaged in the cargo section for a blanket, tucked it around and over her after checking the seatbelt, then slammed the door before rounding the hood and sliding behind the wheel. Taryn started to protest, then relented as her teeth started to chatter despite the blanket and her parka.

"Guess I'm colder than I thought." Blake gave a noncommittal grunt as he started the vehicle and focused on making best time to the hospital.

"That or your adrenalin surge just ran out." Taryn ignored him and looked out her window as she surrendered to the blanket and seat-warmers and tried not to mentally replay the accident and its aftermath. Within minutes, she and Blake were at the covered reception area of the Emergency Room, where she recognized the ER nurse waiting with a wheelchair.

"Dr. Pirelli, we heard you were in an accident and were coming in for an eval. This way. We're putting you in Room 2." Blake helped Taryn into the wheelchair and followed the triage nurse as his phone started chiming with incoming calls. After he lifted a still protesting Taryn onto the gurney, he left to return his calls, ignoring her questions. Taryn fumed; there was going to be a serious come to Jesus talk about the overstepping of boundaries once she was done.

"Name, address and date, and pain level. I know you got something for pain, but my orders were to check you initially every other hour for mental function as well as to follow up on pain management. I got them to run your prescription through the outpatient pharmacy here. You just got the eye reflex check, so I'm just asking for the verbals and not shining a light in your eyes."

"Damn you! Taryn Jenae Carter Pirelli, January 27, 2013, Bend Oregon, the intersection of..." Taryn looked quickly, "Elm and Main, headed toward my goddamn condo in your goddamn truck. Now what the hell's been going on? And if you shine a light in my eyes, I'll stick a fork in yours."

"Nice bedside manner, doc." Taryn huffed and flounced to stare out her window.

It had been an hour-and-a-half before the poking and prodding was done. The x-rays were pronounced officially without acute change, neuro exam within normal limits, and the ER doc gave Taryn the discharge instructions that she could probably recite in her sleep and planned largely to ignore.

"You shut me down while I was getting evaluated, but I know you were getting info. What gives?"

"About what?"

"Argh!! About the accident...and my truck...and why on earth Charlie was there!!"

"Well first, how's your head?" She flipped him off. "Ah, yes; attitude, mouth and wing finger fully functional...definitely same old Taryn as always. Sugar, you ever dial it back for the rest of us?"

"If I let you push easy, who's gonna keep you sharp and on your toes?" Taryn smirked. Blake hid his answering grin, sobering as he briefly took his gaze off the road and rubbed her cheek with the back of his hand.

"You had me worried. I'll show you the text I got later; I'm glad you're safe." Taryn nodded, her initial anger diffusing with his last statement. She didn't realize that she was drowsing until she was jostled awake as Blake pulled into her driveway. The porch and internal lights shone a bright welcome, and a shovel was leaning by the front door. The walkway had been shoveled clear of the newly fallen snow. Blake activated the door opener, then parked his truck in the garage.

"No more coddling!" Taryn pushed Blake away as he

opened her door and hovered as if to carry her in. "I'm awake, and that's Charlie's truck out front...I want the whole story." The two of them walked up the stairs and into the mudroom where Taryn got her usual welcome from Maxx.

Taryn shivered as she shed her boots and coat despite the warmth of the condo heated by the fire. She smiled at Cody as he entered and gave her a fierce, one-armed hug.

"Another of your nine lives just kicked in."

"I'll take lucky every time." She and Maxx followed her friends into the great room where Charlie paced, grim-faced in front of the fire. He watched as Taryn sank into the nearest couch and Maxx jumped up beside her. His expression visibly softened as he watched Taryn settle in, tucking her toes under Maxx's bulk.

"You *were* lucky, young lady. That could have been a lot worse." Blake joined her on the couch, encouraging Taryn to lean her head on his shoulder, but she was full of questions, and unready to wind down, although she accepted a mug of hot chocolate from Cody before he headed for the wet bar.

"Which repair shop did they tow my truck to? And where on earth were the accident victims we were called about? There was a mass trauma alert for a multi vehicle pileup on 97 with injuries, but I didn't see any in the ER. What's going on?" Charlie was silent at her outburst, then shook his head as he glanced at Blake, who uttered a quiet curse as he rose and joined Cody at the wet bar. Blake tossed back his drink and passed it to Cody for a refill while Charlie updated Taryn.

"Taryn, there was *no accident* on 97. Confirmed it with the dispatcher, chief of police and sheriff after I heard your story from the EMT. No one from the hospital admits calling you, or Shannon for that matter. Your truck's in the police impound yard; you'll get it after the evidence collection team finishes. Your steering fluid was essentially dry. What was left leaked out where you got stopped by that snowbank. Your right-side tires were under-inflated; that's why you lost control and ended up in the ditch. Give the police time to gather info, then they'll send it to the service garage of your choice." Taryn frowned and shook her head, "That's not possible...Cody and I had the truck checked out before we drove here; it was in perfect repair. And who would be able to page me as if it were from the hospital?"

"None of it was an accident," said Blake with a sigh as he came over to sit by Taryn. He pulled out his phone, scrolling back through his messages and keying one up before handing it to Taryn. Taryn looked at the text message displayed on Blake's phone, then at the phone Charlie handed her.

"I took this at the scene." The picture was of a note with a single, bolded message, sealed in an evidence bag.

SHE'S USING UP CAT LIVES; HER LUCK MAY RUN OUT, MYERS

Taryn blinked then trembled as she looked at both phones, and the significance of the note sunk in. She hadn't seen anyone near her truck after the accident. She looked at Charlie for answers, as he perched on the chair nearest to where she sat with Blake whose arm was protectively wrapped around her.

"Sugar, I got the text right after the accident, since neither you nor Shannon were out of the car."

"The note was wedged under the driver's side windshield wiper. Obviously, it wasn't there when you were driving. Police are checking for prints and sampling the paper, but they don't expect to get anything useful. Whoever did this is slick, and, we're assuming, also staged the accident. They placed it during the confusion at the scene. One of the officers inspecting the truck before it was towed found it. No one remembers seeing anyone other than emergency assistance and police personnel on the scene after it was roped off. Whoever placed it ghosted away without detection. My first instinct is to advise you to leave and go back to Seattle with Cody."

Taryn shook her head in denial, rethinking her earlier decision to leave the assignment. This was personal now. No way would she leave like a victim or be sent home like some misbehaving, errant child.

Blake ignored her and nodded. "I vote she leaves."

Taryn scowled and drew away from Blake. Charlie shrugged and continued. "I'm not sure that whoever is responsible for this won't follow her to Seattle."

"What?"

"No one there will know what's been going on other than Cody. He's got resources, and your house is probably like a fortress in a normal situation, but this is as far from normal as I can think of." He paused, scrubbing a hand through his goatee as he considered options. Blake had listened to Charlie's musings, then shrugged.

"We're damned if we do, damned if we don't in terms of a response to this." Charlie was silent for a moment before adding, "The pictures of this accident and Charlie's kids means that observation is morphing into intervention. It's getting dangerous for all of you, especially Taryn. Other than the obvious goal of trying to keep Taryn safe moving forward, we should focus on ending your search and get everything to Cy and Tracy to handle from here forward. It's time for the professionals to handle this."

Cody spoke up, concern clear in his voice, "Well if they're devious and slick enough to pull a complex stunt like this, what won't they do? And how're we keeping T. and Blake safe? No offense, Charlie, but both of them have targets on them that neither you nor Cy can remove. Blake got himself canned, but should T even go back to work?"

"What?"

"Company contract terminated...asked to vacate the premises...what the fuck ever...either Cook or Raynor got a hard on, and I'm done there. But I'm not letting them get to Taryn again."

Charlie answered crisply, shaking his head, "Work is the best place for Taryn. Yes, Cook and Raynor are there, but there're also plenty of witnesses, and absolutely no proof that either of them is involved in what happened tonight."

"Who else could it be?"

"I get your frustration, but we have no proof that either Cook or Raynor are involved in what happened tonight. The upside is this 'accident' is officially on record with the police. Not only will there be a police investigation of the accident but one also of everything from the paper that the note was written on, to the source of the text and picture that were sent to Blake as well as all aspects of communication to Taryn and Shannon."

Blake shrugged and nodded. "So, what's the new plan?"

"Depends on Taryn. Do you think you'll be up to brushing this off like it was a random accident? Tracye and Cy are here and will be moving forward tomorrow."

Taryn debated a moment before answering, looking at both Cody, who stared back at her solemnly, and Blake, who was mutely regarding the black screen of his phone. Downing was her biggest concern. She looked up at Charlie.

"I'm not going anywhere. I want to see this through; let's keep going." Charlie gave her a smile and Blake gave an encouraging squeeze to her shoulder. Game on.

CHAPTER TWENTY-THREE

Tuesday Late Night

Taryn shook off her exhaustion and swirl of post-accident emotions as she revealed her information from Harry and Jonas. Everything now pointed towards conflicting information about Downing stemming from his previous job in Colorado.

"Jonas shared his POA directions from Harry. I'll send the info to Cy and his DHS team."

"So, you know about Harry?" Charlie nodded.

"I think you're on the right track looking into Downing's history. I've already sent a current hospital badge picture to their med staff to start. If you're right, we've got bigger issues with Downing, or whoever he is." Blake halted his work with Cody on the Cayman bank.

"*Whoever he is?* How the fuck do you fake being an anesthesiologist?" Charlie sighed, then shook his head.

"It can be done, but I'm pretty sure I can't disclose..."

"Which means it's something related to your time on the SEAL teams." Charlie looked at Blake, then shrugged.

"That's need to know right now. I think we'd best move on to the next issue, which is who knew about Taryn's plans." Charlie shook his head as Blake started to speak. "Not going there, Blake."

"Shannon was with me..."

"Which means someone was watching and knew you two were together." Taryn swallowed and frowned as she re-ran her drive to the Barnes' residence.

"I can't remember anyone following me...but can't say that I was all that observant."

"Not like anyone would have a hard time finding your truck anyway since it's registered with the hospital." Charlie rose to pace before continuing.

"When Blake let me know that someone was moving stock at that storage space, I got the PD to go by there. They saw an unmarked panel truck. We were debating next steps when I had to break off and take Cody's call."

"We need to get back in there."

"Not tonight." Blake and Cody echoed each other as Charlie chuckled.

"Nice we're all on the same page for a change. Why don't we concentrate on looking at what we got from the clones and surveillance of Cook's home network?"

"We got nothing useful on Raynor. The comp Jake picked up was the hospital desktop." Cody ranhis hand through his hair. "I can't figure another way to get access to his laptop or network."

"Cook's info is better than nothing. Blake pushed his laptop back.

"I'm not feeling how we're only getting financials and data on Cook. Smells like a setup."

Charlie shrugged.

"Or consistent with Raynor having more capability or assistance covering his tracks.

Taryn propped her feet on Maxx in her work corner. She ignored the conversation flowing around her as she focused on her work with the duped computer access card. 10 PM PST would be midnight at the Kansas City corporate headquarters of Eagle Pharmaceuticals. "You have a computer access card, Cody?" He stopped his debate with Blake and Charlie to rummage in his backpack, tossing over the bundled peripherals bag to Taryn.

"Timing's right. You making sure no one can follow your back trail?" Taryn snorted.

"Not a rookie. No one will find me if I don't wanna get seen." Cody held up his hands with a smile.

"A reminder...not an accusation. I trust you." Taryn smiled, and engaged the card to access the Eagle mainframe, sifting through the confidential information she needed to help the investigation. Between the pain pills and hot chocolate, Taryn got progressively drowsier despite her interest in what was going on. She persisted, copying files of interest to their cloud account rather than trying to analyze everything she found. She worked quickly to limit her period of access in the Eagle system.

"I've found some suspect video files." Cody was going through the information gleaned from Cook's computer that evening while Blake toiled with the information from the Cayman's bank and Charlie looked over everything they gathered, relaying important snippets to Cy. "They're password protected and encrypted; itching to get at them for that reason alone, given the source. Charlie looked up from his work.

"You think you can get in?"

"Not if... I should have something pretty fast; Cook's no genius with password selection."

"I'm still trying to figure out why you only do this in your free time."

"Less rules more fun." After a few minutes, filled with clacking keys and muttered curses, Cody gained access.

"In! Day-time stamp shows that these files were uploaded today in packets. It's gonna take me awhile to reassemble them into a coherent video...not sure why they're fragmented like that...." Blake slowed in his work on the financial data to peer over Cody's shoulder as he expanded his re-assembly work to an extended screen view.

"I've got things reassembled into a single file...let's have a look."

Taryn padded over to look over Cody's other shoulder, seeing a video showing a dimly lit room with a man tied to a chair spotlit from above. The glare of the light and exaggerated contrast with the inky blackness of the rest of the room made true colors hard to define, but the man appeared to have dark blonde hair, matted to one side of his head by a dark, crusted substance. His face was hidden; his head sagged forward onto his chest. The picture abruptly jumped to show the same man, head up, sweat beading his mottled face and dripping off his chin. His eyes were squeezed shut, and his features were twisted and distorted. A trickle of blood streamed out of the corner of his mouth and mixed with the sweat dripping down his face. He opened his eyes, turning his pain-filled glassy gaze directly into the camera as Blake swore.

"Son of a bitch...that's James! Where in the hell is ...was he?"

"Working on it...I'm zooming in on the background. Maybe we can extract some details." Charlie was on his feet, joining Blake and Taryn as they clustered behind Cody. Cody swore softly as he froze the video feed and enhanced it.

"Cody, run the raw video again." Taryn leaned right to give Charlie a better viewing angle.

"Aside from the first jump in subject position and time, is the video skipping or jumping? Or is it just my eyes?" Cody re-ran the same snippet, squinting as he re-played it with slo-mo, exaggerating the effects Charlie had noticed. "Maybe ... let's put this up on a bigger screen so I can get better definition." He rummaged in his backpack, then tossed Blake a bundle of cables. Let's use the TV as a high def monitor." The tension in the room ratcheted up as Blake made the connections Cody needed. "OK, let's run the original, regular speed, all the way through."

The opening and follow-up images rolled with James was spotlighted as the uninterrupted video showed the whole process of him waking, presumably being questioned, and mouthing answers. The subsequent video showed him being tortured by a man wielding orthopedic instruments, cigarettes and a knife in agonizing, technicolor detail, made even more macabre by the fact that there was no associated sound. No other faces were visible. There were shots of the back of at least two men's heads, blurred shots of hands, and some of the instruments they used on James, but nothing distinctive, likely due to clever editing. The enlarged hi-def video image was jerky with obvious breaks in the action and even image ghosts. The absence of sound meant they were left to provide the sound track from their own individual nightmares as the camera zoomed in on James' anguished face, his mouth often open in a silent scream, eyes wide in terror as the gruesome video kept grinding on. Blood streamed from his increasingly mangled hands and face, dripping and pooling on a plastic sheet strategically placed under his chair. They watched in horrified silence. The only sound came from the crackle of the fireplace. The comforting ambiance providing a jarring contrast to the images on the screen.

Cody put the video clip on loop. As it began to replay, Taryn glanced at Blake, who stood silent, arms crossed as he watched the video repeat.

"Blake, I'm so sorry," Taryn gave Blake's arm a gentle squeeze as she sensed his pain and anger. He stirred, wrapping his arm around her, pulling her close.

"Thanks, Sugar...it's a gut punch actually seeing it, but I knew logically that this was likely what happened." After watching the re-run, he nodded, "I agree with Charlie. This has been edited from a longer recording. One minute...I just want one minute with those fuckers." His eyes glittered and a tic beat in his jaw as he scrubbed his hands through his hair and poured another drink. He took the whisky he poured and walked towards the front of the condo as they speculated and Cody continued to work his magic.

"Why wasn't there sound?"

"Likely because voice recognition, even with the audio distorted, could give more of an indication as to who was participating. Not enough details for facial recognition; no distinctive marks on hands or arms, and no hair. The whole thing looks like it was altered by a pro, who also erased the associated audio.

"Agreed...but there are still things I can work with. Filtering...super slo mo the action after I duplicate the clip. There are some background details that might be distinctive; I can isolate and enhance them. Something about what I'm seeing..." His voice trailed off as his fingers danced over the keyboard.

"Whoever edited this video is wicked slick, but they left some electronic fingerprints I can work with."

"Copy everything to the common account. Cy and Tracye have an AV specialist on their support team."

"Based on this video, we've at got least three people involved with Harris' questioning and presumptive murder, if you count whoever's running the video, along with the two that we're getting partial torso and body shots of. Video came from Cook's laptop; circumstantial if we don't have some proof of him being involved in what we're seeing or get a confession from him. Could also be planted, especially with the recent time/date stamp for video upload.

"Just like Jake got in the admin office, someone else could, too." Blake stood in front of the TV, arms crossed, an inscrutable expression on his face as he viewed the enhanced video now playing. "We've gotta get some concrete info connecting either Cook or Raynor with this damn video....and Eagle." Playback froze.

"Look at the background." The monitor now showed a stop-motion enhanced view of stacked boxes and shadowy walls, along with blown in insulation dripping from pipes and sprinklers.

"Warehouse?"

"Room matches what Taryn and I saw last week. We saw that table and chairs when we were there. Figures that they were moving shit out this evening. Cy needs to get a warrant first thing and get in there before they move everything out. Whadda you think, Charlie?"

"We could likely get in with a warrant...but that wouldn't happen until midday at the earliest."

"This video makes it seem like Cook is being framed as the fall guy. This is all Raynor."

"That still leaves us stuck with trying to get info connecting either Raynor or Cook with a drug supply diversion from hospital stores."

"Evidence of that drug supply diversion, over-shipment of stock from CHG corporate or the individual drug suppliers for the hospital pharmacy would give us what we need. Let me see what I can do to tag some folks at the hospital who might have access to stores and stock info."

***

MAXX NUDGED TARYN; POTTY TIME. SHE YAWNED AS SHE paused her survey of Eagle corporate computers and geared up for the outside, opting to let Maxx do his business in the backyard. Blake looked up as she unlocked and opened the slider off the great room after removing the safety bar from the track, staying in the proximity of the Jacuzzi deck. Maxx padded out and across the deck before trotting down the stairs to the backyard. Taryn leaned on the covered Jacuzzi, giving a wry smile as she realized that she hadn't gotten to enjoy the luxury of soaking in the hot tub with all of the oddities that had occurred since that first weekend in Bend. Maybe...if things quieted down, she could enjoy herself a little more as the assignment went on...*Not,* said the naysayer voice in her head as Maxx came back up the stairs. She was still teetering on the edge of assignment abandonment, especially after the events of the evening. As Taryn sat down, her exhaustion overcame her will, and she slipped into sleep after only a few more minutes worth of work.

She awoke to Maxx pushing a cold, wet nose in her face, and Blake shaking her.

"Up, Sugar...you've been passed out for almost an hour. I just gave Maxx another walk. You need a bed, not the edge of the couch if you're going to make work tomorrow." Too tired to argue, Taryn said a sleepy goodnight to Cody and Charlie, and walked upstairs with Blake and Maxx. After a quick kiss to her nose and a lopsided smile, Blake pulled back the covers of her bed, while Maxx flopped down on his bed. Blake went through another neuro and pain level check, but she was too tired to be annoyed or chew him out.

"Neuro checks and pain management wasn't how I'd envisioned spending time with you, but such is life. I've gotta wake you once more for neuro checks, so I'm staying and helping Cody. Charlie's heading out. The nursing sup called while you were sleeping; no work for you until noon tomorrow, and only if you aren't feeling worse." Taryn nodded sleepily, too exhausted to wonder why Downing or Sherry, the call anesthesiologist hadn't called with her assignment change. She was back to sleep within seconds.

"She was out as soon as her head hit the pillow." Blake returned to join Charlie and Cody.

"Cy just sent the results of that assay on the propofol from her friend in St. Louis. Matches exactly what Harris sent us. Along with the assays on the drugs you two snuck out of that storage space, we have three connected samples. They're getting that warrant."

Charlie checked his watch. "After midnight; I'll head home, maybe tag Cy once more. Blake and Cody walked with him to the door.

"Why were you so concerned about Downing...and not speculating?" Charlie paused in donning his coat.

"I need to work my sources still in the SEAL teams. Infiltration and impersonation can be part of what is done in Special Forces. I need to check things out before I say more."

"What are you looking for?" Charlie paused while on the porch, giving a grim smile.

"I'll tell you when I find it." Cody closed the door, then walked back to the great room, leaving Blake leaning on the door, deep in thought. After a few minutes, he followed Cody to the great room, resuming his seat at his laptop, lounging back in his chair, arms crossed.

"Why do you think we can't find jack on Raynor?"

"He's slick; same reason we couldn't get a clone of his laptop. He's a pro."

"Maybe too slick. Nobody is that stealth without help." Cody returned to his seat and opened his laptop.

"What are you thinking?"

"What if someone very high in the FDA or government is helping him stay under the radar?"

"That would be very bad news for all of us."

THE LARGE ROOM HOUSING THE SERVERS AND mainframe computers for Eagle Pharmaceuticals was deceptively quiet. A series of flags had been tripped and indicated unusual activity and access with a duration longer than one hour was being conducted between midnight and 1 AM CST. The access of the mainframe was just about perfect... except the IDS monitoring program was AI enhanced to identify access card specific unusual activity on the network. A series of emails and alerts were sent to the nightshift network security engineer, noting both the card access information as well as the IP address of the computer used for access. Unlike the hospitals and clinics that Eagle supplied, the corporate headquarters were simply an outfit that operated 9-5, CST with the occasional outlier of early start/late working individuals or teams, which were all logged and noted in advance. The usual security guards had nothing to do with IT and comp security, but received and ignored the automatic CC of the email concerning unusual activity that was also sent to the nighttime systems administrator for the week and the CIO.

The nighttime engineer was roused out of bed by his laptop, tablet, and phone all sending him various electronic alerts and alarms indicating that something unusual was going on with the mainframe. He groped for his laptop, nestled against him in bed, and snagged his phone from the nightstand as he shuffled to the desk in his room with both devices and began his remote checks and investigation. Everything appeared to be nominal; likely another network glitch...certainly nothing that needed immediate attention. The proper card access code had been used and the card matched the list and ID of known remote access cards that he plugged into the program he used to confirm card validity and authorization. Other than logging that he had received the alerts and sending a couple emails to that effect, he decided to wait until the morning to do the complete background research and file his final report. He returned to sleep, taking his laptop with him, sliding the phone back on its charge mat on the nightstand. He quickly fell asleep, unsuspecting of the uproar that would start when the day shift took a closer look at the server, access, and intrusion logs.

CHAPTER TWENTY-FOUR

Wednesday Morning

Taryn woke refreshed, headache free, and unsure of what had woken her. Maxx wasn't around; her phone wasn't charging in its customary place on her nightstand. There was a tap on the door and Blake poked his head in.

"You awake, Sugar? Second time I've knocked...you're due for a final neuro check before you get your day rolling. I swiped your phone so your alarm didn't go off." Taryn rolled her eyes; this was getting old. Blake entered, followed by Maxx, wagging his tail and giving a doggie grin. She looked with interest at Blake, who was carrying a mug of what smelled suspiciously like peppermint mocha.

"Not sure if I should thank you or be afraid about the implications of room service coffee." Blake grinned; he looked better than any man had a reason to so early in the morning. Maxx woofed, and swiped her face good morning before flopping down to take up the rest of the bed real estate. Taryn reached for her coffee, frowning as one corner of Blake's mouth quirked as he kept her coffee out of reach with a shake of his head.

"Neuro check before caffeine." Taryn glared at him, then leaned forward and snatched her coffee before he finished speaking. "Well, then..."

"I don't do bribes." She arranged her pillows and settled in to enjoy her coffee, until Blake plucked it out of her hand, and walked to place it on the dresser across the room. Blake grinned and leaned against the wall.

"You still owe me a neuro check..."

"I heard you...my executive, medical assessment is no more damn neuro checks; I'm fine. However," Taryn tilted her head. "I'd be happy to *demonstrate* full functionality if you're interested." Blake's smile turned into a leer as he pushed off the wall and started unbuttoning his shirt, shrugging it off his shoulders.

"Seduction as a bribe...I'll take it." Taryn's smile grew with his every step. "You surprise me." Taryn flipped back the covers to make room for him as she scooted over, laughing at Maxx's indignant woof as he was pushed off the other side of the bed and trotted out of the room.

"Expect the unexpected."

"That a warning or a promise? Taryn tugged at Blake's jeans. "You're overdressed...lose these...they're in my way."

"Pushy and aggressive in the morning...I like it..." Blake turned a quick kiss into an involved, in depth exploration, winding one hand in Taryn's braids as she cupped his face with her own hand. He paused, smile fading, and released her braids, lightly running one finger down her nose.

"You scared the hell outta me last night, Sugar..." Taryn sobered, replaying the previous evening's events.

"I never imagined the call into the hospital would be a fake."

"Someone knew just the right thing to say and do...and if we thought harder about it, we'd figure out who..."

"So, what are we gonna do?" Blake was silent, eyes distant, then he refocused, and his solemn expression morphed into a leer.

"Why, I think we've got a functional neuro check to do first...phone calls can wait."

"I'm thinking that's a perverted way to do a neuro check."

"Brat.... it's your suggestion."

"And your point is?" Blake huffed a laugh, and Taryn slung a leg over him as she stripped off her nightshirt.

"Where were we?"

Midmorning,
Bend Regional Conference Room

"OF COURSE; I'LL COME STRAIGHTAWAY AFTER THE meeting." The tedium of the monthly Q/A meeting was replaced by panic after Wyatt Cook's admin called. *After what he was told was successful damage control, why would there be two FDA agents in his office investigating adverse drug reactions?* Downing was right; Pirelli had to be up to something. Wyatt Cook's interest in the meeting was irretrievably fractured, but he maintained his outward composure and façade of control. He also sent a series of texts to Ken Raynor asking for advice and assistance. Michael Downing, seated on the other side of the table, smirked as he looked knowingly at Cook, then his phone. For the rest of the meeting Cook checked for a reply text that never came. Downing stood to leave immediately after the meeting was adjourned. Cook, predictably, asked him to stay.

"Aren't you running the board for anesthesia today?"

"You know I am...what now?" As the last person cleared the door, Wyatt, grabbed Downing's arm.

"Did you or did you not confiscate all Q/A reports that James Harris submitted in December?" Downing looked at Cook, then at the hand gripping his arm.

"Careful, Junior." Wyatt paled and quickly released Downing's arm, snatching a handkerchief out of his pocket to blot his sweaty forehead. Then leaned close, whispering as his eyes flitted to the door and the tabletop comm center.

"I've got FDA inspectors in my office." Downing frowned and checked the text alert chiming on his phone.

"Stall....I'm getting new info, and I've got to get back to the OR."

"But..."

"Goddammit, I said handle it!" Downing swore as he stalked out the door, and opened the stairway door, taking the stairs to the operating room two at a time. Wyatt paled, then trailed Downing to the door, straightening his suit coat before making the long walk to the elevator toward the administration suite.

TARYN STARTLED AWAKE AND WONDERED WHY IT WAS SO hot...and why she was still in bed on a workday.

"Ready already for round two, Sugar?" Blake growled as he bit her ear, and nuzzled her neck. The past hour came roaring back in technicolor Imax. She rolled onto her back and looped both arms around his neck, diving into a make out session headed to its logical conclusion...until Cody pounded on the door.

"Okay, enough with the busy! Get your horny asses out

here and join the working! Taryn, you're due at the hospital in an hour. Blake! I needed you an hour ago."

"He always so pushy?" she whispered.

"Pretty much." It wouldn't take *that* long to get ready for work...

"Heard that...I'll just dump your breakfast, then T."

Taryn gave a sheepish grin, then slipped from the bed. "Hey, you get a raincheck. I don't get breakfast, I'm gonna be grumpy."

"CHARLIE LEANED ON HIS HOSPITAL CONTACTS AND GOT confirmation that some of the facilities and distribution staff were involved in moving stock off campus. They've got dates and names; apparently the people involved were low enough in the hierarchy that they just followed orders."

"That covers the pharmacy connection...pathology doc is obviously involved." Taryn ticked the knowns off as she finished her breakfast. "I was fading when I ran into a bunch of Eagle-Raynor emails with subject line 'Ordering'. Take a look; I uploaded everything to the account without looking at them, but they might have the info we need. We're still stuck getting info on Raynor. How're we gonna fix that?"

"Still working on it." Cody scrubbed his hands through his hair, and suddenly sobered. "I even went out on a limb before daylight this morning and cruised by Raynor's house to see what I got with a packet sniffer."

"And?"

"There was activity on his WiFi network, but I couldn't touch it, other than ID'ing the network as KR2."

"VPN in addition to his secured network?"

"At least. It was something at a level of equipment not

available to the ordinary consumer, or even hacker. I'm as impressed as I was frustrated."

"Someone that diligent about security has got to have some big secrets to hide."

"My thought exactly. Where does that leave us?

"You mean other than Dr. Trouble laying low and trying not to piss off Downing for a change," Taryn rolled her eyes at Blake; he grinned and gave her a wink. "Seriously...what's the plan?" Taryn frowned as she leaned back in her chair.

"This is all about connections and relationships."

"Charlie called; Cy and his number 2, Tracye, have started questioning Cook. Raynor's off campus in some meeting and should be back by noon."

"How about looking at professional affiliations and connections?"

"As in?"

"Like those for hospital administrators. Maybe that will give us an indication of how Cook and Raynor are connected. Both of them being here is not an accident." Cody scribbled on a note pad as Blake and Taryn rose to head for Blake's SUV.

"Good idea. I'll dig into that first...and grab your truck when it's ready. The officer at the PD vehicle impound recommended a repair shop." Cody followed Blake and Taryn to the mudroom.

"Let's drop Maxx at daycare. No sense acting like today is any different than usual." Taryn nodded, and whistled for Maxx, who came trotting in from the great room.

"New ground-rules; no being alone with Downing, Cook, or even Raynor for that matter; do your work, keep your head down." Taryn rolled her eyes.

"Yes, Mom." She rolled her eyes and followed Maxx down the stairs to the garage muttering under her breath.

"One of these days, your eyes are gonna get stuck in the back of your head...Sugar. That's just logic and good sense to avoid anyone who you know isn't in your corner." Blake followed her down after looking at Cody, shaking his head.

"He's right, T...just be careful one more day...please?" Cody stood in the door trying to hide the worried look on his face.

"Whatever...Fine." Taryn shrugged, deciding to take Maxx for a walk to escape the smothering blanket of testosterone that had invaded her house.

"Blake, hang on." Blake was headed for the open garage door when Cody stopped him.

"I've got a bad feeling about today. Any way we can get more backup for T at work?"

"We're covered. Charlie worked with Jake to get some agents installed in housekeeping. I flew here with a licensed concealed carry permit and weapon and have no reason to be coy carrying now that I'm not working at the hospital. I've also called Jonas and Charlie. She'll be fine."

Wednesday, Late Morning

"KAT, I HAVE SOME EMERGENCY MEETINGS OFF CAMPUS that I need to attend to before I return. I'll check with you during breaks. Hold anything else that comes in. Reschedule my afternoon for tomorrow." Ken disconnected the call, continuing with the emails, texts and other correspondence that had occupied his time since long before sunrise. He looked again at the email that had come from his superior shortly after he was done with his scheduled call with the Eagle CIO.

Full retreat. Our operations have been negatively impacted by an IT breach at Eagle. You are to proceed to Switzerland, where a new identity is being prepared for you. Execution of above is to begin immediately.

He methodically checked off tasks, single-minded in his goal to survive at all costs, mentally considering and discarding people with the capabilities to accomplish the seemingly impossible. Anthony/Myers had been under observation the previous evening, and had been seen with Pirelli's Seattle roommate, Cody Jennings, in several bars the night before, until both had gone to check on Pirelli after the accident. Since Myers was out as suspect for the breach, the only conclusion that Ken could draw was that somehow, someone else with the clout and technology to duplicate his access card had gained access. He shook his head trying to focus. Time enough later for speculation and retribution. As he worked, he heard the chime indicating that the suite door had been opened.

"What's your problem, Kenny-boy?" Downing asked, as he swaggered into the office and fished a pack of Dunhill Blue cigarettes and a lighter out of his lab coat before tossing it on a chair. He stared at Ken, his hands on his hips. "You yanked me out of the OR and delayed a case until I can get Winger to come in early. This better be good; I got no time for your bullshit."

"Problems and fallout from the Harris affair that I thought were under control. I'm completing some data transfer, and need to be out of town, and out of the country ASAP. I may need your help to make that happen." Ken sorted files as he loaded his briefcase. He tried not to stare at Downing, as he got comfortable on the sofa in the conversation area, crossing his feet on the coffee table, stretching both arms across the sofa back.

"Whatever needs to get done, I'll take care of it. I always do...always will." Downing lit a cigarette then upended a candy dish on the table, repurposing it as an ashtray. Ken watched him light up as some of the candy hit the floor. He compressed his lips into a tight line of annoyance, but said nothing, aware that antagonizing Downing would get him nowhere. "You need anyone to disappear this time or just get you out of Dodge? That ain't no big thing, by the way." He puffed on his cigarette and flicked ashes in the direction of the candy dish.

"No eliminations," said Ken, as he glanced at the stream of smoke curling toward the ceiling, and the smoke detector in the opposite corner of the office, then continued working the slim laptop that he planned to take with him. "Just get me out of town...I'm handling everything else. Only other thing I need your help with is to make sure that Cook's wife does as she is told and keeps her mouth shut while she's in California."

"California, is it? She in on this now? Interesting. The way you're acting, Kenny-boy, I'm bettin' you thinking 'bout tapping that ass sometime soon. How you gonna do that with her man in the picture? Or..." He dropped his feet to the floor and leaned forward, "Ain't he gonna be part of the picture?" Ken Raynor reddened and pressed his lips together at the not so subtle innuendo."

"I'm more concerned that she's not frightened off before she is in place in the capacity and position that the organizers have planned for her," he said mildly as he resumed his work on his computer, rather than display any of the nervousness he felt about Downing's methods or women.

"Not gonna damage the bitch, but she'll be clear about where she stands, and that she'd best do as she's told," grunted Downing as he stubbed out his cigarette, rose and crossed to a cabinet where Ken Raynor stashed a bottle of Scotch to pour himself two fingers. Raynor didn't like the familiarity, but cringed when he thought of expressing his displeasure. He had more important issues to take care of. "What's on the agenda for tonight, beside you leaving?" asked Downing as paced the office, poking items idly, and stopping to light another cigarette. Ken was about to answer, when he received a text message. He read it twice to make sure that he understood correctly, then threw back his head and laughed as he grabbed his briefcase.

"New plan; you help our colleague with his little project before you escort Mrs. Cook to the airport. I can finish my plans on my own."

"*Junior?*" Downing snorted as he stopped by Ken's desk. "With a plan? That fool couldn't find his ass with both hands and a GPS."

"And that *fool* is still your boss, and don't you forget it," snapped Ken, as he looked up. "Now get back to work and do what you're paid to do." Downing drew on his cigarette silently, then blew the cloud of smoke in Ken's face, and smirked, his smile growing into a leer as he spoke.

"Right on it...*Boss*...although I might just take it on myself to deal with the pretty little Dr. Pirelli."

"None of your games..."

"No game playin here boss...none at all." He watched as Downing grabbed his white lab coat, dropping his cigarette on the Persian rug and grinding it out with his toe. "See you later, Kenny boy," he said and slammed the office door behind him.

Ken stopped what he was doing and stared at the closed door, then roused and resumed packing his briefcase.

CHAPTER TWENTY-FIVE

"Blake, get your ass in here...T's found the connection between Eagle and Raynor." Blake had dropped Taryn and work and had just arrived back at her condo to find Cody working three laptops as a portable printer spit out endless printouts. Blake shed his coat then picked up some of the printer output.

"Emails from Eagle to purchasing at Bend Regional, Invoices....everything seems to have been routed through Raynor to authorize quantities and payment.

"T found this last night; I didn't read through the files and put it together until now. She was spot on about the professional association, too. Take a look at this info from the Hospital Admin professional society." Cody slanted a laptop so that Blake could see. "This is a pic of Raynor and Cook at a Membership committee meeting...dates back about five years. Occasion was Cook being elected as chair of the committee to recruit other administrators to join and be active in the organization."

"Okaaaay...I guess I don't follow."

"Membership recruitment for the professional organization...and recruitment of administrators who could potentially be convinced to carry Eagle stock, increase profits, etc."

"Is that a stretch?"

"How do people change policies and practice if not by being influenced by others in 'authority' and influence to switch gears? Especially if they think they get some secondary gain out the other end."

"It's still supposition that Cook used his position in the professional society to recruit for Eagle." The doorbell sounded, followed by pounding on the front door.

"What the hell?" Blake trailed Cody to the door; it was Charlie.

"Tell me Taryn isn't at work." Blake frowned.

"I just dropped her off...what's up?"

"We got the info on the real Downing...who is missing." Charlie shed his parka and tossed it in the direction of the coat rack, then headed towards the kitchen, Cody and Blake trailing in his wake.

"I'm sorry?"

"Just got the scoop from Cy...hoped I could get to you before Taryn went to work." Cody pushed one of his laptops toward Charlie.

"Thanks...gimme a sec." He accessed his email, opening two windows. "First thing is Michael Downing's personnel and Med Staff file from the hospital he was at in Colorado." Both files had a corresponding picture ID attached. Blake shook his head

"That's not Downing." Charlie nodded as he pulled up another file.

"We know that. At his former location, this Downing ran into some harassment complaints that escalated to the point that he was invited to resign his privileges and position at the hospital, as reflected in this letter." Cody shrugged.

"How'd he end up here with *that* history? Someone here had to know that there were issues elsewhere, and that..."

"Raynor was his biggest advocate here, and obviously arranged everything. None of the uncomplimentary info or evals appear in Oregon Downing's files."

"So, where's Colorado Downing?"

"Unknown. Complete police report's pending, but no one local was pushing for answers on that end; no family there."

"He's got the paper cred, but how the fuck can whoever's here fake being an anesthesiologist?"

"How long has he been here?" Blake started pacing.

"Less than a year." Charlie pulled up the ID picture of the person everyone in Bend knew as 'Michael Downing'. "Biggest question is who is this guy, and is he really even a doc?"

"How could Med Staff and credentialing drop the ball on this." Charlie pulled up another set of files, corresponding to the Bend Regional personnel files on Michael Downing.

"This way...they basically took all of the real Downing's information and altered it to match the person who's here now."

"According to Taryn, Harry said Raynor orchestrated everything, including the push for him to take over as chair; good overall performer, excellent doc and addition to the team here."

"Convenient." Charlie looked at a closeup of the most recent picture of 'Downing' and frowned.

"Something about him is something I remember...."

"So, what are we gonna do?" Blake stopped pacing "Whoever that Downing asshole is, he's no fan of Taryn...and she's got no backup today." Blake pulled out his phone to make a call.

"Operator? Put me through to the OR." He paced as he waited for an answer. "Hey Dawn...Anthony...yeah, still here. Listen, is Downing running the board for anesthesia today? When? No...just curious...thanks." Blake disconnected, then faced Cody and Charlie.

"He was supposed to be in charge...but got called away from some emergency; Dr. Winger's coming in."

"There are no coincidences...somethings up..."

"Cy and his team are questioning Cook, right?" Charlie nodded. "I'll text her; make sure she stays away from Downing." Blake snorted.

"How often does that woman ever do what she's *supposed* to do?"

IT WAS AN ODD WORKDAY, WITH MICHAEL DOWNING disappearing sometime early afternoon. A rigidly controlled but furious Sherry Winger was compelled to come in early, with the remainder of the OR cases shifted to accommodate the changes. After several cryptic texts from Charlie and Blake relevant to Downing, Taryn stopped reading the texts in favor of focusing on navigating the rest of her day. Texting Blake when she was done with her workday would be her plan.

Shortly after 4:30, Taryn was finishing up her last case, when she received a call from Maxx's day care. She frowned as she considered the phone but let it go to voicemail. She was headed to the ICU with a marginally stable patient, who had been left intubated because of pulmonary problems in addition to his primary surgical issue. When she finally finished her patient responsibilities in the ICU, she got a chance to check the voicemail. It was a minor problem, but a logistical nightmare. Maxx had apparently been bitten by one of the other dogs at daycare in some very rough play. Taryn tried to call the center directly but got voicemail; it was the end of day checkout rush. The bite on an ear edge would likely need glue and/or stitches, both of which were beyond the abilities of the attendant at the center this afternoon. The daycare had contacted a vet, who had agreed to remain open past her clinic's usual closing time until she could get Maxx to her, but she would be responsible for transporting Maxx there.

Taryn had authorized Cody, and as of that morning, Blake, to pick up Maxx, but with both of them working out of her condo, she was actually closer to Maxx. Cody had texted earlier that he had her SUV back from repairs. Given the circumstances, the best option seemed for her to take a Lyft to the daycare, and the vet, rather than wait for Cody or Blake to drive from the condo to pick her up and then go get Maxx. She'd never be alone, since the driver would be with her the whole time; she could ask him to wait until she collected Maxx at the daycare.

Concerned about her dog, and in a hurry to get from Point A to Point B, Taryn didn't bother changing out of her scrubs. She shoved her street clothes into her backpack and put on her parka over her lab coat and scrubs. The Lyft she arranged met her at the hospital front entrance and she was quickly on her way to Maxx's day care.

"Thanks for agreeing to take me and my dog to the vet... I'll be quick picking him up at his daycare."

"No problems...you sure you have pickup from the vet taken care of?"

"Absolutely...my friends will have time to get there."

Traffic was minimal on the roads, but the parking areas near the daycare were packed.

"Why don't I drop you off, and circle around. No way I'm gonna find a park this time of night."

"Good enough...I'll leave my stuff." During the drive to the daycare, Taryn texted Blake about the new developments, slipping the phone into her backpack before she exited the vehicle.

Taryn was far more focused on getting to Maxx on than her surroundings as dusk settled over the town. As she picked her way through the ice and snow hummocks and approached a truck parked near the entrance, she realized that someone had come up very quickly and very close behind her. Almost as soon as she became aware of the person's presence, he wrapped an arm across her shoulders and poked something in her side as he whispered harshly,

"No screaming means you live, darlin'. Mighty glad you didn't get too hurt in that little accident last night; I'll still put a cap in you if you start squallin'." The words put ice in Taryn's veins, and she frantically tried to twist around to get a view of the man's face. For once, there was no one entering or exiting the day care, or the yoga studio across the street, and that there was no way that anyone inside day care could see her because of the height of the pickup truck and the mini-van to her left beside it; the front seats of both were empty. A small terrier in the back seat of the van yapped insistently at the activity so close to its door but barking in front of the doggy daycare was exactly zero help. Taryn cast her eyes about frantically, looking for help, breaking into a cold sweat as she smelled a distinctive cologne as well as cigarette smoke, and immediately thought of the night that she and Maxx had been walking outside of her condo. Taryn continued to try to twist free, and face her attacker, energized as she realized her predicament, but the man moved easily with her, countering her moves. After a few moments of silent struggle and slipping in the snow and ice, and a muffled curse when one of her elbows struck home, he yanked her braids so hard that it brought tears to her eyes.

"Enough, bitch! Eyes front, stop the bullshit. Walk where I direct you, or I'm gonna get creative." He yanked Taryn closer, wrenching her neck around as he tangled his hand in her braids and jerked her head around, giving her neck a swipe with his wet, slimy tongue, as she continued to struggle for freedom. Her captor gave a raucous, menacing laugh. "Been waiting to get a taste of you since you showed your ass up here."

Taryn's skin crawled, and as she focused on an unmistakable bulge in her back that she could only hope was a gun. She renewed her struggling as she half stumbled and was half pushed toward a sleek Jaguar sedan that pulled in behind the pickup. Despite her struggles , the man outweighed her by at least a hundred pounds, negating both her marital arts training and the fear fueling her struggles with size and inertia.

"Goddam I do like that spirit...knew there was some wildcat under that starch at work. Some spice to go with all that pretty...we may just have to have some quality time alone before we get down to bizness...have us our own party." The man behind Taryn punctuated his words by a thrust of his hips, and a rough bruising grasp of her left breast with a hand that he shoved under her parka. Taryn's eyes teared as she stilled, panting as her heart raced in fear and anger. If struggling was making him more interested, her best option seemed to be staying still, as much as it went against her instincts. She froze, except for a fine trembling as tears rolled down her cheeks When the man pushed her toward the front door of the sedan and wrenched it open, Taryn made one last desperate move to escape, twisting and elbowing her assailant, catching him a solid blow in the stomach. With a grunt of surprise, and a muffled curse, the man slapped her hard enough that she lacerated her lip on her teeth.

"Bitch...you owe me one for that. Get your fucking ass in that car," he growled, then shoved Taryn the rest of the way into the front seat of the car.

"Throw me the goddam tape, Junior." The driver tossed him a roll of gray duct tape as Taryn began to struggle and kick again. Her braids were jerked from behind this time by the driver, causing her to wince in pain as more tears pooled in her eyes. She felt the cold kiss of metal on her neck, as the driver snarled, "Do yourself a favor, shut the fuck up and stay still, Pirelli. I *will* use this." Taryn struggled in vain, as the first man wrenched her right hand down to join her left and used the tape to secure her hands together in front of her, cutting the tape and revealing its reinforcing threads. No way would she get loose easily. As he went to work on her legs, Taryn memorized everything she could see about her assailant, who was the only person she could see...if she could only escape. Plaid barn jacket, hoodie pulled over his head, black t-shirt peeping visible under the partially zipped hoodie...and a ski mask over his face, leaving just eyes, nose and mouth free. He was Blake's height, but muscular. The person in the car used her braids as a control device, torquing her neck to an impossible and painful angle.

"You want her gagged too?"

"No...I'll take care of that later...might be nice to hear her beg....listen, bitch." He punctuated his remarks by another vicious yank on her head and neck, causing Taryn to moan in pain. "If you have a thought to screaming, I'll slit your miserable fucking throat right here and now." So, he had gun *and* a knife? After the first man finished securing her legs, he slammed the front door and jumped in the back seat. As soon as the door slammed shut, there was a decisive click as the locks engaged. It was only then that the driver released Taryn's braids, and she was able to turn and struggle around to find... a man wearing dark clothes, a cap and a ski mask, a knife clasped in his left hand. Taryn's eyes widened, and the man laughed nastily and snapped the knife closed before tossing it in the door pocket. *Switchblade? Pocketknife?* Taryn automatically lunged for her door handle, in a futile attempt to escape.

"Dr. Pirelli, my associate has a gun pointed at your head, and you have no way to move your arms or legs. Two options: Keep wiggling and die here now or stay still and live a little longer. For once I suggest you follow directions, stay still and shut the fuck up." So, the driver knew her... Still no help in figuring out who it was. Taryn tried her only out, which quickly fell flat.

"I've got someone waiting for me; my Lyft driver. He's going to take us to the vet. Maxx is......"

"Your fucking dog is fine, and I'll deal with your Lyft. Watch the bitch," snarled the driver as he lurched out of the car, snatching off his ski mask, shoving it in his pocket before he slammed the car door and flagged down the car with the Lyft emblem glowing in the front window.

"You done made lotsa enemies between work and that big fucking dog of yours, wildcat," crooned the man in the back as he reached to rub Taryn's cheek with a silencer attached to the gun that he held, tut-tutting as she jerked her head away from his caress as her mouth dried in fear and her heart began to pound. She was alone with this pervert and a gun pointed at her head. He continued as if they were really carrying on a normal conversation, caressing her neck with the silencer.

"Damn mutt growled at me more than once ... never could get close to you or your house before last night because of that fucking dog of yours. You done made some real enemies here; everyone thinks you're a big problem, wildcat, and a sneak besides. Course...everyone but me. I been watching' you and hoping for some cozy time; just the two of us. I actually see you as a smart little thing, who follows orders...and I'm betting I don't have to tell you things twice. I bet you train up right quick and nice," as he pointedly fiddled with the crotch of his pants, and nuzzled Taryn's neck, making her simultaneously want to throw up and do something...anything to get free. Eyes wild, she stretched as far away from the gun as she could and tried to get another look at the man. The hoody had partially fallen off his head when he got into the back seat and got a glimpse of what looked like a huge colorful tattoo twining around right side of his neck. "Now ..." whatever bit of perversion the man had planned to say was cut off as the driver's side back door was wrenched open, and the man threw Taryn's backpack in and slammed the door, then opened the front door. Taryn twisted around, hoping for a better look at the driver as he climbed into the front seat. The man with the neck tattoo dashed her hopes when he spoke up.

"You best suit up Junior, if'n you still don't want the good doctor to know who you is." The man behind me tut-tutted. "Amateurs." The driver cursed, then fumbled in his coat pocket, before seating himself with a grunt; ski mask was back in place. Taryn saw a flash of a metal on his right hand with all of the changes in position; watch? Bracelet? Her eyes were glued to his right arm, willing, in vain, the sleeve of his overcoat to shift, getting my wish when he reached to put the car in gear. Watch. She swore mentally as she struggled to recall all the lefties she'd run into in Bend. It actually wasn't something she noticed on most people unless she saw them writing.

"We're ready. Lyft driver's paid; ended the trip on her app and gave him a cash tip. People are fucking ignorant sheep," the man grunted. "Help me get started, then you can go on with whatever errand it is you have to do," and then turned to Taryn and said, "Pirelli, you started all of this by not keeping your damn mouth shut. I'm gonna to finish it." Before Taryn could respond the man in the back seat swore.

"Shit Junior...where's the goddamn phone! Where'd you put it after you finished that ride?" He grabbed Taryn's backpack, as he spoke, and rummaged through it. "And I ain't goin with you. Got my own problems ta deal with. You're on your own; do it right." He extracted the phone and keychain with the Mace canister and waved it at the driver. " I'll meet you two streets over after I'm done with what I gotta take care of. Be good, wild cat." He yanked Taryn's braids hard, but this time it just enraged her, causing her to twist her head enough to pull her braids free of his grasp; done with being manhandled. He chuckled. "Hmmm...love that spirit...hope you still got some later. Careful with her, Junior."

"But I thought..." Whatever the driver was going to say was cut off as the passenger side back door slammed after the man got out. The driver cursed, as he looked in his rearview mirror, then re engaged the locks before Taryn could try the door again.

"We're going for a ride, Dr. I have frankly had enough of your meddling. Your usefulness is at an end; time you went away. And don't even think about trying for that bag...or the door. You make a move for the back seat, and I'm pulling this trigger." He now waved a gun at her with his left hand, then cradled it in his lap and drove with his right. *Where was the knife? Could she somehow get to it?* Taryn was rapidly running through options and not coming up with much that she could do. The biggest problem, other than her taped hands, and feet was that she didn't have anything on her other than her parka and lab jacket. She thought longingly of the taser Blake had given her earlier in the week and collapsible walking stick that was in her car; both useless. and The knife was in the driver's side door pocket was just as inaccessible. She tried to stay calm and think of options as they drove from the light of the business district, to the much darker and quieter area of the adjoining streets which paralleled the river. She concentrated on memorizing details about the driver, seeing that what could be seen of his face shone with sweat. The mask was more of a balaclava than a true ski mask. The wisps of hair visible in the eye holes was sweat soaked; was he *frightened* despite his big talk? Maybe she had a chance after all. Taryn peered out of her window into the passenger side mirror and saw that the man from the backseat had gotten into a black Jeep Wrangler, that she now remembered seeing countless times over the past few weeks, this time, suspiciously without a license plate. Things were heading to the FUBAR zone by the second.

They drove on, with Taryn frantically considering and discarding ideas and options as the 'Fasten Seatbelt' chime pealed insistently, and the icon flashed red on the dash. The plowed streets and walkways gave way to the snow-covered brush and thicket of trees bordering the river-walk as they turned away from the lighted residential area. Taryn was still coming up with nothing for a possible weapon that she could actually reach, until she slid into the door as the car turned and felt a lump in the lump her right side pressed against the door of the car. She frowned, then blinked as she realized what it must be. *She hadn't emptied her scrub pockets before donning her lab jacket to leave the OR, because she was in such a hurry to get to Maxx*. For once, she also thanked the stars that they had been out of male scrub tops that morning in the women's locker room, and she had been forced to wear a 'female' scrub top, which had pockets below waist level instead of on the left chest. She normally despised the pocket placement and overall construction of the gender specific female scrub tops, and refused to wear them, as their construction made it more difficult to tuck her shirt into her drawstring pants. Today, that shirt, and the syringes still hidden in the pocket, might very well save her life. Taryn always carried a stash of emergency drugs in her pocket when she transported sick patients in case they became unexpectedly unstable or lost their endotracheal tube, during transport. Her last patient had been intubated and on nitroglycerin, and gone direct to the ICU, so she had made her usual "anti-death kit" transport thing, and had shoved a syringe of propofol, a syringe of muscle relaxant, sux and a stick of nitroglycerin into her pocket along with a laryngoscope and ET tube before transporting him. If she got the chance, and he was close enough, maybe she could pump her captor full of muscle relaxant in the closest central body part and escape. Sux was short acting and would only temporarily paralyze someone but might weaken him enough buy her enough time to get away, but only if she was only dealing with one person. In the meantime, Taryn needed to stall, figure out what he had planned, and where he was taking her. As she plotted, the phone rang. He answered via speakerphone, the voice sounding like the man who had grabbed her. She craned her neck to look at the display in the car; no ID of the phone listed.

"I'm only gonna be about twenty minutes before I'm back to your location. Get started, and I'll be back to help you. You still planning on parking on that dead-end street nearest the river?"

"Yes. See you there." As the driver ended the call, and made another right turn, Taryn realized that she had a time frame and a window of opportunity for escape.

"When do you expect the product will be delivered?" Cody had been catching up on some of the work that he had delayed during his efforts to go through all of the data that he and Blake had culled from Cook's computer the night before. Other than going to pick up Taryn's truck, he had been busy with activities related to his actual job. While Blake worked with Charlie to sort out the options for who Downing might actually be. Blake frowned as he checked the time.

"Still nothing from Taryn...I thought she said she'd be done by now.' Cody shrugged as he looked up from his conversation with his co-workers. Blake picked up the condo phone on the second ring.

"Myers."

"Is this the Pirelli residence? I'm calling from 'It's a Dog's Life'. We're 5 minutes from closing, and Dr. Pirelli still hasn't picked Maxx up yet. It's not like her to be late, or not give us notice of boarding plans, and she's not answering her cell. Are you able to come pick him up before closing? Or should we board him overnight?" Blake swore silently, already expecting the worse as he waved at Cody.

"On my way now...should take me about fifteen minutes to get there." He disconnected and filled in Cody, who extri-cated himself from his call. "Taryn's missing...daycare is closing; Maxx is still there." Blake called Taryn's last known location, at the hospital.

"The unit secretary in the OR said she was done closer to 4:45...which means that she's been unaccounted for almost an hour. Hold on...." As he listened on the other end, Cody booted up his tablet and started the tracking program he had installed; Taryn's phone was in motion, and according to the map, nowhere near Maxx's daycare.

"I got movement on her phone, and it's not near *A Dog's Life*. When's the last time anyone saw her? She tell *anyone* there where she was going?"

Blake disconnected his call with the hospital and shrugged into his shoulder rig after grabbing it from where it hung on his chair, headed for the mudroom to gear up for outdoors. "We gotta move...she left work right after her case finished and her patient was in ICU; something about Maxx needing to go to the vet for an emergency." On the tracking program, Cody saw that Taryn's phone was moving rapidly out of town.

"This is fucked five ways to Sunday...phone's outside of town proper; it's moving at car speed, towards the airport. We gotta move...call Charlie...I'll head for the airport. Have him or Cy meet me there with some uniforms, and on silent; no lights either. We don't know who we're dealing with..."

"And they don't need to know we're onto them."

As Blake and Cody parted Blake contacted Charlie to update him.

"Taryn's missing between the hospital and the daycare, but her phone's headed to the airport. Are Cy and Tracye still working on Cook?"

"Negative...they got delayed by Cook having to take time to deal with some sort of emergency travel arrangements for his wife. Thought you were keeping track of Taryn?"

"I was until she changed the plan...Cody's got her phone tracking toward the airport...got a bad feeling about this." Charlie swore.

"What do you need me to do?"

"Make sure Cy's got enough people to cover the airport; meet me downtown at the daycare."

"Done."

CHAPTER TWENTY-SIX

C ody fielded calls from Blake as he sped toward the airport, still tracking Taryn's phone by GPS and coordinating with Cy's surveillance team at the airport. Cy was furious that one of his most valuable civilian volunteers was now potentially in life threatening danger.

"Meet Tracye at the airport coffee shop. She's been in and out of pre-security waiting as well as the coffee shop. There's no signs of Raynor. She mentioned she saw Brianne Cook checking in with her dogs. Jibes with the info we got from Cook about some family emergency in California. I'll join you as quickly as I can." Cody continued his mad dash to the airport, miles and minutes behind the moving GPS signal of Taryn's phone. The calls between him, Blake, and Charlie continued with Cody hoping fervently that someone gained a solid lead on where Taryn was. He was encouraged by the fact that after five minutes, the blip representing her phone stopped moving.

"Charlie, Taryn's phone GPS signal is stationary. She's somewhere at the airport." Cody ignored the speed limit signs after he relayed this information to Charlie. When he reached the airport he connected with Tracye, joining her to comb the area in search of Taryn. He began dialing Taryn's phone, hoping that it wasn't on silent.

PAST THE TSA CHECKPOINT, BRIANNE COOK DREW A relieved breath as she sat with her dogs and waited for boarding to be announced for the flight to Portland. She had congratulated herself on escaping after her early morning warning, puzzled by Wyatt's odd request to call some number in the 323/Los Angeles area code. She would soon be free of whatever was going on in Bend. It was a rude surprise that she was under surveillance when her usual limo driver turned out to be a menacing thug, who had been very thorough in explaining that she should expect further instructions and updates when she arrived in California.

Although she was aware that Wyatt had a secondary, demanding set of employers, up to this point, she had not been involved in any of those activities. This new driver had terrified her with the scope of his knowledge of her life and her family's when he recited details of her father's business and personal whereabouts, as well as the addresses of the properties that she and Wyatt had in the Caymans and Venezuela. While unsure of his ultimate goal, Brianne was clear that she should do as she was told, and that there was nowhere she could hide or flee without being found if she didn't listen. After a few moments twisting her hands, she booted up her computer, using her phone to provide a secure internet connection. Her father had encouraged her to make some special account arrangements that she never felt she would need to use...until now. After a moment's hesitation, she initiated a funds transfer from her and Wyatt's joint account, then logged off, and cleared the computer cache before signing out. Just as she began to relax, she was paged to come back through security to baggage claim; whatever could be going on now? Her unease grew even more when she was met by TSA, Homeland Security agents, and a civilian pacing just outside the security portal.

"What was this phone doing in your luggage?"

BLAKE HAD MADE THE DRIVE TO THE DAYCARE IN RECORD time; maybe that was a positive sign. He clutched the gloves Taryn had left on the front seat of his SUV in one hand, hoping that Maxx would be helpful in tracking and finding her, wherever she might be. When he went inside the daycare, Maxx was the last dog remaining to be picked up; leashed and bouncing, he was in his usual good humor. The attendant had no news of Taryn and Blake was stuck waiting for a call or clue with no clear place to look for Taryn. He paced the sidewalk in front of the daycare after putting Maxx in the front seat of the truck, texting and calling his friends for updates, willing the phone to ring with positive updates. Time was passing, and it was fully dark: they needed answers, and to find Taryn.

"Charlie...I've got Maxx. No one here ever saw Taryn. Where's Cook? And his car? And has anyone seen Raynor since his last meeting this morning?"

"Cook's car's still in doctor's parking. Negative on a Raynor sighting of any sort, but residence and car are being watched, and Cy has someone at the airport."

"Fuck! So, Raynor's still unaccounted for, no one's set

eyes on Cook since 4:30, and Taryn's gone. Call me if you hear anything."

After disconnecting his call, Blake continued to drive the streets near Maxx's daycare, his apprehension growing when he scanned the cars parked there and saw a Jaguar sedan with a BRMC hangtag on the rearview mirror. He pulled past the car, sliding into the closest available parking space. He walked back to check the sedan and the area around it, using the flashlight function of his phone. A backpack suspiciously like Taryn's was visible in the backseat. He also saw two tracks that led into the woods that bordered the river-walk, one person clearly wearing snowshoes, the other not. He returned to his truck and paused. *There was a parking hangtag on the Jag's rearview mirror, like the one in Taryn's car, not a sticker like the rest of the cars he had seen parked in Dr.'s parking on the rare times he had cut through. It was unlikely that the Jag was a rental; who could the car belong to?* As he debated, he opened the rear of his SUV and grabbed a battered duffel that held the cold weather emergency kit that he always kept in his car in Denver. He extracted snowshoes and a thick sweater. He swapped his parka in favor of the pullover, buckling his shoulder rig over it, then popping in his Bluetooth earpiece.

After sitting on the edge of the cargo area to strap on his snowshoes, and an adjustable headlamp, he flipped the safety off his handgun and shoved it into the holster, before grabbing Taryn's gloves. By the time he rounded the car to the passenger front door, Maxx had caught his urgency; he began dancing the moment Blake opened the door and allowed him to jump down from the front seat. After unclipping his leash, he crouched down as he looked into his eyes, "Maxx! Find Taryn."

Maxx, in that uncanny way that dogs have, recognized

that this was no game, and with a "Wuff" in reply, took off along a path bordering the woods with Blake on his tail as he called to relay his location and new plan to Charlie.

"I'm parked near the Riverwalk, four streets away from Maxx's daycare, two cars from the corner; following some tracks...and a hunch. Tag anyone you can at the hospital and see if Wyatt Cook is still at work. How fast can you get here?"

"No comprehende...lo ciento," the woman passed by, repeating her question to the couple in the next seat who fortunately spoke English. The man returned his gaze to the blackness of the landscape outside the window. His regretful, sheepish expression morphed into a scowl as he examined his grimy, battered hands, dirt and grease embedded under the nails. Ken Raynor was on his low-tech way to Portland...on a Greyhound bus. While the bus was, in his mind, a galling way for him to leave Bend, he'd gambled correctly. It was also one of the last places that anyone would think to look. The Greyhound was even a step down on the transport ladder from an Amtrak-thruway bus and had a colorful assortment of people who likely had never been on a plane. Before embarking on his own errand, Downing helped Ken transform his physical appearance using makeup, clothing and luggage commensurate with the guise of a mechanic visiting his family. After he boarded the Amtrak Cascades train bound for Vancouver in Portland and assumed yet another identity, he would be rid of the disgusting disguise and to clean the unspeakable filth from his hands and body, not to mention resume wearing his own clothing, which was folded neatly in the cheap suitcase he placed in the overhead baggage compartment. Raynor tipped his grimy Stetson over his face and turned up his collar as he prepared to nap for as much of the way to Portland as he could. He comforted himself with the knowledge of the luxury and ease that awaited him; not on the train to Canada, but certainly on the first-class flight he had booked from Canada to Switzerland under one of his many aliases.

IT WAS INCREDIBLY ROUGH GOING THROUGH THE WOODS in snow without snowshoes. Taryn's hands were taped together in front of her. She'd fallen more times than she could count, and had scratches on her face and hands as she tried in vain to break her fall each time. She was freezing and drenched despite her coat, and wishing like hell that she had her gloves...but being cold was the least of her worries.

Unlike the previous times she'd fallen, this time she was jerked roughly to her feet by her furious, cursing, and winded captor, who despite his snowshoes, was having almost as hard of a time as she. The aroma of his nicotine that choked the interior of the car was as sharp and pungent now as they plowed along the path. The man struggled for breath, panting and audibly wheezing as they continued to trek through the snow and underbrush. *Think Taryn...smoker....out of shape...could this be Wyatt Cook?* Almost as soon as she was on her feet and moving, she fell again, awkwardly rolling to her left as she tried to protect her face. At least it was just snow this time; no branches. Taryn knew she had to change this dynamic.

"Look, I'm not going to be able to continue like this. You've gotta cut my hands loose. I won't run...promise." The man grunted, jerked Taryn to her feet, then shoved her; no chance.

"Walk, bitch... and shut your pie hole." After more falling and floundering on Taryn's part the man jerked her to a stop and finally cut her hands free of the tape with his pocketknife, then wrenched her head back by her braids, and shoved his face in hers. Her eyes watered from the pain along with the stench of alcohol and garlic infused smoker's breath.

"Just because I'm doing this, doesn't mean I won't beat the shit out of you...or shoot you...if you try anything." Taryn's noncommittal whimper of combined terror and rage must have satisfied him because he let go of her braids, then poked her in the back with the gun he had extracted from his pocket.

"Move!" He shoved her forward, now keeping a grip on her left arm. *Knife was in his pocket...gun trained on her.... getting access to either was a long shot...Plan A it was.* "Move it, bitch." Having her hands free still didn't do anything about the fact that Taryn was knee-deep in snow, but it did allow her to balance better. She could also confirm that her syringes and intubation kit were still in the right pocket of her scrubs, and protected by her lab coat, despite all of the stumbling and falling. After a few more yards, her captor tripped, and sank into a depression which had been covered by a blanket of snow that was deceptively level with the path. He struggled to regain his footing while venting a string of curses, but never lost his grip on her arm as he used it to lever himself up.

"Stop!" His fingers dug into Taryn's arm as he pocketed the gun and ripped the balaclava from his face, bracing his right hand on his knee as he bent over and gasped for air. Steam plumed around his face as he wheezed, coughed and attempted to get his breath; even in the moonlight she could see it was Wyatt Cook. As he fought to breathe, Taryn shifted the syringes from her scrub pocket to the more easily accessible parka pocket, leaving the vial of sux and one syringe in her scrubs as she eased the endotracheal tube package out, turning sideways to block Cook's line of sight as she tossed it to her right, near a snow-covered clump of bushes, opting for conversation to enhance the distraction.

"Look...look...Wyatt, whatever it is you want, I'll do it...seriously. We don't have to do this." Despite his apparently compromised physical state, talking and bargaining weren't going to work. Cook tightened his grip on Taryn's arm, clearly enraged as he jerked her closer, grasping both arms as he dropped the balaclava and shoved his face into hers again as he snarled,

"Shut...up... you...stupid...cunt...!" He panted and gasped for breath between each cluster of words, and Taryn twisted her face away from the hot stench of his breath as repelled by the odor as she was frightened. Despite his lack of physical menace due to him being so out of shape, the man still had a knife...and a gun, that he had fished out of his coat pocket again, and now waved near her face.

"You try... something...I'll use this." Despite his threats, Taryn had started to feel glimmers of hope that she could see her way out of this, since he was compromised physically and unused to dealing with a hostage situation. There was an undercurrent of panic in his repeated threats. Taryn trudged on and bided her time, hoping that Cook would forget the balaclava that he'd dropped...and that he wouldn't see the ETT package that she'd deliberately dropped.

Now unmasked, the man she now knew was Wyatt Cook puffed and cursed as clouds of steam surrounded him and sweat poured off his face and matted his hair as he floundered on despite the advantage the snowshoes conferred to him. Taryn continued to randomly leave her version of trail markers as they continued on through the brush, surreptitiously tossing syringe after syringe to her right whenever they reached spots relatively clear of brush; the nitroglycerin syringe, propofol syringe and the laryngoscope, which promptly sank deep into the snow because of its weight. It was a desperate, but poor blaze for a trail, yet all that she had.

Wyatt was more concerned with breathing and retaining his desperate grasp on her left arm than looking to see what she was doing with her right hand. He continued to wave his gun in his left hand, insuring that she didn't stray too far away as they continued through the underbrush. As they continued toward the river-walk, Taryn knew that waiting until they reached the stability and increased traction of packed snow on the path would present her best chance for escape. Without the gloves that she remembered leaving in Blake's car, her hands were turning into blocks of ice and snow was oozing over the tops of her snow boots; she would only get colder.

She ignored it all as she focused on slipping her right hand through the slit behind the pocket of her lab coat and into the scrub pocket, running her rapidly numbing fingers over the lone 10cc syringe and the vial of sux that remained. After easing vial and syringe unit into her parka, Taryn concentrated on flexing and extending her right hand and fingers and keeping them dexterous enough to do what she needed without fumbling. All that remained would be for her to find a way to free her left arm, grasp the vial, withdraw the contents, then inject it as close to Cook's central circulation as she could. The brush began thinning, and she heard the chatter of the river flowing over the rocks near shore as they approached the river walk. Time to bullshit and wait for her chance.

"So now that you have me out here, what do you think you're going to do? Throw me in the river?" It was Taryn's biggest fear, what with the remote location and the certainty of hypothermia. "Don't you realize that killing me won't solve anything?"

"What will be solved...is that you'll be out of the way... we can recover from all of the chaos you and Harris caused," huffed Wyatt as they reached the walk, slowly regaining his breath and composure as they reached firmer ground. Taryn pretended to fall to the right, violently wrenching her left arm out of Cook's grasp, while pushing him with her free hand, unbalancing him and causing him to fall, cursing and swearing, backwards into the deeper snow just off the walk. Taryn's luck skyrocketed when he also dropped the gun; he had no gloves on either. His fall and fumbling search for his gun gave her the time that she needed to draw up the sux, which she did faster than she ever had before. Throwing the vial away, she twisted left, leaned down, and grabbed for any body part close to the head and followed through with the syringe and needle, jabbing deeply through clothing into what turned out to be Cook's neck. She injected all of the contents as quickly as she could as he shrieked in pain and anger. Taryn leaped up and started running up the river-walk, towards town, which eventually would get her back to *A Dog's Life*. She heard Cook struggling and cursing behind her as he tried to recover. She counted down the seconds, knowing that the sux, even as an intramuscular injection, would begin taking effect any moment. Taryn spared a look over her shoulder seeing that Cook had recovered the gun and was attempting to aim at her. She began to zig zag as she ran, until another frantic glance back showed that his left hand was drifting downward as it weaved wildly to follow her. He fell to his knees with a weak, terrified cry. His arm sagged as his fingers relaxed and the gun slid to the ground; *the sux was working!* Taryn stopped running evasively and concentrated on running as fast as she could. As she turned the corner of the river walk, she began to see the lights of the businesses near *A Dog's Life*. She could also hear some noises from the surrounding woods, audible over Wyatt Cook's increasingly feeble moans as well as bobbing lights to her right, headed toward her. She continued to run for the safety of the businesses, surprised when she saw an animal coming up the path. In another second, Taryn gave a cry of delight, at what she realized was a very pissed off Maxx, as he gave a series of rolling barks and ran toward her. She altered course to intercept him and collapsed to her knees to hug him, realizing that if he was here, one of her friends must be also. The shot that rang out behind her and kicked up snow and ice to her right caught her off guard. Cook *couldn't* have recovered so quickly! She turned around, panicking when she realized that the shot had come from Cook's accomplice, who had returned, and was now shooting at her as he came out of the woods near Cook's prostrate form. Taryn stumbled to her feet, panic stricken as she was in the open, with nothing to defend herself with and nowhere to go but back into the woods by the path. Maxx began growling as the man came closer, sniffing as he recognized a familiar scent and started to lunge forward. Taryn grabbed his collar before he could run toward the man and shouted "Maxx! No!" terrified that her beloved dog would be shot. He stayed still, but placed the bulk of his growling, menacing body between her and her would-be assailant, who was distracted by someone who shouted her name as he came running up the path from the direction of 'A Dog's Life'. Blake? He stopped and raised a handgun, and a ruby dot danced over the upper body of Cook's accomplice. He squeezed off a shot from what had to be to be a laser sighted handgun. Cook's accomplice uttered a stream of curses and grabbed his right arm and struggled to re-aim, this time at Blake, but he reconsidered when Blake continued to close in on him. He dove into the woods to avoid Blake's next shot, which went wide. The man abandoned the search for his firearm and took off in the direction he came from with a curse, avoiding the cluster of lights and shouts headed towards the river walk.

Maxx lunged and growled as he moved again to follow the man, but Taryn grabbed his collar tightly and hugged him. No way was she going to risk him being hurt chasing someone who had already decided to run away. He had more than done his job in finding her, then creating a diversion until the rest of the cavalry showed up, in the form of Blake, and whoever was just then breaking though the line of trees opposite her. As Blake ran toward her, he flipped on the safety and pushed his gun back into his shoulder holster. Taryn rose from where she crouched and ran toward him with Maxx on her heels. Tears rolled down her face and she sobbed in relief as the overwhelming tension of the previous hour finally took its toll and reduced her to sobs and shakes as Blake hugged her close. The lights and people emerging from the woods turned out to be Charlie and a couple of police officers. Cody, Tracye, Cy, and two of Cy's men arrived minutes later, the agents with guns drawn, prepared for the worst-case scenario that had come agonizingly close to happening. The drama and strain of the whole situation peaked, and the world around Taryn began to spin. All of the sounds merged — from Wyatt Cook's whimpers to Maxx's barks, and the simultaneous talking of everyone present — finally combining into a roaring noise. Taryn's vision got spotty, her eyelids fluttered, and everything faded to black. The last thing that she clearly remembered was seeing Blake's eyes widen and feeling him grasp her even more tightly as he growled, "I got you, Sugar."

CHAPTER TWENTY-SEVEN

Taryn came to slowly, at first confused as to where she was and why she stared up at stars. Her head was pillowed on Blake's shoulder as he sat cradling her. It all came crashing back to her as she remembered her narrow escape on the river walk. Blake's look of concern changed to a grin of relief when Taryn stirred. Maxx nudged her before giving her face an enthusiastic swipe of his tongue with his usual doggie grin. Cody crouched in front of her, while EMTs hovered in the background. Fortunately, she had few injuries. Blake caressed her cheek, frowning as he saw the bruise beginning to bloom there.

"Sugar, you okay? You're safe. Cody and Charlie are here, and the police. Taryn nodded and blinked rapidly, adding unnecessarily, "I must have passed out...I've never passed out." Blake laughed and shifted her so that she was more upright. Taryn had a brief surge of dizziness, but fought and succeeded in maintaining consciousness.

"You passed out after all the drama was over, but babe you made sure that Wyatt Cook was out of commission before you ran. What the hell did you give him? He was blue by the time Charlie reached him; he actually had to give him mouth to mouth just to keep him going until the paramedics got here." Taryn started to answer, but was pre-empted when Charlie walked up and stole her thunder, holding up the empty syringe and sux vial.

"She gave him a whole syringe of muscle relaxant, which slowed him down long enough for her to get away. We found this by Cook. We followed the tracks from the car to the woods, then started finding syringes and vials — items you dropped by the trail. Effective, if unconventional way to mark where you'd been. He's just now recovered enough so that he can breathe on his own." Taryn looked over Charlie's shoulder, where Cy, the police, and the paramedics were still attending to Wyatt Cook even as they must have been reading him his Miranda rights.

"We didn't get the second guy, but Cook's being charged with kidnapping, assault, attempted murder, and an assortment of other local and federal charges that should result in some quality jail time. He's also facing charges from his activities at the hospital. I doubt CHG is gonna stand by him."

The small group of people initially on the scene was rapidly expanding as various sirens wailed and more emergency vehicles and police began to stream onto the scene. There had truly been any number of ways that the whole thing could have gone south, but it had all worked out. Blake must have been reading her mind as he brushed a finger down her nose asking quietly, "Sugar, what the hell made you call a Lyft rather than calling Cody or me? And why didn't you call or text to let me know what was going on?"

Cody nodded in agreement as he added, "After we got the call from *A Dog's Life,* and found out that Blake wasn't with you, I realized we might be too late to stop whatever was going on. Then we saw your phone heading toward the airport. When we got there and searched outside but didn't find you, we heard the phone playing my ring tone, but coming from the luggage on the cart that was ready to be put on the next flight to Portland. It took awhile, but we finally figured out that your phone was in Brianne Cook's luggage. The only explanation that we could get out of her was that her husband asked her to make a call from the doggy day care when she picked up her dogs. Still, it didn't explain how the phone got there, but Cy ordered her held for questioning. With that info, we decided that we needed to get back to Maxx's day care, since that seemed to be the center where everything had happened."

Taryn looked from Cody to Blake, taking in the solemn expressions on both of their faces, and told them what had happened after she got the phone call about Maxx while dropping off her last patient. She described being grabbed from behind, and ending up in Wyatt Cook's car, separated from her phone, and finally the trek to the river-walk. Although he swore under his breath at various points in her tale, when Taryn finished talking, Blake wordlessly folded her into his arms again, and Cody looked at her soberly while squeezing her shoulder in commiseration.

"We almost lost you, T-baby." Taryn moved to try to stand, and Blake and Cody both assisted her, Blake rising from his makeshift seat on a rock.

"I should have kept you in the loop about everything. I'm sorry, and I promise not to do anything like that again," Taryn said with all sincerity, hoping that her answer would mollify both of them.

Blake shot a hard glance at where Charlie and the EMT's still clustered around Cook, his gaze and expression softening as he looked at her touching her bruised cheek again. "There sure as hell better not be a next time for anything. I'm just grateful that you're safe, and that courtesy of Maxx, we found you quickly." Maxx gave a 'woof' of agreement and leaned against Taryn as his tail thumped Blake's legs, making everyone laugh.

"On that note, I think I'm going to see if Charlie has something for me to do." Cody pushed through the crowd toward the cluster of police and DHS agents.

"Send one of those EMTs here with a cold pack for her face, will you?"

By this time, Wyatt Cook was totally recovered from the relaxant. Blake rubbed Taryn's back as he added quietly, "You almost got killed before any of us even figured out where you were or what was going on. It somehow worked out, but you've *gotta* to learn to think before you act, Sugar," Blake said softly in Taryn's ear, as he tipped her chin up and gave her a kiss on her nose. When he put it like that, she could see how she let her concern for Maxx, who actually would have been safe, even with a torn and bleeding ear, override her common sense.

"What I saw of Cook's accomplice, you wouldn't have fared as well if he had caught you. He's a professional. Probably involved with the torture and murder of James last month." Taryn began to shiver and shake again. This time, due to the cold, and not just adrenaline excess. Blake looked at her and smiled as he shook his head, drawing the blanket an EMT brought over around her shoulders.

"Enough of me bitching; let's find out what the procedure's going to be as far as you talking to the authorities and giving your statement. We need to go home so I can get you warm. And before you say a word, there's no way in hell you're going to work tomorrow." Blake looked at Taryn with a quirk of one brow and his head tilted. The fight was pretty much out of her; excess adrenalin was gone and it had been a hellishly long day and week.

"Okay. Did anyone figure out where Michael Downing was? He left work early; they had to have Sherry start call early."

"He's not Michael Downing."

"What?"

"Long story...tell you details later...Charlie's not even sure who he is...don't know if they will find out...except he's tied up with Cook and Raynor...who's also disappeared. Now let's see about getting you home." Blake continued to circle Taryn's shoulders protectively as Charlie, Cy, and a Bend police officer, joined them.

"Dr. Pirelli, I'm Officer Turner. I know you're recovering, and still need medical attention, but could you briefly tell us what happened?"

Taryn gave a description of Cook's accomplice, wondering if it had been Michael Downing in disguise. Even though it was his second time hearing the story, Blake's arm tightened as she related how she'd been grabbed and manhandled by both Cook and the man who everyone was assuming to have been Michael Downing. A paramedic moved in to check the bruise that had continued to blossom on her cheek. Blake watched with gritted teeth.

"Well at least I shot the fucker. Better still that it was probably that prick Downing. Temporary, partial paralysis was still better than Cook deserved, but it's a start. Wish I could have at him for a bit." She'd forgotten that Blake had shot Cook's accomplice.

Officer Turner, who was completing Taryn's story of the events, which had transpired then turned to Blake. "And sir, how're you involved in this whole situation, and what's your name?"

"I'm Dr. Pirelli's boyfriend, Blake Myers. I've been working as an equipment rep using the name Anthony at the hospital, but also have ties to Dr. James Harris, who died on the mountain last month."

Turner nodded. "We're getting some new info on Harris and how it impacts this situation. What do you know about what happened to Cook, Mr. Myers?"

"Blake, please. I'd like to think that I hauled ass through the woods to get Sug...Dr. Pirelli out of trouble, but it sounds like she did a good enough job on Cook. He was disabled at just about the time that I got to her. She'll be able to give you all the details on him. I did get a shot off and wing Cook's associate; here's my weapon."

Blake stepped slightly away, as he pulled his weapon from his holster, then unloaded it before offering the gun to the officer, who accepted it by indicating that Blake should drop it and the ammo in separate plastic bags. Blake also reached for his wallet and held out a small card, "I've got a concealed carry permit for the gun, which I completed when I arrived in Bend two weeks ago."

As Officer Turner checked the card carefully, Taryn turned to Blake. "You were always sure something was wrong if you planned and brought that with you from Denver.

"James was still technically missing, but I had a bad feeling about this from the start. I never ignore my hunches. Glad I didn't; you've gotta habit of finding trouble."

"And what the hell is *that* supposed to mean?" Cody sauntered up with a grin.

"Trouble follows you? You stir shit up? Chaos is your middle name?"

"Shut up, Cody."

"Man, fuck off."

In stereo. Again.

"You two are trouble, any way you take it...and way too much alike." Cody shook his head as he waved his hand in disgust. "I'm sticking with Charlie," and stomped back over to talk with Cy and his team. Officer Turner coughed to hide his laugh, as he handed Blake his permit.

"Mr. Myers, your permit checks out. I'll need both of you to come down to the station and give us a formal statement about what you saw and did. We'll get your weapon back to you after we do ballistics testing." Taryn wilted a bit visibly as he spoke, forgetting that there was protocol and red tape to be addressed from the police aspect. Officer Turner continued smoothly, "Dr. Pirelli, while I'm more than happy that you're safe, you took a real chance running off without letting someone know what was going on. Given the circumstances, I think we can wait until tomorrow to have you and Mr. Myers come down to the station for formal statements. Hope he'll also convince you not to go off script in the future; your fast thinking got you out of things *this* time."

"Why do I feel I'm being ganged up on?"

"Just safety and precaution, Doctor. Although it's clear from the paramedics that Mr. Cook was the aggressor in this, you lucked way out of what could have been a very bad situation."

Blake shrugged. "Glad someone else sees reality besides me."

Taryn rolled her eyes. "What're you doing to figure if the guy I shot was Downing?"

"Haven't heard from the chief yet...and no signs of anyone down the path, so he was doing well enough to run away."

"When and where did he leave the path? I'm assuming he went into the woods, but Charlie and that agent didn't see him." Taryn shook her head; she had too much going on to even guess at a location.

"I shot him in his right arm, as he reached Cook. The gun spun out of his hand when I shot him." Turner nodded, then waved for one of the uniforms, giving him an approximate area to search for the weapon. After canvassing the area, they found the weapon near the path, and began procedures to collect and bag it, then take it to test it for fingerprints and ballistics. They also found a half-smoked cigarette with a distinctive blue band, which they bagged after some excited conversation that Taryn couldn't follow.

Blake continued, "He'd gotten off one shot as I was approaching while Taryn sat on the ground with Maxx. I shot him before he could fire again; once he dropped his weapon he took off into the woods. I honestly was more concerned with making sure that Taryn was okay than noticing anything else. He was wearing snowshoes, so I'm thinking that he probably managed to get through the woods, avoid everyone else, and escaped in whatever vehicle he arrived in.

Taryn added, "I saw him get into a black Jeep Wrangler near doggie daycare. I also remember seeing it parked at my condo complex."

"I'll check. So, this accomplice is Downing, and injured. He must be presumed to be still at large and dangerous. Dr. Pirelli, I'm not sure you'll be safe staying by yourself tonight. I know that Charlie said that you are staying in a condo with an alarm, but..."

"She and Maxx are staying with me tonight," said Blake evenly, before Taryn could respond. "I'm concerned about her safety as well, Officer, and I'm not leaving her alone anytime soon."

"Blake, it's not like I'll be alone. Cody's staying with me

and Maxx; even though he probably doesn't have his gun with him, I know he'll be able to keep me safe."

"Not a chance...I'm keeping you with me. Taryn nodded slowly in acquiescence, and Blake smiled at her, then gave Officer Turner the revised plan.

"Just let me know what time you want her at the station tomorrow."

"Any time before noon will be okay," he said, as he completed his notes, and gave both Blake and Taryn a card with his contact information. Wyatt Cook, escorted by another officer, walked by cuffed and recovered, on his way to the squad car. The venomous look he gave Taryn spoke eloquently of his mindset, and it rattled Taryn.

Blake gently guided her out of the line of sight. "Come on Sugar, time to leave. I want to get both you and Maxx home. You're done here." On their way to Blake's car, he appraised Cody of the new plan.

Cody gave Taryn a hug and whispered, 'Be good,' as she rethought her evening. "Getting that Lyft was a dumb move... but if you tell Blake I said that, I promise I will make your life in Seattle a living hell." Cody grinned at her and bent down to rub Maxx's head. "Maybe between Maxx and Blake you'll stay out of trouble tonight, huh?" Cody took Taryn's finger of annoyance in good humor then rejoined the conversation with Charlie and Cy, as she and Maxx left with Blake.

Exhaustion descended on Taryn like a thick cloak, and she began shivering as they walked away from the excitement on the river-walk and the dead-end street where Blake had parked. Taryn's feet had turned into blocks of ice due to the amount of snow that had oozed over the top of her boots. They reached Blake's truck in far less time than it had seemed to take when she was wallowing in the snow through the wooded area with Cook. Blake cranked the car and turned on the heater, as well as the seat warmers, so that Taryn could start trying to thaw out. Maxx flopped down in the back seat as Blake stowed his snowshoes in the cargo area. By the time that he had finished, and gotten behind the wheel, Taryn had fallen asleep, her head propped on the window of the front door. Maxx poked his head between the seats, and nuzzled her, then looked at Blake quizzically. He patted his head, then reached across and grabbed the seat belt, and made sure that Taryn was safely buckled in, saying, "Time to go home, Maxx. I think that we got to her just in time. Let's see if we can manage to slow her down and keep her out of trouble, okay?" Maxx woofed in agreement, his tongue lolling with a doggy grin. Blake headed for his home away from home with his new plus two.

As Downing evaded the forces coming onto the river walk and through the woods, he cursed violently, as he realized that not only would he need some sort of medical care, he'd lost his gun and come damn close to getting caught. His carefully crafted cover as an anesthesiologist was blown, and he still had had responsibilities to assure that the scheme would continue to function. His final disastrous act of the evening was not impressing on Cook the importance of keeping his mouth shut, especially since it was clear that he would be arrested and questioned. He had no idea that the fool would turn a sure thing with silencing Pirelli into such a fucking disaster. Salvaging something from the night without getting his ass chewed out by his superiors would be a challenge. His focus? Self-preservation; Raynor was on his own.

He would concoct an excuse before he was due to report, then get treatment for his arm when he was safely away. The field dressed wound burned like fire, and although he imagined giving Pirelli and Anthony some personal payback in the future, he now needed to concentrate on leaving ASAP. He would regroup and play a very personal role in helping plan how they would make both Pirelli and Anthony pay for all they had done. He flexed his right hand, then extracted his cigarettes, taking time to light up before pulling away from the curb, his eyes on the lights bobbing in the woods behind him.

EPILOGUE

Five Weeks Later

B lake and Taryn were on a flight headed back from their trip to the other Washington — Washington, DC — and a closed-door session testifying before Homeland Security major case team. After the circus in Bend, a full, multi-department investigation had been launched to find all of the players and companies involved with Eagle and what amounted to a complex drug counterfeiting and importation scheme. The discoveries that Taryn had made were like key threads on a wall hanging. Following the information and clues was slowly resulting in the unravelling of the scheme, and more low-level operatives, but no one higher than Cook in management.

Cy and Tracye used the evidence that they confiscated from the warehouse for BMC to leverage a full-scale investigation of Eagle as well as implicating and charging most of the upper management at the Kansas City headquarters. Eagle was charged with the use of counterfeit and non-FDA approved manufacturing processes, Customs and FDA inspection subversion, and numerous other charges that would result in years of jail time.

Yet, Eagle was just another company; there were others, as yet unknown sister pharmaceutical companies that were likely gearing up operations as the investigations into Eagle were getting underway. With the small pluses, there were also some very big new questions, centering around the individuals who had disappeared.

The fake Michael Downing had a very distinctive neck tattoo that virtually no one other than Harry and Taryn had seen. The real Michael Downing's body was found in Colorado in much the same circumstances as had befallen James Harris — at the bottom of a high-risk, out of bounds run — with injuries that superficially looked as if they were from the fall. No suspects, no clue about who was impersonating Downing, and no description of him other than that of his neck tattoo and the car he drove. The women who had been attacked outside of local bars had recovered from their injuries were all hospital employees who had somehow gotten in Michael Downing's way. But who was the man really? Harry recovered quickly from his injuries in what was presumed to be an engineered accident as the semi driver was never apprehended...but now the hospital was down *two* anesthesiologists, and having trouble recruiting locums docs due to the drama and intrigue.

As far as Customs and Homeland Security were concerned, the drug counterfeiting was only the tip of the iceberg. The problems with Eagle highlighted the loopholes in Customs and import procedures that needed to be addressed, despite the enormity of the problems patrolling and regulating the trade that came in through ports on both coasts as well as the Canadian and Mexican borders. The borders and ports were porous, and there were constant schemes to breach the security. Case in point? Ken Raynor had disappeared. There had been no sightings of him anywhere in the Pacific Northwest, or anywhere in the country, but with his resources, he'd likely left the country.

The other critical and unanswered issue was who, and exactly where, was the individual in the FDA who was the mastermind? The shadowy puppet master at the top of the power pyramid had managed to ooze away, leaving not a hint or trace about identity or what agency had been exploited to operate the scheme.

To Taryn's knowledge, there were still no clues or theories as to who this person was, and how he managed to avoid apprehension when the feds swooped in and arrested the upper management at Eagle along with Arne Johnnson, corporate CFO of the chain that owned Bend Regional. He had Raynor connections, and had been handsomely compensated for his instrumental role in getting CHG corporate to sign the distribution contract with Eagle in the first place. The only glitch was that Johnsson wasn't talking about any of his contacts in Eagle or how he'd managed to push the contract with Eagle through corporate.

Wyatt Cook, however, was singing like the proverbial canary. Despite his initial attitude and bravado on the night of his arrest, his self-assurance was short-lived once the evidence against him was tallied. A complete search of the BMC storage space revealed a scarf, which Cook identified as his. The scarf was submitted for forensic testing and found to have blood and hair that was a DNA match to James Harris. With this physical evidence connecting Cook with the events in the warehouse, as well as the video that they had found on his laptop, there was overwhelming evidence indicating Cook's presence at the warehouse for at least part of the torture session with Harris. When confronted with the evidence, he crumbled. His legal team started talking plea deals. Somehow, all of the evidence pointed at Wyatt Cook as being the driving force behind the use of counterfeit and smuggled products from Eagle at BRH, despite all of the theories and suggestive information about Ken Raynor, his past and demeanor. In any case, facts trumped impressions.

Despite all of Cook's protests to the contrary, which largely blamed Ken Raynor for everything, he was the only person formally charged for what had transpired, from the kidnapping and torture of James Harris, to being an accessory to his death, and the hospital and FDA issues relating to suppression of problems with the counterfeit drugs. Conveniently and predictably, Cook blamed the MIA Dr. Michael Downing for the majority of actions and the cover up that he didn't push onto Raynor...but had he been framed?

Brianne Cook had finally been allowed to leave for California after Cy's team and the police figured out that she knew nothing about how Taryn's phone had been planted in her suitcase. Other than making the phone call at the behest of her husband, she claimed to know nothing about his plan to kidnap Taryn or what was transpiring in Bend. Since all of the information that was gained confirmed her story, the police had no reason to detain her. The next day, she continued her trip to California, for what was apparently some type of family health emergency that preceded the attempted kidnapping. The shocker came when she filed to divorce Wyatt shortly after charges were filed against him. Despite admitting being involved in the transfer of funds outside of the country to their offshore accounts at Wyatt's behest, she claimed innocence to everything that Wyatt had been doing involving Eagle, and the evidence somehow managed to support that. Cody, more than anyone else, smelled a set up, and speculated that somehow, Brianne would manage to surface again, as would Ken Raynor and the Michael Downing stand in. He beefed up the physical and cyber security for his and Taryn's place in Seattle to a truly insane level. Taryn loved her roommate, but his paranoia about all things Bend was beginning to annoy her.

When the hospital investigation in Bend was completed, the remaining operatives outside of the hospital pathologist were found to be victims themselves with Raynor apparently using the uncomplimentary work or personal information that he had about them to force them to cooperate with whatever actions were needed to advance the scheme in Bend. Bend itself was still reeling from the revelations after the whole incident with Cook, Raynor, and Downing. In very short order, two thirds of the senior administrative staff at the hospital had either left or been arrested.

Within a week after the magnitude of the problems caused by Eagle and its substandard drugs, and the presence of Downing, who no one could even prove was an anesthesiologist, an emergency meeting of all of the major business people in the community was held and a proposal put forward for the community to repurchase the hospital from CHG. Contrary to the initial presentation that the corporate ownership of the hospital was a community benefit, the Eagle/Raynor/Cook association had severely damaged the confidence the community had in CHG and its hospital. Everyone favored return of control of the facility to those in the community who had a vested interest in its success, with Lydia Thompson, a Bend native, unanimously voted in as the new CEO. Blake and his company had their contract reinstated; the issue was Raynor, Cook and company, not company product or performance.

The anesthesia group was likewise back in everyone's

good graces. After he returned from his injuries, Harry was able to reveal the extortionist measures that Raynor used to gain political and financial advantages with the anesthesia group and played a major role in working with Med Staff to strengthen governance by physicians and the hospital board of directors. He also offered Taryn a position at the hospital and partnership in the group, which she politely declined, although she did plan on finishing her locums stint there, which would end sometimes around the middle of April. Without the toxic influence of Downing, they were a great group of anesthesiologists. She additionally had every intention of maintaining her friendship with Shannon and her family and the other people who had made her stay enjoyable; she just didn't want to live there. As they say, it was a nice place to visit, but Taryn didn't see the point of moving there.

As for her and Blake? They were officially entangled... and still trying to define whatever that meant. After Taryn's family found out about her close call on the river-walk, they descended on her in Bend in force. Her parents managed to be in Bend the day after all of the hoopla, arriving not long after she came back from giving her official report at the police department. Her father, Stefano, regarded Blake with wary suspicion, at first, then welcomed him with smiles and slaps on the back after some truly arcane male bonding rituals involving him, Taryn's brother, Marco, Cody, and her sister, Zahara's husband. They started the day skiing and then ended up drinking and apparently engaging in an all-night poker game at Blake's condo afterward. Men! God knows she loved all of the ones in her family, but understanding them was challenge Taryn knew she wouldn't accomplish in this lifetime or universe. Cody's girlfriend, Sina, ended up flying in and joining Taryn's mom, who was fully recovered from her medical woes, along with her sister, and Taryn for spa time on the days she spent recovering from her trauma.

And Blake? Well, Taryn took a deep breath as the fasten seat-belts sign chimed and the flight attendants began their rounds to pick-up last-minute items before the plane landed in Denver. Yup Denver, not Bend. Instead of flying directly back to Bend so that they could finish up their time there, they decided to detour to Denver so that Taryn could meet Blake's family, and the Harris clan, who finally had some answers and closure about what had happened to James and why. Taryn tried to convince herself that she wasn't nervous as the butterflies started up again in her stomach. After all of the stories that she and Blake had shared over the previous few weeks, she felt that she knew them already and was actually looking forward to spending some time with everyone who had played a part in making him the man that he was.

Taryn stared out the window for what seemed like the whole flight, thinking of the changes that had come into her life over the past few weeks, over a decision by Cody to volunteer her for a job as part of a gambling debt repayment. It was one of the best, unplanned accidental decisions that she had ever not made in her entire life.

"Sugar, time to buckle up," Blake said with a smile that Taryn returned as she leaned into his shoulder as the plane came in to land. New adventures... new friends and family.

Somewhere in Canada

THE MAN TRAMPED FROM HIS SNOW-MACHINE TO THE remote cabin, his pack laden with supplies. After removing his outer gear and stowing his supplies, he poured himself a shot of whiskey before opening his laptop and connecting his satellite internet connection. He opened a file entitled *Bend*, with sub-files named *Pirelli, Jennings, Myers, and Post.* The email he opened had scores of attachments, which turned out to be detailed pictures of the high rise where Cody and Taryn lived, complete with building floor plans and schematics. The collection of recent snapshots showed Cody on his way to work, his office, and in his vehicle. The man smirked as he flexed his right hand; almost back to full strength and mobility. He printed out one of the recent pictures, that of Cody on his way into his work office, and pinned it to a scarred wall, then walked across the cabin to a small chest that sat on a side table. He extracted a packet of Dunhill Blues, and lit one while withdrawing a dart from a box. After taking a draw on the cigarette, he clamped it in his teeth, then hurled the dart to strike the long-lens picture of Cody in the face.

"I think I'm gonna start with you, you geek ass son of a bitch."

Gstaad, Switzerland, Same Time

THE PATIENT IN SUITE 239 AT THE EVERGREEN HOTEL in Gstaad had been in a mood again overnight. The nurse on duty for the evening had just given report to the day nurse and warned her about the newest developments, which included the patient's agitation and violent reaction to the news that had come by email earlier that evening. Although their services were fairly routine for most of the patients who had had their reconstructive surgeries with Dr. Michaels, the nurses also knew that a select few of the patients they cared for were, in one way or another, wanted for some type of crime or illegal acts. Those patients actually had surgery to alter their appearance and were also the patients for whom they had very explicit instructions for screening all incoming communications.

While neither of the nurses actually speculated on their charges' possible former activities, they found that some of these men were volatile and easily agitated. Even recuperating from surgery, they had an air that urged caution with both how they were approached and handled, even in a relatively weakened and frequently sedated state. They had been, for the most part successful with Mr. 239 until last night, when he had apparently received an email from someone in Washington, DC in the USA, about some sort of hearing, including a picture of two individuals.

He had printed out the email and picture, and had looked at it a few minutes, before ripping it to shreds, before giving into further venting of his frustration and anger by destroying much of the equipment and furniture in the office area of the suite. The night nurse, Liesel, came to the door of the suite because of the noise, and had immediately summoned help from of one of the male medical assistants on call for just this reason. Somehow, they managed to restrain the patient and prevent him from disrupting the repairs and bandages that covered his face by finding a vein to inject medications that quickly put him into a drug-induced sleep for the rest of the night.

The medical assistant had helped her put both the bedroom and office back in order, and she had taken the time to retrieve the ripped-up picture. In an unusual show of curiosity, she taped the picture back together to see if she could see what was so disturbing. The picture only showed a very attractive couple, the woman with honey-brown skin, her hair in braids and a loose up-do, and the man, much taller and apparently of Native American ancestry, leaving some building, apparently in America, with the title under the picture reading **Washington, DC, 2-27-13**. While both of the people in the picture were glowing with obvious good humor and health, and the man had his arm protectively around the woman, there was nothing particularly remarkable about either one, other than the fact that they seemed to be both very happy and intent on each other.

They weren't celebrities nor prominent governmental officials in Washington, from what she knew of the American administration. But whoever they were, their picture had thrown the patient into a rage. She considered her options, looking at the picture she had reconstructed and then in the direction of the door to the bedroom, before deciding to deliberately fold the picture and shove it in her pocket. She planned to dispose of it outside of the suite at the end of her shift. She left the suite for her office, assuring the medical assistant that he was no longer needed, and completed her written incident documentation and hand-off the report to the day nurse.

She never noticed the glowing screen of the computer, which had somehow escaped the patient's destructive rampage. As she had contemplated the picture that she had taped together, an email popped up on the screen. The message was succinct; the sender line contained a string of x's:

Pirelli and Myers left DC after testifying, and boarded American flight 926, nonstop from Dulles to Denver. How do you want us to proceed?

ACKNOWLEDGMENTS

I'd like to thank my parents first, because they encouraged me to be who I am... which was nothing that either of them had envisioned. I'm still not picking just the one thing, Dad (smile). Thanks also to the friends who supported and encouraged me through all the rewrites and revisions and provided just the right reader critique at the critical times.

There are no good or bad experiences... only writing material! Truth is always stranger than fiction.

DJL

ABOUT THE AUTHOR

D.J. Lee takes inspiration for her medical thrillers from her profession working as an anesthesiologist. Among friends, she likes to joke that she passes gas for a living. Her view into healthcare has influenced her imagination because as she says, "Many unbelievable situations found their way into my stories from my own experiences, albeit slightly differently." Like any good mystery, she has changed the names to protect the innocent...and the guilty. It's true that the strangest things happen in fact, and not in fiction.

D.J. likes living on the fringes of life to explore the light and darker side of humanity. "I have a fascination for looking at the shadows behind and around the spotlights where the good stories live."

She calls the Pacific Northwest her home and hopes readers will enjoy her first offering into the dark and creepy side of healthcare.

facebook.com/DJLeewrites

twitter.com/DJLeewrites

instagram.com/DJLeewrites

pinterest.com/DJLeewrites